READY
TO
CATCH
HIM
SHOULD
HE
FALL

NEIL BARTLETT

READY
TO
CATCH
HIM
SHOULD
HE
FALL

A DUTTON BOOK

DUTTON
Published by the Penguin Group
Penguin Books USA Inc., 375 Hudson Street,
New York, New York 10014, U.S.A.
Penguin Books Ltd, 27 Wrights Lane,
London W8 5TZ, England
Penguin Books Australia Ltd, Ringwood,
Victoria, Australia
Penguin Books Canada Ltd, 2801 John Street,
Markham, Ontario, Canada L3R 1B4
Penguin Books (N.Z.) Ltd, 182-190 Wairau Road,
Auckland 10, New Zealand

Penguin Books Ltd, Registered Offices:
Harmondsworth, Middlesex, England

First American edition published by Dutton, an imprint of New American Library, a division of Penguin Books USA Inc.
Distributed in Canada by McClelland & Stewart Inc.

First Dutton Printing, September, 1991
10 9 8 7 6 5 4 3 2 1

REGISTERED TRADEMARK—MARCA REGISTRADA

LIBRARY OF CONGRESS CATALOGING-IN-PUBLICATION DATA:
Bartlett, Neil.
    Ready to catch him should he fall / Neil Bartlett. —
1st American ed.
        p.   cm.

PR6052.A7543R43   1991
823'.914—dc20   91-10443
                                        CIP

Printed in the United States of America
Set in Walbaum

This book is dedicated to my grandmothers, Dorothy May Bartlett and Edna May Aston.

. . . it is a contradiction, an anomaly, an apparent impossibility; but it is a truth. I am glad to have it doubted, for in that circumstance I should find a sufficient assurance (if I wanted any) that it needed to be told.

Charles Dickens, from the preface to *Oliver Twist*, 1837

CONTENTS

SINGLE

COUPLE

FAMILY

SINGLE

This is a picture which I took of him myself. He was so beautiful in those days—listen to me, *those days*, talking like it was all ancient history. It's just that at the time it all seemed so beautiful and important, it was like some kind of historical event. *History on legs*, we used to say; a significant pair of legs, an important stomach, legendary . . . *a classic of the genre. Historic.* Well it was true, all of it.

I know that though I've shown you the photograph you still want me to describe him to you, this Boy of ours. *What was he like*, you say, and what you want to say is *what was he really like then? Tell me something that no one else knows about him. Tell me something that will prove all of this.* I understand; I mean, you want to know that someone isn't just making the whole thing up when they talk about a man being that special to them. But what can I tell you? That '*I knew the moment I saw him*'? (people do say that about their men, more often than you'd think). I could tell you that he had white skin, black eyes, and black hair, but you can see that from the photograph.

I could tell you that the eyes were so beautiful they could actually make you feel giddy when he suddenly looked up from the floor and straight at you.

That the white skin bruised easily (you could write your name on his back with your fingers, they said). And that the hair was black all over his body, a shiny, animal black, even on his back, at the base of his spine.

But then I don't suppose that would be enough for you, and after all this is Boy's story mostly, he is after all in a proper sense my hero, and you have to have this Boy clearly in your mind before we can proceed. The best I can say is that Boy looked something like, or had something like the feel of, Paul Newman when he's playing the character christened Chance Wayne in that Tennessee Williams film. There's a moment when he looks away from the camera and down at the floor and softly says, *'Nobody's young any more . . .'* Boy often made me think of that particular moment—it was the way he looked down. Except of course that Boy was young, really young. He was nineteen when he came to us.

When you see that film you want to say, *God, he was perfect,* and it was the same with Boy.

And you wanted to hit him sometimes and ask him if he knew what he was doing. He was so young some nights, I mean he looked so young and so quiet, and I was scared for him you see, so scared that he'd get it wrong, that he'd waste himself. Sometimes when I was drunk and I'd see him standing there looking all quiet and black and white and gorgeous, waiting for someone to take him home, I'd get all teary and want to go up and slap him and shout in his face: *How can you possibly understand what it means! You're nineteen.*

So he was young; but his body wasn't smooth and gold, *pure hard gold,* which is what the woman says about the body that you see in that scene of the film. Boy's was white, and furred with close dark hair from the root of his cock to the perfect black, flat fan on his chest, and at the base of his spine like I said. It was not golden; but it was precious. It was a perfect body. A perfected body, not an adolescent one, which was odd, because the rest of Boy was unfinished, and that's what this whole thing is about.

And Boy was as handsome as Chance Wayne, and he smiled as easily. He could smile to order or smile for real, with real pleasure, and it came out just the same, it came out so beautiful that you were sure not to notice the difference. He moved as easily; and like Chance Wayne at the height of his beauty you, or I, would just, well, would just have died for him, stopped in our tracks for him, stopped the car for him, fallen silent if we saw him cross the street or across a crowded bar. Like Chance Wayne when you watch that scene in the film, he made you just want to wake up with him in the room, wake up with him in the bed beside you. You wanted to wake up with him right there in the room and to turn to him and quote the next line of the film right back at him, to whisper it to him, *make me almost believe that we are a pair of young lovers without any shame*, and I don't mean that in some tragedy queen way, but in order to say of Boy that truly I do think that it is a beauty like his that makes it all worth while, and I do feel that if we are fighting for anything, and if I was asked in a questionnaire what it was I was fighting for (and believe me I do feel like I am fighting, more and more I think that), then I would answer, beauty. Beauty or whatever you call it that makes you feel that you have no shame any more, none left at all.

One thing Boy never said, the line of Newman's he would never have used, was *don't call me Boy*. He loved to be called Boy. He smiled whenever the name was used. He loved it that we had christened him and he knew that he was special to us.

And if you still can't quite see him, and this is not your ideal Boy at all, then I'm sorry. Perhaps you think that Boy does not sound too beautiful to you, by which you mean he does not sound your type. Well I have to say

that much of the impact of this story depends upon
your being able to see and think of Boy as beautiful,
admirable and even adorable in the true senses of those
difficult and dangerous but nonetheless precious and
necessary words; I suggest therefore that you amend
my descriptions of Boy and his lover—but I anticipate
myself, that was not to be for several weeks yet; that 'Great
Romance of Our Times', as it became known amongst
us, had not yet begun, its theme tune had not yet been
composed on Gary's piano, its scenario was not yet subject
of our daily gossip and speculation, we were not yet
auditioning for a place in the credits—The Friend, The
Admirer, Blonde Man in Bar, Second Guest at Dinner
Party. But do go back, and amend my description of Boy
so that he is, some way, if you see what I mean, your
type. Make him fit the bill; imagine for him the attributes
that you require. I don't mean that you have to imagine
him as your lover or prospective lover; this story does not
require such strict identification, and I don't see that any
story does. After all, just look round any bar and you'll
see that everybody there, myself included (you too if
it's your kind of bar), has in their time been both The
Boy and The Older Man, both Banker and Domestic,
Ingenue and Other Woman, booted Prince and stirrup-
holding Groom—but I don't mean either that you should
have complete license to make him look just how you
wish; I don't want to think of anyone hearing this story
and grinning and thinking of Boy as some permanently,
conveniently smiling blue-eyed blonde, because he was
not that in any way and that is not what he meant to us.
For instance, don't make him shorter than you are, so
that his eyes must always be looking up at you whenever
you think of him. You might surprise yourself one night
by wanting to feel his arm around your shoulder. You
might want that to happen one night. And I would ask
you, whatever changes you make, please keep him strong,

as strong as he was. When I think about it I'm not sure it makes any important difference how you imagine he looks, I mean who am I to say whether this Boy you are seeing has blonde hair or dark; but I am sure that it does matter what he means to you. Keep him strong, keep him young, and, whatever his colouring, keep him gorgeous.

I apologise if this description of Boy sounds to you like some fantasy and not a real person, a real young man; and worse still, if this looks like a photograph from that kind of magazine which you wouldn't even buy, let alone be seen reading in public, on public transport for instance. But the truth is, if you had ever seen this young man, naked or clothed (and I have see him both, and halfway in between), then you would admit to the accuracy of what I've said. There are such men in this city, and even to see them, never mind to touch them or have them kiss you, or see them just before dawn, or to have them as one of your dear friends, is one of the great pleasures of our life, and it is commoner than most people think. In the part of town where I live I see strangers who I would call truly beautiful at least once a day.

Boy was truly beautiful, when he came to us. I can see him now standing there in the door.

I have this postcard depicting an allegorical figure of Strength. He is naked like a statue, with one knee bent and the other leg straight. He has strong, agile and indeed superb hands; in the palm of his raised, right hand he holds out to you a miniature city, complete with dome, bridges and towers, the freedom of which he is offering you and which he has promised to protect. Now place around the head of this statue angels; place in his left hand a sword; and light in his realistically enamelled eyes a welcome and a promise such as I had never, never in all my years seen. On this figure

*depends the rest of our story; it is on those white shoulders
that all our hopes rest. He is the most beautiful of us all. It
is at his feet that we throw ourselves like the bound figures
which form the pedestal of this statue (one captive looks
upward with adoring eyes). It is him who will attend our
funerals; it is him who will be strong when we are not.*

Actually, I am not sure that I was there on that night of
his arrival, and I don't claim to remember all the details
or to have been as impressed by his appearance, framed
in the doorway, as some people I drink with do; I think
they just want to talk about their witnessing his first
appearance that way—as if he was an angel or something
extraordinary—because of what went on to happen later.
But I don't say that doesn't make sense. I'm sure you have
men you think of in that way too, people you see from a
distance and you think they are angels, or at least heroes.
I think that's a proper feeling. But anyway, one day he
found himself walking in our street, which was different
to how it is now, because not only was The Bar there,
which as you know is gone now, but also there were
different kinds of people living in that part of town then. If
someone was looking for The Bar in those days—because
there was no name written up or sign for it, no lights at
all, and not even a number on the door, Madame liked to
keep it that way even when she didn't have to any more—I
mean when she opened up we may all have been in a sort
of hiding, and not many people knew about The Bar and
our life there, but it wasn't that way later, and now you
know we can have lights and advertising and you see boys
queueing up outside every night, very public, and I like
to see that—but in those days, in those days if somebody
arranged to meet you for a date there, and it was their first
time and they weren't sure how to find us, you'd joke with
them, and you'd say well first there is a wedding, and then

there's a death, and there's the news, and then there's us; meaning, first there's the shop with the flowers, the real ones, and next door to that is the undertaker's with the fake flowers in the window, china, all dusty; and then the newsagent's and magazine shop, and then right next door to that is The Bar. You can't miss it.

THE FIRST WEEK

This is how he came to us.

Boy was walking down the street. Our street, though he
didn't know that yet. And his head was spinning from
walking so far; he walked everywhere, and though he
stopped to eat every day when he was on one of these
journeys of his he did not I expect eat especially properly.
He was worn out. Worn out with his own personal brand
of window shopping; all that staring and never buying
anything, all those shop windows, all those men to stare
at and not dare follow, as if there was indeed a sheet of
plate glass between him and them. And worn out with
all that thinking, thinking all day with no one to talk to,
and thinking because there was no one to talk to. No one
whose advice he could ask. Some days he would follow
a man, a man he'd just seen in the street, for minutes
or for hours, thinking he would *go* up to him and ask
him if he knew the way. I can remember doing that in
my own time. Thinking that maybe this man was the
right man, that maybe it was him I should ask for directions, him who would take me home or wherever it was
I was trying to get to. Boy was like that, he was hoping
that somebody would take him to the place where

everybody else was. Or at least tell him how to get there, or give him the money to get in when he did get there, or at least lend him a map with a cross marked on it, or give him an address.

But he never did ask any man for directions; he walked and he walked. In fact when Boy first came to us he was at the point of exhaustion. This is partly I suppose what made us seem like a destination to him; he was in that simple sense ready to arrive, ready to get somewhere and rest there for the night.

When he arrived it was at a very particular time of day. The actual day's business of shopping was over; for everybody else in the city it looked to Boy like it was time to go home, spent up and carrying bags full of things. The public world was closing down and everybody was going home; it was five o'clock. But for the kind of shopping that Boy was doing there was no five o'clock, there was no closing time.

To reach us, as I have said, Boy had to walk past three shops with windows. The first two were closed already, but Boy looked in the windows anyway; when he was out journeying the whole point was to stop and look at everything. The florist was closed, and they'd put the fresh stock away, so that when Boy looked in through the first window the flowers he saw were of silk; all artificial, but so good that they were better and fresher than the real thing, and certainly more expensive. Carefully aranged sprays and spires of sweet pea and mignonette, tiger lilies and lily of the valley, all in silk, wedding flowers with lots of ribbon in white and pink and pale blue, confetti colours. Next door Boy saw, laid out on the floor of a darkened and otherwise empty shop, a selection of flowers for graves. There were small clumps of purple china roses in the continental style, heavy and sharp enough to be used as weapons; wreaths of laurel, and hellebore flowers in white plastic with glittered stamens. Each arrangement had a blank label or card prominently attached to it. In the next window Boy saw a wall of magazines and papers (in eighteen different languages, including Turkish and black English), as carefully arranged as any display of flowers. This shop was still open, but Boy stayed outside, looking at the window display. In the top right-hand corner of the window was a single magazine whose cover displayed a naked man instead of a naked woman or a smiling mother. Boy stood outside the window and imagined the things he might see inside this magazine, should he ever take it down off the high shelf and open it, perhaps in the privacy of his room or perhaps right there on the street at five o'clock. He imagined small, cheaply staged pictures of sexual tortures involving ropes and wires—the kind of things which Boy had not yet done. He imagined a full-page, black and white photo of two barechested men (their chests shaved), photographed in daylight, walking down the street, gazing squarely at the camera, holding hands, one of them holding an alsatian straining at a leather leash. He also imagined men photographed in colour, sprawled alone or holding each other, doing extraordinary things but in ordinary rooms, living rooms; doing things on sofas, on sheepskin rugs, stretched across a coffee table. He imagined the personal messages which appear in the back pages (usually on cheaper paper, and often coloured a dull pale yellow or pink) of such magazines, and he imagined writing replies to these messages, imagined exactly what he would say, even imagined meeting some of these men. And then (as he stood and stared through the window at the magazine) Boy imagined sleeping with these men, actually sleeping, sharing a bed with them for the night. And then Boy could imagine having a cup of coffee with them in the morning, but he couldn't imagine anything else after that.

*

And now Boy was truly tired, end of the day tired, dog tired.

He wished that the geography of the city was different. Often at this time of day, when he felt the day's journey should be ending or reaching a destination, but knowing that it was not, knowing that what he was looking for probably happened after everybody else had gone home, he wished that he could end his days walking at the edge of a sea or a lake so big that you couldn't see its other shore. He wanted very much to walk out onto a pier—those constructions built so that people who have come to the sea to get away from their place of work can, for a moment, almost leave their working life behind, can go to the very edge of their week's holiday and then dream of going further. Constructions built so that people who cannot afford to leave or sail away can feel that they are almost leaving. Boy would have been happiest to stand on the end of a pier from which big ships, real proper ocean ships, embarked; but he would have settled for just an ordinary pier, a small one—so long as it was big enough for him to walk away from the city, into the wind, turn his back on everything and stand there looking west at an empty sea, or a far horizon, and think about America, or somewhere.

And next door to the window full of magazines was not a window, but a black door.

Over the doorway was a small plaque. It said, *In this house* (and the ceramic of the plaque had broken and the name was missing) *stayed on his first visit to the city, and it was here that he wrote the opening pages of his greatest work.* There was no name painted up over the door. We just left it blank most of the time, because The Bar was always changing its name. It's had about ten or twelve names since I've been going there, though some of them were just for one night, just for a party or celebration, and even then the name was never written up anywhere, you just had to know that tonight it was The Lily Pond, or The Jewel Box, The Gigolo, The Hustler, The Place (no, I think that was somewhere else), Grave Charges (I loved that one)—or The You Know You Like It, I remember that year especially. Just now we didn't have any name for it at all, and it was just The Bar, like it always was, the bar.

There were three bells by the side of the door, and these did have names written by them. It was as if these were the names of tenants or people who lived upstairs, but in fact no one lived upstairs except Madame. The bells didn't work and I don't know who put the names there, they've just always been there. The first bell was labelled *San Francisco*; the second *El Dorado*; and the third *Timbuctoo*. Underneath the third bell someone had also written, using a biro on the paint of the wall, *Ethiopia*. Also there was a cluster of messages on small adhesive labels, like the ones Boy had seen stuck in phone boxes near the railway station, and he bent down to look and read all of these. They said: *'Big, strong man gives sense of direction in life'*; *'Boy seeks Angel of Death'*; *'Blonde boy seeks older man with Fast Car for mutually satisfactory crash.'* One of these labels or messages was dated, and it said, *'Thursday afternoon August 12th, Kevin Come back Darling.'*

This doorway also had a display of flowers arranged behind glass. On the wall to the right of the door was a small illuminated case with the label *'Appearing this week'*, and below that a selection of coloured photographs was pinned to a board covered in cheap red plush. The pictures however didn't seem to be of artistes of any kind; they were just of anonymous, handsome young men, the sort of photographs that Boy had seen in barber's windows showing the kinds of haircut you could get. The colours were a bit faded and it looked like no one had

rearranged or replaced the pictures in the case for some
time.

The door was shut, locked in fact. Boy could see the
scuff marks around the doorhandle where other men (Boy
knew it couldn't be *people*, he just knew it was *men*) had
opened and closed it. On the black paint of the door was
chalked a message: *eleven o'clock*.

The street was empty. Boy had an erection. He promised himself that he would come back later no matter
how tired he was.

I can see that people must have thought we were being
very mysterious then, that we were a bit of a mystery, that
The Bar was a very strange place; but it never seemed that
way to us. To us, it was as normal as home.

And because it was so normal to us, it is very strange
now trying to describe it to you. Giving an account of
it like this makes me feel as though you're asking me
to account for it, explain it for you. Explain our lives
there—as if they needed explaining, and the whole point
was that when you walked in the door of The Bar you
knew you didn't have to explain anything to anyone who
was there, not anyone.

Our lives there were promiscuous, I can say that for a
start. And though that was where I felt most private often,
it was a very private place you see, even at its busiest, and
it was busy, I mean it wasn't small and quiet, I don't want
you to think that, it was very public. A very public kind
of life. *'Promiscuous, public and semi-professional'*, it said
in one of Madame's books about the lives of the great
courtesans, and I think that's about it. Some of us were
great courtesans very definitely, certainly Stella sitting on
her stool at the bar, you'd think she was in pearls the way
she sat there. But even the less dedicated of us, *public
and semi-professional*, I think you could say that of us all

really. And I will say that myself I was very promiscuous sexually, I will say that because I think a lot of people want to leave that out of the story, well not me thank you very much.

But, very strange it must have seemed, certainly the first time you walked in. For instance you had to know the names, the cast list. On a good night you'd have Ron Ackroyd; Terry and Bobby (and Bobby's Mother); Sandy and Eddie; Big Janet (she was always in); That Awful Hugh Hapsley; Teddy, Tiny, Leaf, Minty, Winter; Madge, also known as The Troll; Miss Public House; and, of course, Mr Mortimer. Stella I've mentioned; Stella I was her full title, she would be sitting at the bar, and then later, Stella II would be sitting there beside her. I shan't be telling you all about these men, but it does give you some idea, the way we were, the chorus, the bit players in this romance which is what I really want to tell you about.

And there was the way of talking, as well. Nobody talked like that all the time, of course, but you have to imagine what sort of an evening it was when all these things were said, what was really being talked about when we talked like that:

Stella (to Noel, who looked like an air steward, but wasn't): 'Will you do us a favour? Come over 'ere and sit on my face and go to sleep.'

Stella again: 'Good evening, Sean. Remember what I told you; the first lesson's free.'

Sandy and Eddie at two in the morning, surveying the evening's crowd and explaining who was who to a newcomer: 'You see that one in the white vest, that's his affair in the denim. They've been together for fourteen years, they met at school. And you tell me, how fabulous is that.'

Sandy, at three in the morning, watching Boy: 'If I was built like that I wouldn't wait until three o'clock to take my shirt off.'
(*pause with music*)
'In fact I don't think I'd even wear a shirt.'
(*longer pause*)
Eddie, lighting a cigarette; 'I wouldn't even buy shirts.'

Greta—Greta was a cook. She used to show you a collection of photographs which she kept in her wallet as if they were family photographs, but in fact these pictures were all pictures of men's cocks, she used to make them stop on the way home at the photobooth in the entrance to the station, she'd make them stand on the stool with their trousers down, she never got caught—Greta, on seeing me leave with an especially handsome man: 'I hope you're on the pill.'

Miss Public House: 'I can't stand any more trouble.'
Now this was a line from a film, and he was always using it. He'd be talking to some man all evening, they'd be getting on very well indeed as far as we could all see, but then Miss P would still be there alone when the lights went on, and the man would have gone. And he was never especially unhappy about it, and I rather admired that really. I think Miss P had a real point; you do have to know when you just can't stand any more trouble, not tonight anyway.

When I very deliberately try and remember it like this I know I end up remembering it and describing it being like a bar scene in a musical, where everyone that the camera pans past is a very definite character, and they're all so eager when the camera is on them, clapping and laughing and tapping their feet to the music so convincingly. Well that was how we were; playing our scene for all it was worth. People criticise this style and say it's all a lie, they take one quick look in through the door and they say that we are all acting madly to conceal some great sadness from ourselves. All I can say is, I think they must never have spent a night in The Bar if they think that, or never a good night. I want to say to them, when they talk like that, *well, where do you go in the evenings?* Playing like we played wasn't lying at all, it was nothing to do with lying.

What did you expect us to do? Sit around and be depressed? Madame always had a little stage set up there at the end, and I remember thinking at the time, well, seven nights in a week and seven different acts, it's one way of dealing with the situation. One night there was a little backdrop of a painted garden, and in front of it two new boys were doing a strip routine to the original 'Let's Stay Together'; but then they got carried away and ended up just leaning against the wall together, leaning up against the painted flowerbeds and the little painted bridge, just kissing and making love right there, for at least forty minutes, nobody minded. It was lovely just watching them you see. And the next night the backdrop was 'A Night in Spain', and there was Stella II, it was his very first night, all done up in black and gold lace with an underskirt of violent red, a red Elizabeth the First wig for some reason and a real red rose, it was sensational, and it was his first night too, Stella II doing 'Te Amo' till the tears ran down his face. And there was the original Stella up on her stool not being able to believe what she was seeing, going mental, screaming, *That's my sister, it's my long lost fucking sister.* And all that in one week, it must have been one of Madame's special amateur talent weeks I suppose.

As a background to all this, The Bar was basically black inside. Black was always fashionable with us. Whether it was being referred to that week as The Tea Room, The Oasis or The Hole (I liked that one too), it was always basically night inside, A Good Night Out; not black as jeweller's velvet exactly, except on a good night, but always when you stepped in off the street it was truly night inside, a night dark enough to dream in and on which to meet strangers, whatever the variations on where and when this particular night had fallen. (One time we did scrape the black paint off the windows at the back and we served tea and pastries in the afternoon and had no music, but that wasn't a great success with us. We would rather have gone somewhere else if that was what we wanted; it wasn't quite right somehow and so we painted the windows up again.) Against the black walls there were of course changes in fashion, changes of music, changes in drink; for instance for a couple of years you could get little liqueur glasses of violently alcoholic black coffee with pyramids of whipped cream on top after one of the barstaff had come back from an affair with a real sailor (or so he said anyway) in some German port, Germany somewhere. And sometimes Madame would just decide that we all needed a change and there'd be paint ordered and people would come in during the day and work for a couple of days and the whole place would be done out for a party or a festival. And suddenly we'd all be in Amsterdam or Paris or something like somebody's idea of America for the evening, or else it would still be our own dear city, but from very definitely another era, all striped Regency wallpaper and framed Angus McBean photographs of Vivien Leigh; or another time there'd be nothing but opera on the sound system for a whole week, there'd be complaints of course but Madame would say, *I'm just trying to give you boys an education*, and Gary at least would be very happy. But then it would go back to the usual music, the old pictures would go up again and it would be back to the black paintwork. Basically you see The Bar was always the same. It could be relied on.

And whatever else the decor was or the show was that night, whatever city we were all supposed to be in, one thing that was always the same and that Madame never got rid of was the ceiling. The design of the ceiling at The Bar was very wonderful. She'd had it inlaid with a hundred, several hundred small white fairy-lights, and it gave the effect of a real fantastic night sky, especially on a good night. I always loved that. The bulbs weren't just scattered, but were arranged in the correct patterns—so that if you looked up you could see (if you knew which star was which), up there amongst all the dragons, bulls and poisonous scuttlers of the Heavens, right in the centre you could see the constellation which I always thought of as being our special one, a solitary man walking with his faithful dog, the high summer constellation of Orion, the Hunter, stretched and striding above us. But I never knew what all the other stars meant, just that one constellation. I didn't know the full map. Gary would sometimes see me staring up at them, and he'd say, *you know, it's no good trying to read the stars up there . . . the only real stars here tonight are those two making out on the dance floor. Well I for one am shocked,* Gary would always say.

On certain nights, when things got very late and very heavy, Madame would go to bed and leave us to it there under the stars. And of course the door was shut then, and there'd be just seven or eight of us left on the dance floor. There would always have been a few men who had been dancing barechested all the evening, dancing with the fierce attention of the tango, or the *apache*; these were the ones who stayed on late. And now they would be dancing, as we said, *dancing right down,* with the elegance and economy of movement that only exhaustion brings, the careful and expert moves that only come at that

particular time in the morning. The music by now would
sound so fractured and sophisticated that only they, the
real dedicated dancers, could still hear its rhythm. They
were evidently hearing something different from the rest
of us now, for we would watch them slow-dance to the
fastest beat, and then, on the next record, see them
execute perfect and elaborate improvised arabesques,
all fast footwork and impassioned arms, in the gaps of
a slow blues. And sometimes, towards dawn, the music
would be at full blast and there would be hardly any
movement at all, nothing left except maybe just one
couple kissing—and yet that looked like dancing too.
There was something about it that was scandalous.
Two men kissing to music under the stars . . . or Little
David, the barman, would bring out his famous white
gauze and feather fans and send them gliding across
his sweating chest and face (you don't see this any more
these days)—as if the secret thoughts that were normally
hidden behind that odd smile in his eyes had escaped
and taken flight; as if, I used to think, it was magic, as
if some oddly attractive boy had unbuttoned his flies for
you and brought out not a fat red cock but a blinking,
blinded, delicate, fluttering magician's dove, releasing it
into the roof of the dark theatre to fly crazily over your
astonished head . . . and above all this was that ceiling of
shining stars. And on a good night the stars would seem to
brighten; if you looked up it was like a clear winter's night
in the city, one of those nights when you find yourself on a
dark street, one without streetlamps, and for once you can
see that the stars have different colours; they are like still
fireworks.

This moment is very private and is rarely if ever seen
by outsiders, not even glimpsed through a window.

And then the lights all came on, and it would be like
the hardest-to-bear dawn ever.

*

What else can I tell you about our nights there? Yes, you could have sex there, in the toilets, but only according to certain rules. I should say, really, that you could live just how you wanted there, according to certain rules. But the point was, they were our own rules.

And so it was into all of this that Boy made his entrance.

At the moment of Boy's arrival, at the very moment that he was standing there framed in our doorway, hesitating (which makes such a good entrance, though Boy wasn't doing it deliberately), at that same time on that same first evening there was a terrible attack on one of the men from The Bar.

It's odd that I should remember that now, because I didn't connect the two incidents at the time. I heard about the first one pretty soon, the next night in fact, because everyone I knew was talking about the arrival of the new beauty. The second I didn't hear about for four days and even then not from a friend but from the free paper which used to be given away in the bars once a week those days. The details were all there; they'd used a knife, and they brought it down on his face four times. It was strange then, all these things were happening, and the thing was, sometimes you didn't hear about them until much later, even if it was someone you were used to seeing all the time.

THE FIRST MONTH

'That Boy's a bit exclusive today, isn't he?' that was what we used to say, the joke being that actually Boy was there nearly every day right from the start; and every day that he was there, he went home with someone. In fact, Boy quickly became quite a regular at The Bar. He didn't waste any time.

And every time he came in Mr Mortimer would say, 'Oh, so you've turned up again, Boy.' This was another one of his quotations. Back in 1961 it had been, briefly, a very famous line, and a very tragic line too. It came from a scene set in a bar not unlike ours, and was said just after everyone in the bar had turned pale at the sight of a particular young man, a regular, entering the bar after a week's absence; the thing was, they were all wondering how they were going to break the news to him that there'd been a terrible suicide, they were all wondering who was going to be the one to take this boy to one side and tell him what had happened to his friend, and why. And now, you see, the thing was that we could see Boy walking into our bar, pausing in the doorway, and we could just say the line and laugh.

That laugh was our sweet revenge on those bitter times. And you could say that Boy's life in The Bar and in fact his mere presence there began somehow to be for us our revenge on that poor boy in that terrible, bitter, unhappy scene in that famous film.

I know, I know, I hear you say, this precious Boy of yours surely has no imagination if he is content with the first place he finds and the very first crowd of men that he runs across. But I know, and you should know, that imagination is not what counts at this stage of a young man's career; what he needs is application, study, repetition, diligent imitation and sincere admiration of his peers. You have got just to find some place and stay there and get stuck in. Boy knew this without being told. Or perhaps he felt he had no choice, perhaps he didn't know about the other places in the city which he could have gone to; anyway he became a real regular, and soon he was there most nights, in fact every night, six nights a week, The Bar being open every day of the week except Monday, usually from the afternoon and always until three a.m. (at least officially). Every day except Monday which was, as we said, our day of rest.

People talk about how much of a shock, a wonderful shock, it is the first time you realise that there are places like ours that you can go, but for Boy I had the feeling that coming to The Bar didn't feel like that much of a change in his routine. He was used to walking all over the city, as if searching, as if dedicated to the act of searching, every single day; and now he came to The Bar every single night, and did his searching there. Of course now he didn't have to walk quite so far to do his searching; but a similar kind of dedication was still required of him, for The Bar contained in a way the streets of the whole city, there were men there from all the different parts of it. What Boy had to do now was not walk down those streets, but stand still and choose amongst their inhabitants, choose the right one to follow, the right one to lead him in the next stage of his journey or wandering through the city. And journey he did; from The Bar Boy would be taken home and driven at night down all those same streets down and round which he had once walked by daylight. He already knew most of the city's different districts and its short cuts, its sudden changes of place and people; it was just that now he would see the shop windows shining at night instead of by day, see them gliding past from a car or taxi window as he was driven home for the night.

Every night Boy would wear the same thing, a white t shirt; and every night he would throw that t shirt down on a different bedroom floor.

His special trick was to look at the floor a lot. That way people could stare at him as much as they wanted to and as much as he wanted them to; then at the crucial moment he would lift his face and turn those famous eyes on his chosen suitor for the evening. People thought he was doing this deliberately, because people never really believe that the beautiful lack confidence; looking back, I think that to start with Boy must have been frightened almost all of the time. He was always silent; always waiting to be asked, and never asking. Of course being nervous he often drank a little too much, so that when he finally looked up at the end of the night it would be with something like desperation, a fear that no one was going to ask him to leave with them; but the way he looked at you also meant that you knew he would never say no, if you did ask. This made him easier to take home for the night; people who would normally never have approached such a beauty felt that they could.

Boy went home with someone every single night, he'd go home with anyone really.

And he always learnt something.

*

Lesson by lesson, Boy learnt how to behave in the
company of men. He learnt how to talk in the car on
the way home, even when he didn't want to; he learnt how
to take a shower in somebody else's bathroom without
embarrassing himself. He learnt that he could make love
and come both in haste and with impressive slowness, for
five minutes or for three hours, without asking either for
more or for less time from his partner but fitting in with
their timing. He learnt how to make love in complete
silence or to talk all night if that was what the other man
wanted.

In one of these early lessons he was very lucky in
his teacher; Miss Public House took him home on one
of his first nights—she who usually never could be
bothered—and in one exhausting night Miss P taught
him everything he knew about how to make love without
getting hurt or hurting anybody (remember that in those
days we were still getting used to the idea and still
elaborating our repertoires of what you could and couldn't
do, which was very hard for us, for me anyway, since we
had spent so long trying to forget the very word *couldn't*).
And Miss P told him that if ever any man tried to mess
him about or to make him do things he didn't want to
do then he should come right back to The Bar and tell
us, and we'd sort the man out for him. When Miss P
said this to him Boy realised that he couldn't actually
imagine a man proposing something that he wouldn't
want to do, or wouldn't at least want to try just once,
but he understood what he was being told and he learnt
that lesson well, thank God. I am sure he had no idea
how lucky he was.

He learnt all the signs and conventions, very quickly,
not only because he made himself student to so many
tutors, but because he watched so carefully everything
that each one did, with that strange, silent, exhausting
attention of his.

Boy never refused an invitation. He went home with a couple who had been together for twelve years, not because he wanted to know what it would be like to be made love to by two men at once, but rather to see how these particular two men lived as a couple; specifically, what they did together in the morning before going to work. He got himself invited to a large formal dinner party at which one man served the wine and another served all the food, and was tired and irritable, like a wife; Boy observed all of this very closely.

He went home with a single man whose mantelpiece was crowded with framed family photos—partners, holidays, weddings, babies, graduations, christenings; the man (who was gorgeous) told Boy that he worked in a photo processing lab, and that none of the photos were of his own family or lovers, but were all stolen.

He went home with a man who made love to him very violently on the living room floor, wanting to fuck Boy face down on the floor, and straight away, without any kissing; the floor was covered with scraps of glittering sequinned fabrics. This was Madge, who made costumes for the rest of us to wear at the party nights. Boy was not surprised at the kind of sex they had, because he had already learnt never to assume that people made love in the same way as they talked.

He went home on the Saturday night of his third week with someone who invited him to stay for Sunday lunch. The lunch was to be a Christmas dinner, even though it was the middle of May. The living room ceiling was hung with bunting, the kitchen smelt of roast turkey, the house was full of people who all knew each other intimately, the videos had been ordered and the sideboard was laden with drink and in fact everyone behaved just like it was a real family Christmas, except that Boy had sex with two other men in the bathroom, and they didn't even bother to lock the door because they knew that no one else there would mind, knew that they didn't have to hide what they were doing from the rest of the party.

He went home with a man who had wallpapered his living room with seven hundred copies of the cover of a Sunday colour magazine showing a white-skinned 22-year-old Glaswegian photographed wearing the second, whiter skin of a gymnast's leotard; his hands and wrists were also powdered dead white. In the middle of the sex this man whispered in Boy's ear, *you're just like him, you know, you're just like him you are.*

Although they were all very different (Boy spent a lot of time noticing the differences in their physiques, techniques, cars and living rooms), they were also all the same in one respect. Boy only ever went home with older men, men older than himself, men who had stories and careers and sometimes even families and children of their own. *I'm always giving myself away*, that was how he thought of it. Sometimes he thought that he needed to feel like a woman, a younger woman or at least The Other Woman; certainly he needed to feel like The Young Man. He especially liked to be taken to the home of a couple, to sleep securely between them if they'd let him, and then in the morning to ask them questions about their house, about the furniture which they'd chosen together. He was still amazed and fascinated by the fact of two men being together at all; he was almost overwhelmed by the idea of two men actually living together. He never ever thought that he might live in one of these houses; he always cast himself as the honoured young guest.

Only once in this period did he sleep with someone of his age, and on this occasion he chose someone who looked almost exactly like himself. On that night he watched himself in the mirror all night, and for the very first time he was the one who asked for things and who made things happen in the order that he wanted them to. He made his partner change roles and positions constantly, every few minutes, until they hardly knew which body was which, which was giving and which was taking. That night, because he could see himself, Boy thought about himself all night long.

In all of this Boy was trying very hard, so very hard that it was touching to watch. We all talked about him, of course; his name was now 'The New Boy', *so how was The New Boy?* we'd say. Sometimes we would even just refer to him as 'The New'. Whenever he was shown a new sexual technique, he would use it the very next night on his new partner. Whenever a man smiled at him he smiled right back. If someone touched him from behind on a crowded Saturday night he would push himself back onto the anonymous hand, just like a cat would, without turning round to see who it was. And when he began to have the confidence to talk to us, he would have long discussions with people about films which he had never actually seen, but which he could pretend to have seen, since he made a point of reading all the reviews of the new films and musicals when he found out that that was what people liked to talk about on first meetings. You could say that he was doing all of this so that he'd end up behaving like one of us. He even began to sing along quietly when Gary played. He wanted so much to be one of us, you see. (Boy would never, of course, have used the word *us* at this time. And there's lots of men won't use the word *us*, still.)

And of course sometimes during this apprenticeship Boy knew that what he really wanted was not to be taught to be one of us, not to be taught how to be a man at all, but to be reassured that he might somehow remain a boy forever. When he realised that arriving at The Bar meant he was still only just at the start of his wanderings or journey, he ached some nights to be told that he need go no farther than this.

One night (this was in the second week after he had arrived, and about nine or ten weeks before The Romance really began) the man who had driven him away from the Bar had done so in a big, warm, expensive, deep-seated car. He had played classical music on the stereo, which Boy had assured him he liked, and it was true; Boy had never heard music like this before and he thought it was wonderful, a sound as big, and as warm, and as expensive as the car; a sound as exciting as the sensation of being driven through the night by a stranger. It was a starry night that night, and by leaning against the cold window Boy could see the stars, not the stars of The Bar ceiling now, but the real ones. The man said:

'I live a long way out of town.'
and Boy said, as he always said:
'That's alright.'

Soon they were driving almost through countryside, there were no street lamps any more; and Boy suddenly found himself saying, *stop the car.* The man pulled the car into the long, wet grass by the roadside. He turned the lights and the music off, and because there was no other traffic on the almost-country road at three in the morning, there was complete silence. Boy wound down the window so that he could see the stars better, and then he made the man kiss him, right there.

Then they drove on, freezing, because Boy kept his window down so that he could see the stars. He tipped his seat back and zipped his jacket right up and he asked for the music to go on again, and he lay there in the dark with the music on, feeling warm in the middle of the freezing night, and he could feel himself smiling. *I want to be like this*, he thought. *I want to be like that . . . I want to be this,*

*I want to be that. I want to be rich and handsome. I want
to be a rich young man, if wealth is what it takes to buy
this feeling; a young lord leaving the city after a night of
riot ... I want to be nineteen for ever. I want never to
arrive. I want the dawn never to come. I want the stars
never to fade. I want to have this man drive me in his car
all night long, for us never to arrive anywhere ... but if
we should, then let the gates swing silently open, let there
be a long gravel drive, let it be like when the young master
comes home from school. Let the man lift me from the car
still asleep and wrapped in a tartan blanket, let him lift
me and carry me up the stairs to my bed, let him gently
say, 'we're here' ... let him lay me down to sleep. Let him
kiss me when I'm half asleep, kiss me once, and then again,
and again, as if half wanting to wake me. Let him take his
chauffeur's cap off very slowly and say softly to me, 'oh sir,
I don't never want to work for anyone else, never'; let him
kneel by the side of the great bed, in the moonlight, and let
him lean over to kiss me gently on the lips and to run his
leather-gloved hand tenderly across my cheek, across my
lips, through my hair, saying all the time, 'oh sir, I'm here
sir, I'm right here, I'm right here by the bed; was you calling
me sir, did you call me?'*

It was nearly four in the morning by now, and Boy was
ready to sleep; not exhausted, but content, knowing that
the night was perfect just the way it was. And in fact they
never made it to the man's house in the country that night,
because Boy made him stop the car twice more. The first
time, he asked the man to make love to him right there in
the car, not to take him home yet but to do it to him there
in the car. They did it, very slowly and tenderly, and then
drove on again; and then Boy made him stop the second
time, in a layby with the first lorry headlights going past,
and the man took Boy's cock in his mouth again, and
masturbated Boy again so that he came a second time,
and then they drove again. And by then it was nearly

dawn, and this time, the fourth time, the man stopped
the car without Boy saying anything. He just stopped
the car on the the top of a small hill, for they were right
out in the country now. And they sat in the car with the
windows down in the freezing dawn and they watched
the distant city lights going out under the dawn at five in
the morning, they sat there for a full half hour, looking,
and thinking how beautiful the city looked at this time
and at this distance . . . *All the shame, the desertions, the
exposures of their life there* (this is what the man was
thinking of as he sat silent by Boy's side), *all the slow
hours and cruel thoughts and disappointments of the night.*

And this half hour of sweet silence was the greatest
pleasure that night, it was its crowning moment (Boy
thought, *this is as good as coming together*), the precious
moment from which Boy was to go home exhausted and
almost jaded with pleasure, the moment to which all the
overtures of the night had led.

When it was fully light the man said:

'It's no good, I have to go to work soon. Can I just drop
you off?'

And so he drove Boy back to where he lived. They
got there at half past six in the morning. The man
stopped the car for the fifth and last time, and there,
right outside where Boy lived, they kissed, passionately,
scandalously, because by now people were up and there
was traffic passing, the first buses and freight lorries on the
Commercial Road; people could have seen them. They
said goodbye to each other and promised not to ignore
each other the next time they met.

And when Boy got home to his bed he was too tired to
sleep or to speak. He loved this end-of-the-night sensation
of hardly being able to think, just feel. He slowly took off
his clothes and the smell of the night with them, and stood
there naked in the morning light by his bedroom window,
and he smiled. Smiled to himself and just for himself. Boy

thought that this had been in some ways the perfect night, the best that he had ever had since he'd arrived at The Bar.

You see sometimes Boy, like all of us, sometimes Boy just wanted to be taken care of without having done anything to deserve it. The way that sons always are, the way they always expect to be taken care of.

The bed that Boy climbed into that morning, knowing that he wouldn't sleep, but wanting just to lie there a while, was on the twentieth floor of a council block right close by the river on the east side of the city. When he'd first arrived he had lived in a succession of bedsitting rooms on the west side, for which he had been charged extortionate rents by landlords who he never met; the third night after coming to The Bar for the first time he had slept with someone who knew of someone who had a spare room at a much more reasonable price, and Boy had moved in. The rent on this new place, like the rent on all the places he'd lived in since he arrived in the city, was paid for by the Social Security. And apart from that rent Boy hardly had any money. That was why he had walked everywhere on his early journeys; and now it was the main reason why he was so happy to eat the food which men prepared for him either before or after they had sex, to sit at their dining room tables. He himself lived off fruit with sugar, yoghurt, cereals, eggs, instant coffee, and he often ate toast three times a day. So you see he was very happy, very flattered to be bought drinks in The Bar, and this life with hardly any money at all was why listening to other people's classical music on their expensive sound systems was a real and true idea of luxury to him.

Because it was on the twentieth floor, the flat had an amazing daytime view of the great and glittering river; by night, it was the great towers of the financial district to the west that glittered.

Boy would sometimes sit staring at this view with a guide to the city open on his lap. He'd use it to identify and locate all the landmarks which he had stared up at during his exhausting explorations, now seen from a very different perspective; he knew the names of all the streets where the distant, anonymous towers of the banks and finance companies were sited, having worn himself out many times by walking along them, fascinated by the scenes glimpsed behind their mirrored, darkened or tinted glass windows and walls. Now he'd sit and stare at those same walls made transparent by all the lights left on at night. From his local library he got photocopies of the maps of his district for 1811, 1843 and 1871; he'd sit there and try to work out how the changes in the maps related to the view at night; where the darkness of rookeries, courts and tenements had been replaced with the darkness of lampless parks and public gardens. He worked out where The Bar was on his maps, and then checked this perspective against the actual view—from where he saw the city it looked like The Bar was right in the middle of it, not hidden away at all like it was on the map. He also got a copy of the underground railway map, and tried to trace that invisible geography over what he could actually see; he would even try and trace the map of the flightpaths of aeroplanes over the city, deciding which direction indicated which distant country. Boy thought he would like to see the city under heavy snow; then it would look like a real map, all in black and white, the river a thick black ribbon, or, if frozen as he knew it had once been, a clean white ribbon, the only space in the city without streets, names, lights or indeed owners.

The man who actually had the lease or paid the rent anyway on this flat was a man who worked sorting for the Post Office. Boy was his lodger I suppose.

Boy as I said lived during the days on sugar, yoghurts, instant coffee and toast; then every evening the man would cook up a big casserole, one big casserole filled with fish and lots of potatoes, tinned sweetcorn, something like that, and they would eat that together in the kitchen every night at seven o'clock, before the man went off to work—he worked nights you see. The other time that they used to sit down together was for a cup of tea or coffee at six in the morning, which was when the man got home, and often as not that was when Boy got home too. They'd sit in the kitchen with a pot of tea just after dawn, their very different labours finishing just as the rest of the city was going to work. Boy used to think, *I suppose we both work nights, really, it's no wonder we're as tired as each other, we've been up working all night.* Then the man would go to bed for the day, and Boy would stay up, dozing but mostly watching the television. The fact that he lived with someone who slept by day, and the fact that his own life, centred around The Bar, was more or less nocturnal, made it seem quite normal to Boy to always consider the life of the city around him from the perspective of the night. He never felt that he quite belonged to the life of the daylight hours.

This man Boy lived with went swimming every other day, kept the greying hair on his body clipped short with an electric razor, made a long phone call to a lover in another city every weekend, and kept a photograph of this lover visible in every room of the flat, even the bathroom, so that he was never out of his sight. Of course Boy had seen inside a lot of different men's houses, but this was the first man's life he had ever watched at such close quarters, the first time he had ever seen a man taking care of himself, the first time he had ever seen another man living day after day after day.

During the days, while the man slept, Boy would sleep a little himself, in a chair, in preparation for his nights at

The Bar; but mostly he would stare out of the window at the city, or stare at the television. This sounds like an idle life I know, but these long hours of staring were no more idle than Boy's long journeys around the city on foot had been aimless. Boy looked through the glass of the living room window, or at the glass of the television screen, with the same fierce attention that he had stared through the shop windows. If you had asked him, I suppose that he would not have been able to give a very convincing answer as to why he was walking, or looking, or watching in such an apparently random and obsessive fashion. He might have been tempted to say, *it's sort of a job* by which he meant, *it's something that I have to do.* The one thing he would never have said was *I'm looking for someone.*

None of the television which Boy watched for so many hours made sense in a conventional way, because he watched television as if it was one continuous programme. He watched a disgraced politician's confession on a Wednesday; on the Thursday a party broadcast made no reference to his disgrace, but was followed on the news that night by edited highlights of his arrest. In the middle of this, Boy switched to a documentary made by a group of prostitutes which showed married men sitting nervously on the edges of beds in hotel rooms, sitting on neatly flowered bedspreads and having difficulty (they were embarrassed by the female camera crew) saying exactly what it was that they wanted to do for their thirty pounds. One man just sat there in silence, looking at the camera, grinning and folding and refolding his six fivers. Then Boy cut to a black and white film in which a good man comes back from the war in uniform and finds his wife hostessing a party in black satin with orchids, and he throws out her gin-drinking friends, and she says to them, laughing but then not laughing at all, *my husband would like to be alone with me. He probably wants to hit me again.* And then Boy cut back to the man on the bed, who was saying (actually it was a different man in a different room, Boy realised; the sofa and the quilted nylon counterpane were in a different colour in this room, though the man sitting there looked just like the last one), the man was saying *I like your shoes, please take off your shoes;* and Boy cut backwards and forwards between this man and the politician beginning to lose his self-control and saying *I would just ask people to forgive me really and to forgive my wife as well.* Boy watched all of this as if he was seeing fragments of one, continuous and baffling programme.

He would sit there all day doing this, sleeping sometimes in his chair but never turning off, trying to make all these pieces of television fit together in some way. Sometimes the effort overwhelmed him and he failed and gave up. Watching the final scenes of Jean Harlow's last film, the ones shot after she had died, defeated him in this way. In these scenes an unknown actress, impersonating Harlow's voice, speaks the lines with her back to the camera or with her face hidden by a wide-brimmed hat; at the sight of this, Boy simply got up and left the living room, left the end of the film unwatched and just sat in the kitchen with a pot of tea. Why, he thought, had they been unable to abandon the film, to leave it without an ending, as a memorial to her death? Why hadn't they just put a notice up on the screen half through the scene she was shooting when she died, saying *this has to stop somewhere?* Why did the story have to be finished in such a bizarre way—Boy was suddenly overwhelmed with the thought of things never being allowed to end. The idea that one person was interchangeable with another suddenly appalled him. But he did not admit defeat to the extent of turning the television off; he simply left it on and went into another room.

The man used to say to him sometimes, when he saw him sat in front of the screen:

'I don't know how you can watch it like that. How can you concentrate?'

And Boy would say:

'I can't, that's the reason; I can't concentrate. That's a good reason to practise, isn't it?'

Sometimes, over their early morning cup of tea, Boy would tell the man about what he had watched, in the way that people often like to describe the highlights of their working day once they get back home to their partner. One morning he said (the man didn't talk much during these early morning cups of tea, he was too tired, but he was happy to listen):

'I watched a whole film through earlier, it was really good. There was this scene right at the end where the woman lights a cigarette after she's left the gas on the cooker on and everything goes up in an explosion; and then in the very next advert there was a car driving through a field, and the whole field went up in a sheet of flame. And now every time I see an advert, or just anything, I expect things to explode.'

The man didn't usually comment, but this time, after a pause, pouring himself another cup, he said:

'Oh I've seen that one. We saw it together. She's just got him out of prison after making all that money and going through all that shit for him, he finally comes home, and all he wants to do is watch the match on the telly, and all she can think of to say is (and here he mimicked a heavy filmstar accent which actually was nothing like the actress in the film at all, because the woman in the film is an ordinary, decent, hardworking woman), "Oh dahlink, I 'ave missed you so much," and then the first thing she does after waiting for him to come home for seven fucking years is to leave the fucking gas on while she's making his coffee, and then of course she's so tense that she just can't wait for a fag, she lights up, there you go; bang. Silly cunt. It's not my idea of a happy ending.

D'you want more tea? I think I might go out today after
I've had my bath.'

And Boy thought, *oh, I see, he's thinking about his lover.
He's thinking about how if his lover comes to live here, then
that's not how the story will end. That's not what he thinks
would or should happen, the day his lover finally arrives.
The day his lover finally comes home from that other city.*

Boy thought about this reaction to the film all day, but
in the end he found it unsatisfactory, both as a form of
interpretation and as a form of enjoyment. What worried
him was that the man was somehow rejecting the film,
announcing that he didn't think life was really like that.

Just to see what it would feel like, Boy tried hard to
copy this attitude during the film he watched the next
afternoon. He tried hard not to admire or approve of
the heroine, tried to imagine that life was not like that
really. He argued with her silently, pointing out that by
any normal standards she was doing all the wrong things
and was allowing her story to end badly or wrongly. When
her father was being stern with her, and she hid her face
from the camera in the pillow on the morning before her
wedding, he thought of all the arguments that he would
have used to persuade her to get up and face the situation.
When, in well-cut white satin and glycerine tears, she
sobbed, *Oh but Daddy I do love him, I do love him,*
he still tried to reason with her; but then when he saw
her hitching up the satin and running across the lawn,
throwing off the veil, scattering the astonished wedding
guests as she ran, and when he saw her jumping into
a truck, not caring that she was getting petrol stains all
over her *broderie anglaise,* jumping into a truck and not
with the man they all expected her to love, but with the
one she really loves, and then driving off with him in a
cheap pickup truck to a motel in Wisconsin, shouting out,
Goodbye Father, Goodbye Father! as she goes; well when
he saw her doing that then Boy could not bring himself

to disapprove. He said to himself, *but I do think life's like that.*

And that night of course in The Bar we were all saying, *oh god when she jumps into the truck, how fabulous was that, it just makes you want to cheer;* and Boy thought again, *well that is how life is, that is how I feel, that is how I feel when I'm leaving the bar with my husband for the night, my husband-to-be, that's just what I think when I'm getting into his car, Goodbye Father, Goodbye.* (Of course, Boy would never have used that word, *husband*, that's my word. But then, I'm old-fashioned, I mean, we used to talk like that all the time. What word do you use then?) The next day Boy thought about the film again, and while he still felt very approving of the woman in the film, Boy knew that the man he lived with would have disapproved very much of her whole attitude and the whole way her story had been told, would probably not even have stayed to watch the end of the film. All Boy could think of to explain this was that the man was older than he was, and that he actually had a husband in a sort of way, and not just for one night or a few nights, and so that had to be why he felt differently about the films he watched. Boy never thought that anything on the television was ever about anything except his own life.

Boy had dreams in which he spent all his money and most of his time shopping for and carrying home bulbs, seedpackets, leafless vines and small, bare-branched trees. In these dreams he would never use a basket for the shopping, but would cradle the roots and bulbs in his bare arms. Back home, he dreamt, he filled the whole flat with buckets of earth, even filled soup dishes and the kettle and the wineglasses with soil, and spent hours watering them and moving them carefully around every day, carrying them from room to room so that they would

*be struck in turn by whatever sunshine came in through
the different windows at different times of the day, making
sure they were kept warm. He would be deeply moved and
encouraged, in his dreams, even by the smallest and most
ordinary bud; his nostrils got raw and caked with fine dirt
as he knelt down and sniffed and sniffed to try and catch
the first smell of green life. His favourite word, the one that
he heard again and again in these dreams, was spring.*

*Did Boy ever ask himself why he didn't dream about men,
when he got home from The Bar—why he had instead these
strange dreams of shoots, bulbs and roots; roots kept in the
dark, waiting to flower, needing a gardener's attention?
After all, if you had asked him, Boy would probably have
said, for the first time in his life, yes, thank you, I am very
happy.*

WEEK FIVE

Every night when he was in The Bar, Boy wore his black shoes. He had bought them when he arrived in the city, and they were the only shoes he owned. They were good value, because they were in a style that he could wear anywhere and they were strong enough for all his walking and kept his feet from being bruised on the city pavements, for when you walk as much and as far as Boy did at that time you can hurt your feet badly. These shoes had stood him in good stead.

They had come in a good strong box, which Boy had kept.

The box was always somewhere on the floor by his bed, and was tied up with a bow, as if it was a precious parcel or a gift intended for a special person; the bow was tied from a length of scarlet nylon ribbon which Boy had seen in the dustbin outside a florist's, and had stolen, and taken home and ironed, having sensed at once that its splendid colour made it suitable for the tying up of this very special box.

In the box Boy kept a few books and a lot of letters; apart from his clothes these were about the only things he had in the flat that were his own. The letters were written on several different kinds and colours of paper, airmail paper, headed notepaper from hotels in several different cities. Each was in an envelope; the envelopes all bore Boy's name, and the addresses of the twelve different places in which Boy had briefly lived since he had arrived in the city, before he had managed to get this place where he was resident now. There were however no stamps on the envelopes and no postmarks. Some of the letters were in ballpoint, some in a big fat lazy hand in heavy black ink, only twenty-six words on the page, some typed (some well-typed, some mis-typed); but despite these differences, each letter began with the same phrase: *My Dear Boy*. The letters were all signed with different names, each in a different handwriting. Some appeared to be from famous historical figures; the signatures on these were *Oscar, John A, Edmund, Edward Morgan, James*. Others were signed with names of characters, either characters from films or works of fiction, or the kind of people that you meet in our kind of life in our kind of city, and they're so large, or so strong, or so infamous, that you say of them, *she's a real character*. These letters were signed *Carla, Bette, Yvonne, Rose-Marie*; one (on airmail paper and from an American city) was signed 'Love from all the Family', beneath which were four signatures: *Mom, Dad, Eugenia and Auntie B*. There was a set of letters tied up in a bundle with a violet silk ribbon and all written in the same ridiculous and now-faded violet ink; they were scented with old makeup (each one bore at the bottom of its last page a lipstick kiss in *Nuits de Paris*) and were on expensive and indeed pretentious notepaper as thin as an onion skin. These were all signed *Fanny*. They formed a sequence, dated from 1903 to 1927, detailing the changing fashions of that period—*my dear, we never showed our legs like that. Might have got more trade if we did I suppose.* The letters from 1915–18 were missing.

These letters were full of details of makeup, hair and gossip; advice on how to make the best of oneself when just beginning one's career.

Some of the other letters in the box (the typed ones) were much less elegant, and seemed to have come from strangers; they contained advice of a different sort, instructions about where to get sex and how much to pay for it if necessary, often these were just plain filth like *I'd like to do this to you and then I'd like to do that to you, be at the top of the park in your grey school trousers and I'll show you what a real man can do for you. I'll make you listen to the sound of your own voice saying, 'Yes, please, I want you to do it.' I'll get you on your knees. I'll get you so you won't even recognise your own body but after we've done it you'll be grateful to me that I made you do it and you'll enjoy it and you'll get better at it and one day you'll thank me for doing this to you.*

In some of the envelopes in Boy's shoebox were photographs. Some of these were old portraits that Boy had bought in a street market early on a Sunday morning, wing collars and moustaches printed in sepia; some were cut from pornographic magazines or bodybuilding magazines (in colour); some were cut from newspapers (these in black and white). On the back or across the front of these photographs were signatures duplicated from the letters; John Addington Symonds, Baron Corvo, Robbie Ross, *for Boy with kindest regards from Reggie Turner.* There had been no attempt to make these signatures credible; the words 'for my Dear and especial Boy, with affectionate regards from Mr Arthur Bloxam' appeared across a faded nineteenth-century portrait; but they also appeared scrawled lavishly across a portrait of an eighteen-year-old boxer torn from the sports pages of a recent newspaper. A reproduction of the famous 1886 Sarony portrait of Oscar Wilde in New York had *fuck you anytime, Denny* written across it. A commercially-produced greetings card, with a colour photograph of a handsome and well-muscled man blindfolded and tied to a pillar, had clumsily printed across it: *You made me love you.*

The photograph that Boy looked at most often and which he sometimes even left out of the box and kept on the floor beside his bed as he slept was one that looked like a photograph of Boy himself. It had the same dark hair, the same white skin and the same extraordinarily inviting eyes. But the face was framed by the stiff collar and strange beribboned cap that the Foot Regiment of the Scots Guards wore in 1915. The portrait had been taken against a painted canvas studio backdrop depicting a road winding across chalk hills beneath a summer sky; the stage property milestone against which the soldier had been posed, leaning, bore the inscription; *to France.* Many such photos were taken in 1915 and kept by wives, girlfriends and lovers as mementoes of the men who went to Flanders. I never did find out if this was in fact some relation of Boy's, his Grandfather perhaps, or whether the resemblance between the now-dead soldier and Boy was merely a coincidence. If it was, I don't know why he kept it or what exactly it meant to him.

The box also contained letters which were hardly letters at all; small unsigned notes on pieces of paper torn from notebooks or the backs of envelopes. These just said, *darling, I'll see you tonight,* or *Darling, it's going to be alright, really it's going to be alright, everything is going to be alright, everything is going to be alright.*

On the rare nights that he was not in The Bar Boy would lay out all these papers in a circle on the floor around his bed (he had this affectation of keeping his bed, a mattress on the floor, in the centre of his small but almost empty room). He laid them out like they were a pack of cards spread out around him for a game of patience. He'd lie on his bed at three or four in the morning just looking at them with rapt concentration, not reading them, just laying them out, changing which one was next to which one, as if determining some sequence or some relationship between the writers. He was making couples, choosing partners, arranging meetings in a café where they could all talk, all those men who never had had the chance to meet. Sometimes he would lay out in a row the seven or eight letters from the seven or eight men who he would most like to meet and talk to when he got to heaven. He knew of course that he never could meet them, but he wanted so badly to talk to them that he would get out their letters and pictures from his box of papers and talk quietly to them anyway.

Boy did not keep in this box the letters that arrived once a week at his flat, regularly, on a Tuesday morning, letters which also began 'Dear Boy' or 'My Dear Boy', but which were all signed 'Father'. Boy did not throw these letters away; he kept them all, and indeed read them not only on the day that they arrived but again and again during the week before the arrival of the next one, but he did not keep these letters in his box, and he did not reply to them either.

SIX, SEVEN AND EIGHT

The Bar was not just a place, but also a person; The Bar *was* Madame. Madame was there every night, she was The Bar and she was also the reason why so many of us went there all the time.

Madame had not always been Madame. I have seen photographs of her (looking it must be admitted not much younger than she did at the time in which this story is set), across which she has signed herself 'Mademoiselle', and sometimes 'Miss'. In the days when it was briefly fashionable to be seen around with black people she had also been known as 'Missy', and she'd had a black lover then. And, since you asked, she once went for a policeman with her stilettoes as he tried to bundle a black man into a car outside a dance hall on the bottom of the Tottenham Court Road (derogatory remarks in that department were still more likely to earn a black eye than a black look in The Bar). That was after the war; during the war itself she had been known as just *M*, wherever she went. I think she must have seen a lot of things at that time which had made her the way she was, seen things in the blackout and in the underground stations. You still hear about it; the women fighting like cats to stay together, the couples making love in the park and up against walls; the uniform boys in the arms of the Soho queens, the Americans in Piccadilly. And she'd come out of all that and she'd opened her bar, at a time when there were hardly any. She had her reasons, is what I'm saying.

It was in memory of those days that she had given The Bar its first and now largely forgotten name, *Babylon*. And then after that it was *The Mandrake Studios* (I know the man who's still got the nameplate, a brass nameplate it was, very discreet, like a private doctor's). The very first film that ever had a room full of homosexuals and no one else, that was the name of the place where that scene took place, you see. And that was the film with the scene of the boy coming into the bar that I said I thought of when I saw Boy coming in sometimes.

Once or twice I have heard her begin to tell the story of those days to some young man, but then halfway through a sentence she would go white with anger, knock back her gin and go silent. *Don't talk to me about what it was like in those days*, she would say. *The truth is*, she would say, *I'm still looking forward to life beginning*.

After all that, she'd been just 'Madam' for a while, which might have indicated that she was getting older or grander, except that she always looked just the same, never any older. *That Madam*, Gary used to say, *she's been forty for as long as we've known her*. And she clearly intended to stay that way.

And then at a certain point she felt, and we felt, that Madam wasn't quite enough; and so just now, anyway, she was known as *Madame*, and no one in The Bar ever addressed her as anything else.

Madame was our constant; against the fact that she never changed her style or her outfit (it was always the same dress, every night) you could measure the changes in all the other faces and bodies that you spent the night scrutinising—faces subtly altered by a recent bitterness or passion, a body sagging under the pressure of losing a partner or made alert by the proximity of a new or potential one. In the centre of all these changes, supervising them and sitting straightbacked above them on her high stool, was always Madame, the central figure in the composition of whatever new tableaux we rearranged ourself into. Madame, with Madame's Waterford crystal tumbler always placed just at the same place on the bar; Madame, in position, on guard, ruling the night. Do you know what that meant, and means, to have someone who was there every night like that? Sometimes I wonder that she didn't collapse under the sheer weight of how much we needed her, of how unreasonably we all admired and needed her.

When she had opened The Bar, Madame had kept up the costume in which she'd worked when she was just an entertainer in other people's places—she'd worked in them all. It was this outfit which made her age so hard to determine. The dress (*the* dress, because as I said she wore it every night) was full length. It left her back and her strong arms bare (she powdered her arms white) and it was close-fitting everywhere, showing off her large hips and her large breasts. It was white, very classic, with lots of silver in the brocade and lots of sequins and real crystal beading. The effect was very Palladium, very 1957, I used to think. But I've seen pictures of Holiday in a beaded sheath just like that, taken well before the war, and publicity shots of some of those French singers or chanteuses coming down staircases in just the same sort of thing even earlier in the century. Crystal beading, brilliants, feathers—or plumes, really—that was the look: Madame often wore feathers in one way or another, a marabou-trimmed cape, or a fan, a real osprey if she was feeling very upmarket. One hundred and fifty years of glamour sitting on a stool right before your very eyes, that's what she was. And the face didn't date, either. Madame's hair was dead black, scraped back like a dancer's in the daytime and at night done up in coils with big silver pins. Every night she greased her face, whited everything out and redrew it just as she had always done; a heavy coat of pale powder, black mascara, black eyeliner, heavily pencilled black eyebrows, and then, finally, her famous scarlet lips, always perfect, always done in the same shade, *Rouge Extrême.* It never changed.

Once I heard a very stupid queen say, *How old are you, Madame?* (god that one must have been out of it).

Madame replied:

I am old enough to know better.

Madame drank water all day, and gin all night, always in that same Waterford crystal tumbler. I never once saw her drunk and think it may have been water in the evenings too, half the time. She always had a cigarette in her right hand, and her right hand was covered in rings.

I must say again that it is very odd for me to have to describe all this for you. I mean, everyone knew Madame. Her dress, her rings and indeed her whole style were common knowledge. The Bar was, as far as we were concerned, the only place to go. So everybody went there, all the time. And it's so odd, it's hard now when somebody says, 'What was it like?' or says, 'What did she use to wear?' because of course we all saw her all the time and thought nothing of it, saw her at the very least once a week (*missing service*, it was called, if you went a week without visiting, and it was certain to be discussed amongst the congregation when you did finally show up), it's just very odd for me to think that you were never there and that this is all strange to you when to us it was just an ordinary life. It was daily life. You were never there, you never knew her, you never saw her, you know nothing of our lives then, nothing, nothing, nothing, it's extraordinary to me that.

Anyway, since you ask, the rings were black and there were ten of them, all on her right hand. They were mourning rings, real eighteenth century. Little black cameos of urns and weeping women all mounted in real old gold. She had names for them all, and would count them off sometimes like a rosary. Sometimes it would be *Bessie, Billie*, names we'd all heard before and knew about; her favourite fistful, the one she would recite just before she got up on stage, was *Mae, Marie, Maria, Anna Mae B, La Miss, Marian* . . . I forget the other four now. *Marian* I know was Marian Anderson, the black singer, she sang on the steps of the Lincoln Memorial on Easter Sunday morning in 1939, it was freezing, they'd locked her out of the concert hall she had booked. But even when they were famous names like those, Madame used to recite or whisper them like they were the names of lovers or at least the dear departed, girlfriends, people she had actually met.

On the other hand, the left, was the diamond. This was very big and very real. Madame believed in money.

The outfit may have been grand, but it never stopped her from working. I've seen her behind the bar in that dress, many nights. And she'd go on the demonstrations in it too, I've seen her at a rally in a park dragging that beaded hem through the mud. She had put an old cardigan over the top, and she'd rolled up the sleeves and she was shaking that bucket. When Madame shook the bucket you turned out your pockets even if it meant walking home. I've seen her angry in that dress many times, but never as angry as when some man said to her, *I don't see why we have to keep on giving money like this.* I've seen her in that dress with the whole of the bar top covered in loose change, laboriously counting the coins, bagging the

silver and copper coins separately. We blunted our fingers
counting coins in those days.

And I've seen her, done up and looking her very
grandest, reach into a small-feathered evening bag, take
out an antique cigarette case with an M in brilliants on it
and offer a surprised young queen a condom. *Something
for the weekend, sir*, she said, stopping him just as he was
about to leave with another young man—you see she'd
noticed that they hadn't talked before going off together,
they'd just started kissing and were going to drag each
other home without discussing anything, and they were
young, really young, eighteen. Madame's was one of the
very first places to have condoms for free. *I can't keep on
fishing in this bag*, she said, and then she had a holy water
stoup put up by the door, and filled it with them, you just
took some on the way out.

And of course I've seen her blazing in that dress of hers
when she kicked off against someone. Madame kicking
off? Well, for instance; one night Stella went crazy and
assaulted a visitor who had called Stella II a skinny black
bitch right in the middle of her rendition of 'Te Amo', and
he meant it, right there in the middle of his number—well
Madame not only showed her approval of the assault by
conspicuously buying Stella drinks every night for the
whole of the following week; as soon as she saw the
fight starting she got off her stool, yanked out the plug
on the sound system, hitched up that frock, got straight
up on the stage while they were still on the floor (she
knew Stella would sort him out) and she went into an
unforgettable aria of abuse against this stranger which
culminated in her eschewing all her usual magnificence
of phrasing and just standing there shouting *fuck off* at
him, screaming *fuck off, if you don't like it you can fuck
off, E,X,I,T, there it is, you came in through it and now
you can fuck off out of it, fuck off out of it why don't
you you stupid bastard* (and by now of course someone

had dragged Stella off and we were all up on our chairs cheering while the disgraced stranger made his slow and humiliating exit through the parting crowd) *why don't you just piss off and insult someone who doesn't have the balls to answer back because you've picked the wrong girls here darling, fuck off that's it, fucking fuck off, fucking fuck off right through my front door and don't you ever, don't you ever, don't you ever step on my fucking frock again.* God she was heaven when she went off like that. No one goes off like that any more. The whole bar was up on its feet to watch even before she had finished laying down the opening phrases; by the time she was into the full fury of the aria, with its demanding coloratura decorations, its elaborate breathing technique and its famous placing of the pauses, we were all applauding and whistling. For the closing phrases, by which time she'd completely lost it and was just plain screaming, we all fell silent, because it was awesome; and then when she had finished the victim of her fury slowly exited right on cue in complete silence, complete silence except for Madame's heavy breathing and the sound of Gary playing recitative on the piano, for he had been playing along under her rage all the time, as if to support it, as if this really was music to our ears. And then Madame stood there in her dress and took the applause and cheers just like she'd done 'Casta Diva' or something,

Once on holiday I saw a supposedly miraculous statue of the Madonna brought back to her resting place after making her annual tour of the capital city. The Virgin wasn't in silver and beads, but gold, with real diamonds; and I say Madame, in her dress, was just as splendid.

At the end of a special evening, or rather at its high point, you would hear Gary playing a certain intro, and you'd hear the whole bar going quiet as people recognised it.

That quietness was typical of us; we had a very strong sense of etiquette you see. This intro on the piano was in its way a very formal announcement, and people would hear it over or under whatever other music was on, and the bar staff would turn the tapes down and then off, without anyone having to say anything, they would just do it. And everyone knew that now it was time for Madame's famous song.

Over the intro Gary would always give his little speech, very quietly—almost to himself. We had after all all heard it before, it wasn't as if this number actually needed any introduction. *Ladies and gentlemen,* he would say, *Ladies and gentlemen, now it gives me very great pleasure to introduce the woman who is responsible for holding this whole show together; the woman who first understood all those years ago that there was crying need for a place where all you lovely people could gather of an evening, the one that we all know and love, and so . . . would you please welcome on stage, the very lovely, the very talented . . . once again . . . our very own . . .* and sometimes he would fade out, and not even say her name, and he would pause, he would make us wait, he would suspend his elegant hands over the keys; and then, in that silence, he would play the first notes of the actual song itself. And to the sound of those notes, to the sound of the first simple phrase of that famous melody, Madame would lift the hem of her beaded silver and white dress and she would place her silver-shoed foot on the first of the six steps to the stage.

Word would have gone out that she was going to do it again tonight. People would even bring flowers, but she never accepted a single bouquet, not one. She said, *keep them for my grave.*

Because of the way she did it, they said of Madame, 'That woman knows what she's singing about,' and this expression became a common one. If someone was making a confession about an unfaithful lover, and was on the edge of tears, people would often say, *listen, darling, this woman knows what she is singing about.*

She couldn't actually sing I suppose, but when she sang, she meant every word. She would as often as not weep during the song, and these were not glycerine tears, and they were not, except in the later years, produced to order. Her performances were legendary, and I am at a loss to describe them now. You'd be better off spending time seeking out the great women of your own day, young man; turn off that radio. Or at least make sure you are listening to the right station. Or talk to anyone who saw her on one of the nights when she was worth seeing, and ask them what it was like. I can't do it properly. Ask someone else to justify how much it meant to us. How much it meant to us when she brought her Waterford tumbler up onto the stage with her, settled her feathers and her sequins and then looked calmly round until there was complete silence. And then she would look to Gary for him to begin the piano again, and she would look us straight in the eye for as long as possible, and she would sing:

> *All of me,*
> *Why not take all of me,*
> *Can't you see—*

and even this early in the song, I have often heard Madame falter and stop, and just open her arms towards us, palms outwards, in a simple refusal to sing, just letting Gary carry the phrase on the piano—and of course we all knew the words anyway and so could hear them even when she wasn't singing, sometimes you'd hear the whole crowd singing almost inaudibly along with her. And indeed I can still remember that strange whispered singing, all those men singing, I can remember it, and I can remember every single one of those words even now,

and I've often quoted them to myself when I've needed to.
I have walked down the street crying and said those words
out loud:

All of me,
Why not take all of me.

I've often wanted to say that to a man, *go on, take all of me,*
why not? And I've wanted to say that to someone who's
just staring at me, just go up to them and say, *all of me,*
the whole fucking thing, take it.

Why not?

There were six steps up to the tiny stage, Gary would
be playing the intro, and with each of the steps Madame would say a woman's name, fingering one of the
rings. She would dedicate her song to them all. Here
again, she knew what she was talking about. Madame's
room above The Bar had a large glass-fronted bookcase,
and also a high bookshelf running right round the
red-lacquered ceiling, and they were both stacked with
biographies and autobiographies of financially successful
women; courtesans, couturiers, financiers, novelists, ac-
robats, madams, actresses, mistresses, singers and wives.
Madame had once heard one of her customers castigating
another for spending all his money on a faithless younger
lover: *you're such a Camille,* he said. Madame interrupted
with a seven-minute lecture summarising the economics
of the real Marguerite Gautier's career, explaining exactly
how and why she had made her way through the Paris of
the 1840s with such skill and courage . . . Madame could
not help but admire any woman who had gained access
to enough money, either early or late in her career, to
be able to laugh and to leave people. Her studies were

remarkable; as a young woman Madame had filled
eighteen notebooks with summaries of these women's
careers, reading them very literally as sources of practical
advice, in much the same way as she had taught herself
to understand stock management and how to do her own
accounts. Her favourite line was Bernhardt's, and this she
copied into the front of each of the eighteen notebooks, at
least the five of them that I still have; *Oh well, I'll just buy
the theatre.*

She didn't just pin them up on her walls, these women,
she studied them.

And she carried them all up on stage with her when she
climbed those six steps to sing her song. (Of course we
understood none of this really, we just thought she was
fabulous; when she left us, simply left us, taking only the
jewels, we were terrified and had no idea of how to keep
things going. We had not watched closely enough; we had
simply paid our money over the bar and hoped—without
knowing it—that Madame would always be there to open
the doors and close them behind us. We thought that our
evenings in The Bar could simply be bought. Of course we
tried to keep things going—after all, we knew, vaguely,
how much we needed that place, needed our evenings
there together, but after seven months of enthusiasm and
mismanagement The Bar closed. The place which now
bears its name is in quite another part of town and is
run by men who didn't even know Madame. Men with
more sense than we ever had. I suppose that means that
we are learning.)

Those were the nights, with Madame singing her song.
And Boy listening.

NINE

At Madame's right hand, on the stool next to her, hardly ever talking to her but always right there beside her, was the man that we all called O. I deliberately haven't told you about him yet. You'll see.

O was only one of the many names that we had given him, but it was the one that had lasted. His actual name, as it happens, was Hart (like the poet), Hart Price. Because he sat most nights on his own and looking very much removed from the whole crowd, very dark-browed and quiet, we speculated endlessly on his story. When he first appeared he was known briefly as The Broken, referring to his christian name, and to the way he looked so grave, even grief-stricken sometimes in an odd way. And then, because we admired his beauty so much, someone would often say of him, as we were sizing up and judging the night's array of talent, one of us would quietly say, The Price Is Right. But this didn't stick, and because his style was as I have said to always sit and wait, and never to make the first move, we began to call him The Older Man; and then this became just *Older*, and finally just *O*.

You never thought of O as someone who was with people or who went home with people, and he never seemed to be looking round for someone all the time, which is how most of us must have appeared. However, O was no celibate; several of us had slept with him. But his style was always to seem self-contained. He may have left The Bar accompanied, but you never saw him following anyone, gazing after someone or persuading them to come home with him. Asked exactly how O took people home, you'd have to say that O just summoned his men to him somehow.

They said that O had been an alcoholic. Nowadays he just smoked all night (the same brand as Madame) and kept a glass of iced water constantly beside him—Little David would keep it fresh and cold without being asked. I always thought that was extraordinary; a man like him sitting apparently alone all night with that one never-empty, unintoxicating, frosted glass, as if it was the sign of some great abstinence or purity. It was all the more striking because O had such a body; he was magnificent. Forty-five at least, with grey in his black hair, and magnificent. He always wore a plain white shirt with the sleeves rolled back off his splendid forearms, and he had eyes dark enough to look truly black in the lighting of The Bar. With those looks and that air about him I sometimes thought that he was a Prince really.

We all assumed that O was a man with a past. If someone asked you, *who is that man?* you said, *oh, she was wounded in the war, you know.*

A major part of the mystery was that as I have said O sat on Madame's right hand all night every night; and he never left without kissing her goodnight, formally, on the cheek. If he was taking a man home he would keep him waiting while he did this. Because of this ritual we wondered if Madame was privy to his secret, if she knew the story, if she sat by him because she knew that O's great self-possession and his quietness were in fact the signs of a pain which had to be kept hidden, a pain which stayed fresh and so had to be controlled every hour of the night.

Pursuing this theory, we attributed to him some great and unhappy love, and then surmised that he had only ever confessed it to Madame, perhaps in the days of his terrible drunkenness. We placed in that magnificent chest a magnificently broken heart; we imagined that without Madame's support and proximity he would break down, order whisky all night, then howl out some great and vivid grief before collapsing on the floor of the Bar before our very eyes. However this convenient explanation of his style bore no relation to what we did know about O's past life with other men. For all his silence, he was passionate, not desolate; if there was a sadness or loss there, it was bigger or deeper or stranger than the loss of one person.

And if Madame stayed close to him, it can hardly have been because she thought he needed looking after.

Talking about him with the others, I did find out that several other people had had the same experience with him as me; that his lovemaking was done in silence, that he never said a word (in fact with me he hardly looked me in the eye either, just stared at his own hands as he moved them over my body, not stroking so much as seizing and kneading me, holding me down too); but then later in the night you would wake to hear him talking to himself, lying there fast asleep (O always asked the men he fucked to stay with him all night long, always), fast asleep and talking out loud in the night, talking in a fast, furious, hushed, hollow voice.

O's whole way of making love was strange; he worked on your body until you couldn't stand it, but it was impersonal somehow, as if he was digging inside you to find someone else, something else, something he'd lost or wanted but couldn't find words to ask you for. (This was very strange for me and I found it hard to talk about. We didn't use to talk about him like we did the others.) When he got you home he would strip at once, taking everything off right there and laying his clothes down on the hall floorway as if he had to be naked at once, methodically removing every item. No, not every item; he kept on his locket. A gold locket in which two small photographs lay face to face. One photograph was of a very beautiful man. As I lay on O's chest something moved me to snap the locket open, and I remember I asked, *who is that?* thinking maybe this was the solution to the mystery, and he said, in the same voice that he talked with later in the night, a sleepwalker's voice, without taking his eyes off the ceiling he said, *I don't know; I just found it in a magazine. I think he is the most beautiful man I've ever see. I'd give it all up, for him.* The other picture was of an unrecognisable small boy, holding a cat up to the camera, wearing shorts and standing in front of a privet hedge on the edge of a lawn. *And who's this one then?* I said, and O said, *that's me. That's me before I was who I am now.*

I can't remember if the picture of the man from the magazine looked anything like Boy.

One more story about O: he told me (it was as if he was trying to explain the oddity of his lovemaking to me, as if he was trying to account for or apologise for the way he'd treated me, or perhaps to reassure me concerning the effect he'd had on me, I don't know), in the morning he told me that there was one man, this had been just a couple of years previously, there was one man who had summoned him to his bedside to be counted amongst a farewell gathering of lovers, dear friends and great passions. When O had arrived the dying man had ostentatiously sent all the others from the room, leaving just O and the flowers. He had called O to the side of the bed, taken hold of his hand and then quietly said to him: *please take your clothes off. I wish very much to look at you one last time. You were the most perfect, the most beautiful, the best I ever had.* And O said to me, *the thing*

was. I couldn't remember. I didn't even know he still had
my address, it all happened years before, we barely even
had an affair. We never talked. I know we were drunk
together, but we were never close, never intimate.

Never intimate; that was O.

And what I wanted to know was, why had O and Boy
never been seen to look at each other? After all, they were
our two greatest beauties, surely they deserved each other.

TEN

Every night that Madame stepped up onto the stage in her dress, Boy would be watching her; he always stayed for that. And of course O would be watching her too.

Madame had this way of pausing between every single word sometimes. The phrasing got so slow and emphatic that you knew that she wanted you to listen to and weigh up every single word; but you couldn't tell if each word was freighted with anger, or bitterness, or joy; it just came out with great, quiet force, and you had to work out its tone for yourself. This slowness gave Madame plenty of time to address phrases or just lines to individual people. And now, often, it would be Boy. Madame would see Boy there, she'd look at him and she'd give a whole line straight to him (*Can't you see . . . I'm no good without you*). And then Mother would look from Boy to the other man who was also there every night and never took his eyes off her when she sang, O, and she'd sing the next lines to him, *take these lips, take these arms . . . can't you see?*

When I saw this happening I began to watch more closely, and I saw that some nights even when she wasn't up on the stage Madame had her eye on these two and would often look from one to the other and then back again. She was of course famous for her powers of observation; she was better than any of us at using the mirrors which she had had installed everywhere to keep an eye on everything that was happening, or was about to happen and might need averting. Even when she was talking to you or giving you your change, you could feel her smile going somewhere over your shoulder as she took in the whole room behind you. She always knew exactly who was in and who was missing; and if you were missing, Madame probably knew why, and with whom. All night long she made mental notes of all the transactions being made, the profits, the losses, meetings, separations, the wanting, having, getting, seeing, the excess, the moderation, the negotiations; all those men trying to work out what they wanted, what they could afford, what they needed. *God*, thought Madame, when she added up the night's takings, *one week I should write down who's having who as well as who's drinking what. There would be two columns in the ledger: Tonight's Takings, and Tonight's Givings.* Sitting up straight-backed on her stool, she could flatter two men at once and still be watching a third in a mirror; she could keep tabs on the whole shifting choreography at once. She could confess, absolve and advise two erring lovers in the same weekend without either of them knowing that the other had collaborated with her in engineering their reunion. And now she seemed to be planning a new use for those skills as I watched her gaze, fixed on Boy, or shifting from O to Boy. The way she looked at them was odd, because there was no story here as yet, no drama whose next development or twist of plot or big scene we were all awaiting; remember, they had not yet met or even looked at each other. I don't think anyone but me was taking notes at this stage of the proceedings.

*

Of course Madame keeping an eye on O was nothing new. She always had half an eye for him; sometimes I thought she watched him as a tamer does a tiger. Madame had you see known him in his alcoholic days, when indeed such calm must often have been the prelude to him lurching into an argument, or falling heavily from his stool. In those days Madame would never stop him from drinking, would never put her hand out over his glass like a good or responsible woman is supposed to in such scenes; Madame would give him the whole bottle, and say, quietly and sincerely, *I hope you know what you're doing*. But now there was something new about the way she watched him. If you had not known who O was you might have thought that Madame was planning a seduction, or wondering whether he was a suitable candidate for a job—her new barman or doorman.

And now it wasn't just him she was watching. She was watching two men.

She was singing her chosen song. She was matchmaking. She was eyeing up a potential couple. She was smiling and making money and catching people out of the corner of her eye. That woman was thinking all of the time. Do you know what I mean?

She had clearly decided, without ever speaking to him, that Boy (she concurred in the popular choice of name) was an asset to her establishment. She knew nothing about him (none of us did), though of course she could see both how he looked and how we all looked at him. And she knew that he had been to The Bar over thirty times in seven weeks now. She did not know his real name, and did not ask either Madge or Mr Mortimer, both of whom had already taken him home, what it was. Madame didn't need to know; she trusted profoundly in appearances. Madame wondered how long it would be before Boy got his hair cropped short so that he looked just like the others. And on several nights Madame, looking from O to Boy and from Boy to O, noticed, as several of us had, their remarkable similarity of colouring. Their bodies were very different, although Boy's showed promise, and could indeed have been a version of, a study for, O's magnificent musculature, twenty years earlier. But their colouring was identical; white skin, black hair, eyes dark enough to look black beneath our artificial stars. They made, as Madame was later to remark to Gary, a handsome couple.

I told Gary he should have said, 'And they must make you so proud; everyone can see where they got their looks, Mother.'

I have said that when Boy first entered The Bar he was exhausted; exhausted, walked off his feet. And there was still an extraordinary shadow of tiredness on his face, as if his eyes were ready to bruise with exhaustion, he often looked like that. But under the tiredness he was forcing himself to stay awake, stay alert; his eyes were alive with hunger when he looked up into your face. He was always looking for the beginning of something, and he had the energy of someone starting their career. When I looked from his face to O's (my eyes often followed Madame's) I saw an older face, one I thought had been weathered by sex and by that indefinable sorrow of O's into a quiet, strong silence. I suppose both of them were silent; but I thought that O looked as though something was almost over, as if he was ending somehow. That's it. Boy was beginning, for all his exhaustion; and O, for all his strength, was close to ending. One ending and one beginning. I think it's like that with a lot of couples.

*

I was there the night that Madame made the first move
in what I now see was a careful campaign to prepare
Boy for this romance or meeting. She had sung her song
that night. There was an edge of anger in the song, as if
she didn't see why we hadn't understood it yet. Boy was
listening of course.

She waited until he went to pass her to reach the
door and leave at the end of the night. Boy was a bit
shamefaced, a bit embarrassed, because that night he
was going home alone, having tried very hard but not
succeeded. Perhaps Madame had waited for just such a
night. She stopped him by resting a hand on his arm, and
spoke to him—it was the first time.

'I hate to see you going home empty handed,' said
Madame, and she gave him a package tied like a cake
in neatly folded greaseproof paper.

'Goodnight,' she said

'Goodnight,'—Boy was not sure if he was yet allowed
to address her by her name, didn't know if he yet had that
right.

The first thing in the package was her letter:

> *My Dear Boy,*
> *I don't do this for everyone. You will probably realise*
> *that these books are precious; they are also, some*
> *of them, worth a considerable amount of money. If,*
> *in addition to the few notes which I have taken*
> *the liberty of enclosing, you feel that you need any*
> *advice, then please ask for it. I would however prefer*
> *that you got as much advice as possible from the*
> *books first. When you've finished these (you may*
> *want to read some of them twice), I'll give you*
> *more.*
>
> *Also, all your drinks at The Bar will in future*
> *be free. You are an asset to my establishment.*

If you wish to discuss any of the above in private,
please feel free to call me—after one, which is when
I rise, and before four, which is when I begin work.
Yours, M.

This letter of Madame's isn't entirely accurate . . . True,
she went to bed late, and was often at her desk until
four a.m., and so might have been expected to rise
well after midday, and luxuriate over breakfast before
beginning her day's work at one in the afternoon. But
in fact Madame was often back at her desk at ten a.m.,
having already spent an hour tending her body, her face
and her hair.

Beneath the letter was a xeroxed newspaper article
listing all the bars in the city. Some of these simply
had written across them, NO. Boy assumed that it was
up to him to find out if these bars were closed, were
unfashionable, were dangerous or were simply too expensive for him to visit . . . Beneath that was a leaflet
with the number of the switchboard (837 7324) and
then eight pamphlets dealing with sexual hygiene, four
of them coming from America, ones which Madame had
got hold of before anyone else. Fuck knows Madame was
a tower of strength at that time. Madame, you see, never
assumed either ignorance or experience.

Below the leaflets was a list. This I have kept, with the
letter, and I still have it:

1) *Accept all the advice you can get, courteously. After*
   all, they've been doing this longer than you have.
2) *REMEMBER, YOU HAVE LEFT HOME NOW.*
3) *Never make love badly.*
4) *Remember who you were this time last year.*
5) *Protect your body.*
6) *'Money is everything, right?'*

7) *The moment after he's come, just after, that's when you really see his face how it is. Whip out your instamatic and take his picture and keep that in your wallet.*

8) *Mother speaking of a great gown: 'If you can't afford it, steal it; if you can't steal it, copy it; if you can't copy it, buy a postcard of it and dream about it; if you can't afford the postcard then get your fucking act together.'*

9) *Mother says: If someone does something, it is probably because she wants to.*

10) *Mother says: People only lose because they're not strong enough, not because they don't want to fight or aren't good at fighting.*

(This, incidentally, was the first time that Boy had heard Madame refer to herself as Mother.)

The rest of the parcel was books.

The first book was a novel about nurses in the Second World War, a pair of lovers in a training hospital—Boy assumed that Madame had lived though this.

The second was a paperback, a romance set in Ancient Greece. Although it was full of period details—greaves, chitons, how to anoint your lover with olive oil after wrestling—it was also clearly a thinly-disguised account of life in this country in the year of its publication, 1948.

The third was a lengthy and dully-written biography of a late nineteenth-century general. Boy looked at the pictures of the moustached and uniformed characters with some relish; but he couldn't finish the text, and so missed the single paragraph that Mother had circled in black ink. She wanted Boy to know that for all the book's nine hundred and forty-eight pages the author had seen fit to devote only one ambiguous and insignificant paragraph to the fact that this great man had lived forty-one years of his public life accompanied everywhere by a handsome and dedicated working-class servant.

The fourth book featured a scene in which a man planned to write a letter to his Father and Mother telling them of his new-found happiness, but he never could bring himself to write the letter. Boy remembered this scene.

The fifth was a biography of a famous writer, which Boy read twice with great fascination. At the age of sixteen, this writer had slept with an older, married friend of her Father; she had arranged to meet him in a churchyard after dinner and they made love on a tombstone. At seventeen she bore his daughter, but it died. Eleven months later she bore his son. Four months later she left the country and travelled constantly, following her lover wherever he wanted to go. Four months later her sister committed suicide. Two months later her lover's wife committed suicide, and two days after that she married him. To please him, she travelled, learnt languages, read all the guide books to the cities he insisted they visit, became a sexual virtuoso, developed opinions on the classics and on contemporary literature, and learnt never to voice them at the dinner table unless asked. She then wrote a best-selling novel, which is full of dead children and pointless travels; its subject is the education of an unkillable, stubborn, ignorant and horribly-deformed woman. She was still only nineteen when this novel was published. By the age of twenty-four she had published her second novel, given birth to and buried a second daughter, buried her first son, given birth to a second, and received a letter describing the death by drowning and the cremation of her husband. The cremation in particular was described in great detail. There was no proper funeral, as there had been no proper wedding ceremony; they simply hauled the waterlogged body onto a bonfire of driftwood, and even though the sea wind at dawn had made the fire hot enough to break the stones of the beach, it was six hours before the body was gone, and then they had to wait a whole day before they could rake the ashes for his bones and send them to her. She returned to England on the death of her Father; she did not attend the funeral (in a picturesque little English church), but did become his literary editor and published the first and most authoritative biography. She wrote eighteen more novels, none of them distinguished or now read, enabling her to live alone in relative comfort for sixty years and to give her only son the best upper-class education that her country could provide at that time.

As I've said Boy read this narrative twice, but still he could not understand why Madame wished him to study it. He did not know who he was supposed to be—the child-wife, the monstrous heroine, the burner of men's bodies, the woman of independent means, the beloved and expensive son?

The sixth book forced Boy to think again about this problem of not knowing who in a story to be. It was as if Madame had deliberately placed this story underneath the story of the authoress's life. It was completely fantastic, yet had a simple, conventional plot about love and marriage running through it; her story contained every deviation from the conventional storyline of marriage possible yet was, in every detail, true, and so in that sense not fantastic at all. This sixth book was entitled *Lady into Fox*. The lady in the story (as plainly told as it is titled) inexplicably turns, halfway through an ordinary afternoon, into a bright-eyed vixen; and the man in the story, equally inexplicably, Boy thought, remains faithful to her and loves her dearly even when she leaves him in order to raise a family with another animal and he even, in the end, goes mad with love for her.

The fourth book had, as I said, impressed Boy with its famous scene of the unwritten letter, which he thought must relate in some way to his own collection of letters. In the seventh book he found a letter which he in fact copied out and added to that collection. He was delighted that it was already, even before he did this, addressed to him. It began:

> *My Dear Boy, my greatest fear is not that I shall never again touch you, but that when I return I shall no longer be able to hear your voice. The most casual obscenities, the most hackneyed endearments, coming to me from your rose-red lips, are worth more than the sagest advice of all the old men in the world.*
> *I fear, my dear, that I'm going deaf . .*

Boy loved this letter not only because the man it had been sent to shared his new name, but because it was addressed by an older man to a lovelier, younger one.

Madame's letter, and her books, were put into Boy's shoebox to join his collection of letters and photographs. In fact he couldn't get them all in, and he acquired a second box, a small tea chest he found, with metal corners. When he'd stored his new acquisitions in it there was still lots of room left for more books and papers. This excited Boy; he thought, *I am acquiring a library. I must have a future.*

When Madame had given him her advice, she didn't interfere. In fact they never discussed what she had given him; Boy sensed that this was a private matter, something to think about but not talk about.

She left him alone to get on with it and fuck around.

*

If only Boy had known, there was lots more where that
came from; there was lots of advice which Madame might
have given him, but didn't. When she was in her room,
when The Bar was closed, she had a recurring fantasy in
which Boy's black hair was long enough to reach down to
his waist. She would imagine calling him up to her room
every night before he went home to bed with a man, and
taking her silver hairbrush from her desk and brushing
his hair out like a daughter's, one hundred strokes every
night. Madame imagined that while she was doing this to
Boy she would tell him everything she knew, she would
talk to him quietly each night whilst brushing his hair
before bedtime. She would tell him where to place the
pillow under your back, how to put on a condom for
someone else, how to dry tears quickly, how not to be
afraid, how to go down, how to let go of someone because
it's not the end of the world. How money is the most
important thing. What to take with you when he leaves
you.

She wanted to rehearse all her wisdom out loud to
someone so that she could find out if she still believed
it herself.

ELEVEN

We knew that something was about to happen. We knew that something was going on, because it was in this week that Madame changed her name.

She had in fact been referred to privately as 'The Mother of Us All' for some time. But now she announced that she wished this title to be publicly used. She made the announcement, of course, from the stage.

'The recent change from Madam to Madame,' she said, 'though it has doubtless raised the tone and general tenor of proceedings in this low and benighted place, has not quite succeeded in erasing the traces of squalor and indeed sleaze which cling to that title in the popular or gutter imagination whenever it is applied to a hard-working woman. We are, after all, no longer in the Dark Ages. I am not, after all,' she said, looking around her domain with a distinct smile, 'running a house of ill repute, which is what I fear the present title of Madame seems to suggest, along with bead curtains, red velvet plush love seats, champagne buckets and other such fittings and accoutrements which are not our style at all these days. I should hate anyone to think that I am,' she said, looking around her at us all and smiling again, 'that I am in the business of catering exclusively for prostitutes, tarts, working girls, slags, bitches, cunts, whores, studs, pimps, rent boys, butches, nellies, queens, masseurs, escorts, one-night stands, ex-models, ex-policemen, ex-Armed Forces, ex-boxers, security guards, tennis instructors, so-called businessmen, tourists and those poor unfortunates who simply come here to pass the time and meanwhile do some shopping; oh, no, let it never be said! Bearing this in mind, the title of Madame will no longer do. It is too redolent of rooms upstairs and days gone by. I have decided that as from tonight I will be reborn under a different star,' and here she gestured upwards to the constellation over her head, 'I will be rechristened, I will come down those stairs tomorrow night fresh to the world and glistening with a new name; from now on, you will kindly refer to me, both to my sainted face and behind my back, as Mother. Thank you, and Goodnight.'

And so from then on, when you left the Bar, it was 'Goodnight, Mother', 'Goodnight, Mother', from all the Boys.

THE LAST WEEK

In the final days before they met, Mother's face began to harden when she sat and watched Boy and O, as if she was trying to push them together by sheer force of will power. Mother, she who had seen so much, wanted one last triumph; one final casting coup. When she spent all night every night watching her clientele, her boys, it was for this; she was waiting for her chosen ones, the last of her protegés, her perfect couple, her two to see her through the dark times. *This time*, she said under her breath, *I want to see them fucking perfect.* She added another scene to her fantasy of brushing out Boy's long black hair. Now she had both men in her room upstairs; she had them standing naked before her. Taking in every inch of their bodies, she said, looking from one to the other, she said, in her famously well-timed drawl, *That's just how I want you. You two are so* (pause) *fucking* (pause) *perfect* (drag on the cigarette). This fantasy was so vivid to her that she would even rehearse this line out loud, looking at herself in her mirror as she smoked the last cigarette of the night, after she'd taken her face off, after all the noise was over and we'd all gone home.

Maybe she felt that if she couldn't do it now, she would never do it; maybe that was why her face hardened as she watched them, still apart, and imagined them, together.

And indeed she left it to the very last possible moment; she almost missed her chance.

Let me describe how it was, exactly.

The fact is, as he later told Boy, O almost quit The Bar that week. He almost gave up on us. It was on the Thursday, the very night before he met Boy. It didn't show, of course; he showed very little, was always still and dark-eyed and dark-browed. The way he explained it to Boy, it was one of those moments of giving up, one of those moments when you throw away your still half-full packet of cigarettes as you walk home in the drizzle and you say out loud, *well that is it, that is the last time*. Or like the time when you say, right out loud, *that's it, I could have been at home sleeping*.

All that we saw on that Thursday night was O going home on his own once more; though if we had watched closely we would have seen that he simply left his stool and did not say *Goodnight, Mother*. And we would have seen how her eyes followed him to the door.

But we didn't see any of that; we didn't notice that, as O later put it, his eyes weren't just dark that night but almost blinded, blinded with grief. He did not know why he suddenly felt this way; he was not angry with himself, or with us, and he was not crying. It was just that suddenly he felt he could not look up, that he couldn't, as he put it, *either stand it any longer, or stand any longer*. He left The Bar in a hurry, and with his eyes cast right down.

All he saw was the street under his feet; the escalator at the station suddenly yawning under him; the signs in yellow paint saying: 'DANGER'.

I should say here that O was a grown man, a strong and handsome man. These were not the bad nerves of

the lost or the young; O was well used to the life of the
city at night. It is just that some days, and at some times,
often in the early hours of the morning, sometimes this
is what it feels like; sometimes it gets me too. It often
gets me when I am in a high building or can look down
over the city, or sometimes at a station when there is
another journey to begin. Sometimes the tears come for
no reason (by which phrase we mean that someone is not
crying for a particular reason, for something or someone
in particular, but that they are crying for everything). And
when the tears come like that I think it is better to retreat,
to go home, to go to sleep, to leave wherever you are and
try to just sleep.

That was O's instinct on this occasion. He was leaving,
giving up, going home. Even though it was only ten
o'clock.

He did not look up until he was right down in the station;
and it was a sound that made him look up.

For some reason there was almost no one else there.

The poster at the end of the tunnel was so large and so
perfectly lit that it seemed to O, looking up at it suddenly,
that the tunnel did not end in a wall, in fact did not end
at all, but led to the green fields of France. Green fields
through which a road wound, not tiled like the tunnel
floor but just as white (the deep white dust of chalk hills
in August) so that the tunnel floor seemed to carry on and
meander into this summer landscape. Across the perfect
sky hung, inexplicably, the words 'Don't You Just Wish?'
There seemed to be some other words at the bottom of the
landscape, but O could not make these out.

The sound that had made O look up came from a man
who was sitting on the floor, leaning against the wall
of the tunnel, looking not much like a beggar, but just
someone worn out; perhaps he had collapsed there and

was resting. But he was singing; people only do that either if they are drunk or if they are trying to collect some money, in which case they will sing and sing all day, having no other means of getting it. So O decided that he looked like a beggar after all.

O also thought, because of the man's posture, and the huge overcoat in which he was wrapped, that he looked like a queen in a tragedy which O had seen, who in a terrible moment of despair had sat down, not on a throne or on the marble palace steps, but just right there on the floor. She had gathered her robes around her, sunk to the ground and then had lifted her hand to her face (so painfully it looked as though her wrist was broken) with exactly the same gesture with which this man now covered his eyes.

O remembered that the line which had accompanied this action was *O, intolerable.*

O stopped to watch. And he was sure that the man was begging now, for he was holding out his other hand with the palm upwards; except that then O thought that maybe the gesture had another meaning, maybe the man was extending his hand in the hope that some passer by might take it, grasp it firmly and pull him to his feet.

He was singing quietly and hoarsely; unintelligibly. If he was begging, he seemed hardly to expect that anyone would give him money for making such a noise. It was almost as if he had chosen this quiet tunnel in a relatively quiet station so that he could sing to himself undisturbed, carry on singing without having to admit to himself that this was a hopeless task, that he wasn't going to get anything.

O listened. As he listened he could smell the man; and he could hear that the song was almost turning into a sob. Sobbing and singing both come from the diaphragm.

He could see that the singer wasn't especially old or badly dressed under the coat.

O stared, he didn't know for how long, at him and his outstretched hand, wondering whether to grasp it, fill it with change, or knock it away; and then he looked up, because he heard his train coming and also because he felt the hot wind on his face. When he looked up he saw two other people in the tunnel with him. He looked up and he saw two people walking or appearing to walk away from him down the white road of the tunnel and out across the green hills. He had not heard them pass him; he had been too intent on watching the singer. The woman was in black stilettoes, walking slowly and evidently in pain—as if she had walked into the country in inappropriate shoes and was blistered and had a long way to go, as if this hot summer wind from the chalk hills was almost too much for her. And in each hand she had two heavy plastic carrier bags of shopping; they cut into her hands and threatened to split. They were evidently too heavy for her to carry. She put two of the bags down for a rest, and used her free hand to push her dyed black hair back from her eyes. Straggling behind her was a small child, about four or five, O couldn't see what sex the child was. Without meaning to, O found himself staring at them too. The Mother waited for the straggling child to catch up with her, and then she bent down, shouted something to it right up close against its face, and then hit it hard across the face with the back of her right hand. The child sat down, more from surprise than the force of the blow; the woman picked up the shopping bags and walked on; she knew that she was in danger of missing the train now. She was shouting *come on, fucking come on.*

The bags were of that thinner kind of plastic they use for the bags that they give away at the supermarket, the free ones; and now one of the bags in her right hand split and she just stood there helpless to stop them as three cans fell out and rolled across the concrete. She was stuck there with the bags, she couldn't leave them to go and pick the child up. All she could do was raise her voice higher, the train was coming in now, and she screamed at the child, screamed at him *Come on, Johnny, fucking come on.*

The child didn't move, and just sat there looking at her as if astonished.

And the child didn't cry.

The woman stood there with the bags at her feet and said out loud, to no one, not to O, not to the child, not to the singer, just stood there and threw her head back and stood there, framed against the blue sky and green hills of France, with the train leaving now, she screamed out loud, over and over, *oh fuck, fuck, fuck, fuck, fuck.*

And at that moment the man who was singing turned his song into the sob it had always almost been; the stretched note was broken by the efforts of his strained, knotted stomach into a series of high, senseless yelps. His begging hand was still outstretched but his other hand now fell from his face so that O could see his gasping mouth labouring with the hard, near-fainting breath of extreme grief. O was horrified to see that the man was actually crying.

The woman had left the bags and O saw she was walking back to the child, he heard her heels, but O did not stay to see what she did to the child (and so he did not see her pick the child up in her arms and hold him tight); he turned quickly, and left the station as fast as he could.

Like the three kings in the story, O went home another way, feeling that in some way he had just been warned about something.

He got himself back to his flat and he turned the lights on in every room. He stood in the middle of the living room and took off all his clothes, leaving them on the floor where they fell; then he inspected his naked body, front, back and sides, in the full-length mirror that he had on his living room wall. This was a variation on the routine he would put himself through every time after a man he had just slept with had left the flat; he would check his body for scratches, bruises and teethmarks. On this night he did not then go straight to bed. He walked into the brightly-lit kitchen, opened the fridge, took out a bottle of pure water and opened it. He ran a glass under the kitchen tap, then returned to the living room and, looking at himself in the full-length mirror all the while, stood there naked, shaking violently as if with cold, and poured himself and drank three glasses of water without stopping. Then he put the bottle and the wet glass down on the floor, walked into the bathroom and turned both the taps in the bath on full. Then he walked into his bedroom and sat on the edge of his bed with his head bowed while the bath filled, breathing deeply. While he waited for the bath to fill he went through the whole scene again in his head and congratulated himself for staying so calm. He began to speak out loud over the sound of the copious running water; he congratulated himself for not crying in public, he congratulated himself for not getting hurt, for not letting himself be assaulted on the way home, for not letting anyone corner him or get him down on the floor or up against a wall but for keeping walking instead.

Then he went back to the bathroom and turned off the taps. He waited until the surface of the water in the bath became quite still, like a pool, like a swimming pool before the very first swimmer enters it early in the morning, and then with one quick move climbed in and lay right under the water with his eyes closed. The water had in fact run cold from both taps because O had not had the heating on that evening, but he did not notice. He held his breath under the water; then climbed out again (leaving the bath full) and walked dripping back into his bedroom. There he crawled naked and dripping and wet-haired into his bed and pulled the sheets and the duvet tight around him. He was not cold, because his body, despite the water, was burning and almost feverish. He went quickly to sleep with the lights still all on, his body hot and rigid, curled up into a tight ball, and his eyes screwed up tight.

O did not talk in his sleep that night; all his dreams were silent films about shooting people. He had his own gun and he killed four men and two women, shot people for looking at him, never mind saying anything, shot them like on television, with no blood, no noise and no justice.

The next day, which was the Friday, O didn't work and he didn't eat; he woke up late, stayed in bed until it was dark, got up at nine and dressed in his white shirt just like always and he went to The Bar looking for his heart's desire one very last time, and that was the night that he met Boy.

Of course I didn't know at the time that this was to have been O's last night in The Bar; and I knew that it wasn't Boy's first visit to The Bar, I mean he did not see O the very day he walked in, their eyes did not meet across the bar on that very first night. But let me say here that that was just how it looked to me at the time; that there was a nice logic to it, that Boy's beginning matched O's ending, that Boy's first night was O's last, or it certainly would have been his last if Boy had not fallen into his arms.

They were not expecting anything is what I'm trying to say. It was an insignificant moment, no one there would have thought that it was to be the first movement in such a great drama, not only for them but also for those watching.

And if it was so insignificant then why can I still see that first kiss even now? Why am I still able to describe it? Why

are they so special to me, these two, why do I remember
that one kiss out of all the other romances I knew about
there in that place on that particular Friday evening, why
do I remember it, do I actually remember it all or just want
to?

This is how it happened. They didn't chat each other up,
because Boy still didn't know what to say half the time,
and O didn't want to say anything, not any more, he
had said too much to too many men. It was three or
four a.m. and the music was very slow; and usually at
that time Boy would have gone, or have found someone,
or have been found by someone. But on this night he
was making one last move through the crowded bar,
and at that exact moment O was making his way to
the door. And they passed. And because the Bar was
still crowded for some reason they were literally pushed
together. And the contact turned into an embrace without
either of them looking at the other or talking, they just
put their arms around each other. And began to dance;
the embrace turned into a dance. There was no kissing
yet, though Boy did at once lay his head on O's shoulder.
And then O placed his right hand in the small of Boy's
back and put his left hand up behind Boy's head and
he kissed him right there and then. That was the start
of it.

No one noticed, or seemed to notice. There was after all
nothing remarkable about seeing two men kiss in that way
at that time of the night. But I looked at Mother as they
were kissing and she had seen all right. She must have
been watching because she smiled, or rather tried not to
smile too obviously—she tried to conceal her pleasure
in witnessing the beginning of her triumph by pressing
her lips together, but the smile came out anyway. And
I was watching them, and I got an erection I remember.
I could just imagine how that felt. I love it when they put

their hand right there and you can feel their fingers in
your hair and pressing into the top of the back of your
neck. I've always liked men who kiss like that. It's dead
romantic.

I do not know if they talked or if they went to bed
together on that first night. For a long time they just
held each other there under the stars. And people say
they noticed how tightly O was holding Boy, pulling
him closer and closer to him, as if he was clutching at
him; and how he smelt Boy too, taking in big draughts
of the air around him, as if he was a man just escaped
from drowning holding onto something and pulling the
sweet night air down into his lungs in great grateful
gulps.
    They were almost the last to leave; as they were leaving
they paused, of course, to say goodnight to Mother.
Some of us had stayed just to watch this happen. All
three spoke as though the moment were of no real
consequence, but I know that for Mother and for O at
least it must have been a strange and moving moment.
O said:
    'Goodnight, Mother,'
and then Boy said (for the very first time):
    'Goodnight, Mother.'
    And then she said: 'Goodnight Boys. Don't do anything
you wouldn't want your Mother to hear about.'

And just as they were about to leave, as if to make a
grand exit of it, O kissed Boy again, very publicly. It
was as if he was making a declaration: *I am taking
this Boy home, this Boy of ours, and this is how I feel
about him.* And it was as if Boy was now suddenly the
drowning one, and O was the lifeguard; O slapped him
twice around the face, pulled his head back by a handful

of hair and placed his mouth over Boy's before he had time to speak, and kissed him right there in the doorway of The Bar.

And when we saw that we all started talking about what might be about to happen between these two.

And at three or four a.m. that morning, as O and Boy
kissed for the second time, the blade of a Stanley knife
sliced for the second time across the cheek of a man (I
don't remember his name, it wasn't anyone I knew) who
was at that time on his own, not with anyone, just waiting,
on his own, at a bus stop, waiting for a night bus which
was due at any minute.

COUPLE

_____

Neither dark nor dumb ceremonies, but . . . so set forth
that every man may understand what they do mean, and
to what use they do serve.

From 'Of Ceremonies: Why some be abolished
and some retained,' *The Book of Common Prayer*

Sunday

Dear Boy,
I'm just sitting down with a drink and the news
before dinner. I've had my bath, after a satisfying day
in the garden, and so I thought this would be a
good moment to put pen to paper.

I've been deadheading the roses; there is such a
wonderful profusion of colours this year now that
the new bushes have settled in, especially the big
white one which I'm sure you remember. I haven't
cut the lawn for two days but tonight the garden
smells of freshly mown grass nonetheless because next
door have just done theirs. Actually, Helen and Geoff
are away (with the children, of course, it's Spain
again this year I think), and Mr Davis's boy Kevin
from the house on the corner is keeping an eye on
things and doing the garden for them. At this time
of year of course it's all go, what with the beans
and the tomatoes and the soft fruit coming on all
at once. There is so much ripe fruit that I just ask
people to come in and help themselves, also I get
to see everyone that way and hear all the news and
of course the children love it. That Kevin is certainly
growing into a fine young man, he has been working
with his shirt off in this weather and you can see he is
going to be just as much an athlete as his father was.

My back is much better. Everyone here sends their
love as ever, and asks about you.
yours, 'Father'

PS I enclose a photograph of the wedding, and also
last week's christening. It was so good to see every-
body there.

Sunday

*Dear Boy, It must be very difficult for you sometimes
I expect not having anyone and having to do all
the shopping and cooking for yourself, I know that
when I was working I certainly could not have
managed on my own, coming home tired and then
making dinner your own dinner and then going
upstairs to do some more work, what sort of life is
that, though I know all about that because of course
I did do that for three years almost, and I know
how much happier I was when I knew there was
someone waiting for me and having the dinner ready
and keeping the house clean and all those things,
or perhaps you people don't think those things are
important. Anyway I wish you well and send my love
to you as ever, 'Father'.*

MEETING

It was a full week before they reappeared in The Bar; we
hadn't seen them for six nights and there had been much
discussion. Someone said that O had not been seen at his
job in the video hire shop for the whole week either.

Of course when they did reappear the predictable line
'And on the seventh day he rested' was much used.

If Boy had been quiet before, now his quietness had
become silence. All he really wanted was to be next
to O; and you could see that the whole time he was
listening, watching. Also for most of the time at this
period in their affair Boy was either slightly drugged, or
drunk, or exhausted; and he was in a permanent state of
sexual tension, for either he had just come from O's bed
or he was on his way to it. He found it hard to think, never
mind talk; all he could do was wait. All he could feel was
his body, trying to anticipate the next touch.

Boy was of course no virgin, but he had never spent
a whole week with one man before. He had never had
someone say to him, at half past eleven in the morning,
let's go back to bed now. He had never been with a man
who wanted to take him out at three in morning and stand
him up against a wall in a dark street and jerk him off, not

because there was nowhere else to go, but for the pleasure of doing it like that; he had never done it again and again with one body. In fact Boy had never done it more than three times with anybody.

We were not surprised to see Boy behaving like this; in the week of their absence, we had decided that their lovemaking would be extraordinary, legendary. Since so many of us had made love to either O or to Boy we felt that by comparing notes we knew a great deal about how they behaved when making love, and so when we saw them reappear so obviously as lovers we were pleased to see that our predictions had been correct. We had assumed that their affair would in some way be a violent one, because O was known to be violent, and because Boy made you feel strange when he gave himself away to you, a strangeness, and a feeling that you always wanted more, that often came out as violence. And now here to prove our thesis was Boy, silent, stunned, clearly exhausted. His eyes glittered. He looked quite extraordinarily tired, ravaged by intimacy, shattered by sex, dazed with sex.

When a young man looks like that you think about the phrase *Still waters run deep*. And also we had our own adaptation of the phrase 'She's out to lunch'; in such extreme cases as Boy's, we would say, *Darling, she's gone to the Opera*. 'And,' added Gary on this occasion, 'it looks like she's not coming back.'

As well as the silence we couldn't of course help noticing the bruises. We were, let me tell you, impressed. Boy was bruised badly around the mouth, and had red burn marks around both of his wrists. Of course we weren't about to ask, *what on earth has happened to you*, since we knew it could only be O who had done this to him. And we wouldn't even have thought of asking such a question. It was a point of honour, in The Bar, to behave as if nothing, not anything, was extraordinary. No sexual perversion, no possible error of taste in the choice

of erotic or romantic partner was considered odd. To cry
for no apparent reason was not considered odd. Nothing
anyone wore was odd. The strangest of stories (*And of
course when I told her that, she just threw me out of
the house, my own Mother . . . well, Goodnight Mother,
I can tell you*) were treated as entirely credible. So we
said nothing, and noticed everything. The bruises on his
wrists showed like diamonds beneath Boy's cuff; he was
wearing one of O's white shirts, with the sleeves rolled
down. When someone finally did ask, How are you two?
Boy smiled, and then winced slightly, because his lower
lip was split, and then he took a sip of his beer and he
smiled sweetly and said, *In love.* What he actually wanted
to say was, *I'm struck dumb with love.* (He smiled, and
thought, *I'm just a dumb kid.*) But he realised that that
wouldn't make sense, since a man cannot be struck dumb
and then speak of that condition, so what he said, when
we asked him how he was, what he said was, very slowly,
In Love. In Love with Another Man.

They spent that first night of their return to public life just
standing close together in silence, like they were a couple
of lovers; but they weren't, of course, not yet. Six nights
together does not entitle you to be lovers in that sense of
the word. Occasionally O would take hold of a handful of
Boy's black hair, which was still long all over then. We
noticed that they touched each other all evening, shoulder
to shoulder, knee to knee, nothing obvious, although I did
see O raise Boy's hand to his lips once, and later I saw Boy
rest his head on O's knees, just lay it there for a moment
like a dog. When I saw that I wanted to be him, or one
of them, or both of them, but anyway I was just so happy
to watch them together. Like several of us in The Bar at
that time, when I made love, or masturbated by myself,
I often used to have fantasies about doing it with either O

or Boy. Now that I'd seen them together like that I started
to have fantasies of being invited to watch them together,
or to take photographs of them. My biggest fantasy I think
was to be a sort of assistant, a nurse, holding Boy's hand
while O worked on him. Stroking his brow, holding down
a thrashing arm, holding Boy's precious and sweating
head in my two hands on the pillow and whispering
to him, *go on, push, push, breathe, push, breathe, that's
it, push, push, push.*

We were all waiting for Mother's reaction to their
reappearance. Mother, of course, was allowed to say
anything to anyone. She left it right to the end of the
evening. When they went to leave, having sat in silence
all night, O paused to speak to Mother. She said;

'Goodnight, O,'

and then she turned suddenly to Boy and said to him,
very pointedly:

'And what on earth have you done to your eyes?'

This was a trick question, because of course no one does
anything like that to themselves; both of Boy's eyes were
as black and blue as if he was still wearing yesterday's
makeup. And also it was a trick question because Mother
knew full well what had caused the bruises; she was
just testing his nerve. Boy paused before answering, and
looked at himself in one of the mirrors. I think Boy
thought about everything he ever said. Then he spoke
to Mother, but didn't look at her; when he replied to her
question he was looking at O, and O was looking at him.

'It's alright,' he said, 'I don't think he'd ever do anything
to hurt me.'

And then they left, hand in hand.

(In fact Boy hadn't been hit in the face by O. As I said,
that white skin marked easily, and Boy's eyes were in

fact just bruised with fatigue, with six sleepless nights in
a row. Boy had spent half the hours of each night awake,
listening to O talking in his sleep. Boy didn't complain
about being kept awake in this way. Boy did not complain
about anything ever.)

When they had left, when she had watched them leave
together, Mother allowed herself a moment of exultation.
That night she was perched on her stool wearing her cape
trimmed with marabou over the dress. Occasionally when
she was wearing this she had a trick of lifting it like wings,
or ruffling it as if it was her real plumage, and she'd
declare: 'My dears, I am preparing for The Flight—into
Egypt, to the islands, to the New World—who knows!'
      And now she lifted the cape and she said, to no one in
particular:
      'I am taking those two under my wing.'

*If that woman had wings, they were splendid. More
splendid than her antique fan of* ombré *ostrich plumes
or her green-black coq feather boa, more splendid even
than the towering aigrette* à la Pougy *which she wore
sometimes to go with the diamond. They were the wings
of Argos. They were the wings of the riddling Sphinx, they
were the wings of the Archangel Michael as he descends
with his sword shaped like a flame; the wings of the angel
who watches, a single tear on his left cheek, as Adam and
Eve make their staggering way out of Paradise.*
      *Or they were the wings of that sweet-faced Gabriel who
appears in so many pictures, whose scarlet plumes brush
the ceiling of the bedroom in which he has alighted; whose
shadow fills the whole of the bedroom wall, whose robes
cover half the bedroom carpet and whose single, beckoning
finger silences the virgins of history, making them forget*

the books which they have been surprised reading, and sends them sinking to their knees. Gabriel's wings are as silent as those of the barn owl; he can fly right past the back of your head on a summer's night and you'll never know. He comes to your chamber unbidden and unheard.

EXCHANGING NUMBERS

After six nights in a row with O, Boy spent the seventh
night on his own; he went to his own place. He slept
immediately and deeply, and then got up at six a.m. to
turn the television on and make the tea ready for when
the man he lived with got in from work. They had their
tea, then Boy went back into the living room to watch the
breakfast television, which was sport, and then the phone
rang. It was O, calling Boy up for the very first time.

The man took the call, in the kitchen.

He was surprised, since for all Boy's nights out, during
which, as the man correctly assumed, Boy had sex with
many different men, he never received visits, calls or
letters from the men he had been sleeping with. The
man did not think that Boy ever gave his address or phone
number to anyone. He wondered sometimes if Boy even
told people what his real name was.

And now here was someone on the phone saying, *Is Boy
there?*

The man dried his hands and took the phone through
to Boy, then walked back into the kitchen. Then he heard
Boy say 'Yes,' and then he heard the TV change; Boy
had got up and turned it over to a boxing match, which
was something Boy never usually watched. Wanting very

much to hear (because he was sure that this was a lover calling, from the voice), the man used the boxing match as an excuse, and he came and stood in the kitchen doorway with a wet plate and the cloth in his hands, and looked at the television. And on the screen was a blackhaired, whiteskinned, nineteen-year-old boxer. His lip was split, and he was bleeding.

What had happened was that O had been at home, not sleeping, thinking about Boy at six in the morning, and he had called up and said, 'Are you watching TV,' to which Boy had replied, as the man had heard, 'Yes,' and then O had told Boy to turn over to the boxing; he'd just said, 'Get up and change to the third channel. I'm watching it, and I want you to watch it too, It makes me think of you.'

Though it was so strange and so cryptic, Boy understood this call, because he began to understand now that there are different kinds of wanting someone. He thought, there is wanting to go to bed with someone, which is really just an erection; and there is the kind of wanting which extends beyond the night into the day, the kind where you spend all day waiting, sometimes several days. Sometimes you are waiting for a phonecall and sometimes for a touch. You think about the person all the time, *I think about you all the tine*, that's what you say. And you begin to say things that don't make any sense to people who don't know what's going on between you, but you know that the other person, to whom what you've said is really addressed will know what you mean, even though he may not actually be there.

And also, as he watched the boxer on the television, Boy began to think that there are two kinds of sex: the kind of sex where you say *do this, do that,* or you manoeuvre yourself into position for a particular kind of pleasure; and then there is the other kind of sex, where you want to say, *do anything. Do anything you want to me, you can do anything you want, I give you entire permission over me.* This feeling and especially these words cannot actually be spoken, because the words are too shaming; but for the men I know and for myself certainly I know that it usually comes out as *fuck me, please fuck me,* though that may not be exactly what you mean. I mean it is not necessarily about wanting to be actually fucked this feeling. It's more to do with the way my women friends use the word 'fucked', when they say, *I fucked him,* or *I didn't want to fuck him*—for us it still means literally I fucked him, he got fucked by me. What I mean is, sometimes you are on top of him, you have the back of his neck in your teeth, and you still find yourself wanting to say to him, fuck me, go on, go on, even though you are on top of him.

This is all so hard to tell someone, so you try to do it with your body. When you see a man bury his face in his pillow, he is doing it to avoid saying all this; to escape from the words he hears himself wanting to say, to silence himself, because he knows that your face is just six inches from his but still he cannot look at you or say what he means.

You noticed this when O and Boy were out together in public. They were always very close to each other, but would never seem to be able to look one another in the eye, as if afraid of some terrible blush. They avoided each other's eyes in different ways: O would stare away as if checking out some man across The Bar; Boy would often as not still look down at the floor as had always been his habit, as if he were indeed living up to his name, as if he were indeed some young and inexperienced boy who O had just fucked into the ground. As if he was unused to having his body turn on him and shame him by admitting that it wanted these things to happen to it. As if reluctant to acknowledge in public that it was indeed his body and not someone else's body that had done those things the night before or the afternoon before. As if he was not responsible for his actions. As if suddenly he might not be able to help himself and suddenly right there in the middle of The Bar he would say out loud: *Fuck me. Please fuck me, take this body of mine right down into the deep with you, pull me under the earth, drag me under the sea; pinion my arms, put your mouth over mine and pull me under these heavy waves I'm feeling, drown me.*

When O put down the phone at the end of this first call, he did not know how to say goodbye to Boy; he did not know what name to use. He would remember this later, this not knowing what to call him, *Boy* or *Darling* or whatever. One night, later in their affair, O woke up in the middle of one of his long and noisy dreams and lay there for a long time looking at Boy's face as he slept. And then, very deliberately, as if this was what he had decided, O said, very quietly, but very definitely, out loud, *baby.*

This time there was no knife, they just got him on the
floor and it was just a fist which had come down on the
man's face again and again. And it happened just two
streets away from The Bar. He came into The Bar with
blood everywhere. He was trying not to cry, and he kept
on saying, *I'm shocked, I'm just a bit shocked that's all.*
He wasn't as badly hurt as he looked, actually, but it was
enough to make us all think at least twice.

People say to me that I must be keeping a list of all the
attacks I hear about. They say it's morbid, they say what
are you trying to prove anyway. They say why do you have
to talk about that just now. They say to me, how many
of them do there have to be before you think you've got
enough on your list. They say when are you going to stop
it, and I say, when am I going to stop it, when am I—it was
the second night they were in the bar together after their
week of absence I remember. When the man had had his
face washed (by Stella) and been given a drink, and one
of the barmen had called for a taxi, Mother got right up
and got on the stage and told Gary she was ready for her
song now. She did her own intro. And if ever I thought it,
that was the time that I thought that Mother knew what
she was singing about.

First she dedicated her song that night to the man who was bleeding (he was still in The Bar, the taxi hadn't come yet), and then to the men who had brought their fists down on his face just two streets from her Bar. Then she went on and dedicated her song *to all those men here tonight who are still hunting, all of those who are unhappy in love, all of those who are putting up with second best, all those who are not getting what they want. Don't waste another night,* she said; *if there is somebody here you want then you go right up and tell him about it, you just tell him, because he may not be here tomorrow night. If you want him to beat you, then you ask him; if you want him to stop beating you, then you tell him. If you want him to take you home, go up right now and ask him, sure he will.*

She then proceeded to recite a bitter list of all the failed marriages which we had in our midst or knew of. She named the names of all the broken hearts. She dedicated her song to all the boys who had really regretted doing it, all the men who have ever said, naming no names, *it took ten years of my life, and now I can truly say that I never want to even talk to him again, never to see him.* And then, just when people were looking genuinely shocked by what she'd said—remember that this man, who we all knew, was still sitting there with the blood just washed off his face, as if to remind us that she wasn't joking—then she said, *don't be scared Boys.*

She said, *don't waste any time, Boys, because you don't have any to waste.*

She looked right at O and Boy when she said this and it was as if she was trying to scare them in particular, even as if she was trying to frighten them away from each other, as if she was saying, to them, and to all of us, *this is what you have to go through, right?*

She said, *I want you to listen to this song very carefully tonight. I want you to note that I am not singing just 'Take my back, because it is my best feature'* (in the mirror we could see her beautiful strong back in the low cut of the dress, and of course we could see ourselves too). *I am not singing 'Take my body'. I am not singing 'Take my head and my heart and all my bad habits but by the way I'm sorry that you have to put up with all that but they're just part of the package you see.' I am not saying take me on my good days. I am not saying take me like I look tonight and pretend that's all you've got to take, I am saying take me when there's blood on my face. What I am saying most specifically is take all of me*—and here of course Gary began the melody on the piano and we all smiled and then she sang, sang her song, and believe me we did all listen to the words that night, we knew that the man who had been attacked was there, and we knew that O and Boy were standing shoulder to shoulder in our midst, we saw them in the centre of the mirror, saw ourselves standing beside them and standing by them and give me a drink now because I had such hopes of a lover of my own on that evening and here I am.

Give me a drink. You know I have always wanted to get married, not for always, but just for once in my life I wanted to live out my love for a man like they did. I suppose you think I mean I want to walk down the aisle in white with my friends watching, but that's not it, that's not what this feeling is to do with. Or not all of it, because of course I would love to do that. But that's easy to laugh at. What I want is to hold his hand in public. And what I want then is to hold his hand in front of the television for several evenings a week, and if you don't understand that, if you don't know what that feeling is, if you don't know why it's like that then you know nothing, nothing, nothing.

I'm sorry.

I mean, Gary says you dream about marriage the same
way you dream about someone coming down your throat;
it's not something you're going to actually do, not these
days, but that doesn't mean you don't dream about it. It
doesn't mean you can't actually almost feel what it would
feel like.

COURTSHIP (1)

They had such a formal courtship. They would meet as
arranged. They would go out to dinner together. They
would go for walks at the weekend (and of course they
were also sleeping together, I mean, this was not a
courtship that involved having to wait for anything). They
would go to the pictures together; but when they watched
a film together it was usually at O's place; he would bring
tapes home from the video shop. Boy found it a bit strange
to sit there and watch a whole film in silence, without any
advertisements or changing the channel. But because he
knew that these were films that O had chosen for him, he
would watch them as intently as he had read the books
Mother had given him earlier.

They hardly ever talked.

They gave each other breakfast. When Boy had O back
to his place the first time, he gave him toast and instant
coffee; at O's place, O brought real coffee to the breakfast
table in an antique silver coffee pot, almost boiling; it was
wrapped in a white linen napkin. In the middle of the
breakfast O lifted Boy physically out of his chair, kicked
the chair away, moved Boy to a wall and held his left arm
up over his head, hard up against the wall, keeping a firm
grip on Boy's wrist. Boy was still naked that morning; O

ran his thumbnail down the tender inside of his lifted arm, down across his armpit, just cutting the edge of his left nipple, down his ribs, across his flat groin and the front of his thigh, leaving a trail that was first white and then turned red. Then he explained to Boy that he wasn't going to fuck him, then he pushed him face down on the floor and then he pressed his cock along Boy's spine from the back of Boy's neck right to his arse, till Boy hadn't been able to stop himself shuddering and gasping. Boy didn't know if O always served coffee in an antique silver coffee pot wrapped in freshly laundered linen, or was just trying to impress him, and he felt the same way about the sex. Was it always like that, he wondered, always that skilful and passionate and unexpected and close to tears? As I said, they never really talked much; there were long silences. Talking is not how they found out about each other.

Their daily, repeated intimacy at this time was astonishing for Boy because it had never happened to him before. And it was astonishing for O, because he did not really think that this was ever going to happen to him again. When O was in the bath, he would call out to Boy, *put that record on again will you?* or *Put some music on, whatever you like*, and then he'd leave the bathroom door open while he towelled himself dry. This was so that he could hear the music, but also so that Boy could see him naked if he wanted to, just as he was, just naturally naked from the bath, not for some pornographic scenario this time. In fact both of them found that sort of scene extraordinary, though in a way of course these were the most ordinary moments of their intimacy. Boy would find O's cigarettes in the living room, where he'd left them the night before, and he'd take one and light it without asking, and O wouldn't even comment, just take one as well, and they'd smoke together, and Boy thought that that was real intimate too. When you're nineteen, being accepted like that, getting up in the morning and having a bath and a cigarette together as if it is the most natural thing in the world for two men to do that, that is extraordinary to you.

And they'd come into The Bar together like that was natural too, as if they were really already a proper couple. And when they did that Boy tried so hard to feel and behave as if this was natural for him, but all the time he was looking so calm and assured, with the so-called natural sureness of the young and the handsome and the desired, Boy felt that his heart was a bird; or a tree or a shop full of birds. His heart was like a crowded birdshop, and O was walking between the high stacks of cramped cages running his fingers along the bars, and each feeling of Boy's at this time was a different species of bird in a different tiny cage, each bird hopping and flitting in a different direction. Some flung themselves against the bars, blunting and splitting the feathers at the ends of their wingtips, breaking their wings even; some still sang resolutely. Two lovebirds sat in a silent huddle. One old parrot swung from its perch like a mad, balding, demented angel. Boy wanted to choose just one bird, just one bird, just one perfect tiny yellow bird, guaranteed to sing sweetly, and to give it to O. Just one perfect feeling that he could take and hold in his hand, and then offer as a gift. A bird so small and delicate it would die if you were to hold it too tight, as a clumsy child would, squashing its small bones until its beak gapes and it dies. *Some birds must eat their own weight in food every six hours if they are to live, did you know that?* Boy wanted to say.

And since this story seems to be moving so swiftly towards a great and happy romance, let me ask you what you think of the rest of Boy's life at this time.

This period of their courtship went on for some time, and of course they were not together for every single day and night of it. Do you think Boy still saw (that is, not only looked at, but laughed with, went home with, lay down with, kissed, licked) other men? How do you think they arranged that side of things? Did they in fact arrange it, discuss it, come to some agreement, ask each other's permission? Do you feel that Boy should, at this stage of his life, have been seeing other men? Should he, on the nights when O was working until eleven and not getting home until twelve, on the nights when they had not arranged to meet up, should he have gone out, this Boy, and leant against the back wall of The Bar with his eyes mostly on the floor, and have stood there until some stranger, someone who didn't know his story, finally found the courage to come and stand by him, and then to stare at him, and then, finding his stare returned, to kiss him, and then to be surprised and delighted when the first small kiss was quickly returned by longer, deeper, expert kisses?

Whether you think he should or not, whether you think he did or not, he did.

He kissed his strangers deeply and well; and in public. Right there in The Bar, where everyone knew that he was at this time courting O. He went back to their rooms with them and made love to them with almost as much enthusiasm and skill, and with the pleasure that he also gave, later in the night, or the next evening, to O. It was not, of course, exactly the same kind of love that was made; Boy never cried for these men, only cried out with pleasure; he never quite reached the bewildered depths of pleasure that he did with O, never floundered and gave up and felt truly like a Boy, as he did with O. But he smiled his devastating smile, gave himself away, made his suitor for the night feel almost shocked by how much he gave and how quickly.

Do you think we should have said something?

Do you think Mother should have said something to O about all this?

We didn't, and she didn't. We knew about this; we knew it wasn't easy, or done lightly.

And she may not have said anything to him, but Mother never took her eyes off Boy on the nights when O wasn't there with him.

So Boy continued to sleep with other men. In fact this was the time at which he found he was unable to sleep properly without another man in the bed. When O wasn't with him he would try filling the bed with pillows. One night he woke to find that he had pulled the duvet off himself in the night and was not covered by it, but was hugging it, had one leg and one arm thrown over it as if it had been a man he was trying to gently wake by pressing his morning erection against the small of his back.

I have talked to several people who were chosen to fill the space in his bed and who did sleep with him at that time; they all told me very different stories although all agreed that a night with Boy was a night in heaven. It seems that Boy's tactics were chameleon. The man who wanted him to be tender was delighted by how sweet he was, by how simple sex could be again after so many nights of deliberate sophistication ('Just hold me,' Boy said, 'just hold me, that's all I ever really want.') The one who wanted to be dirty was amazed that someone so lovely could be so expertly depraved, by the way he came crawling towards you on his hands and knees with nothing on but the boots you'd just watched him lace himself into. The way he hardly winced when you tightened the straps. The way he said, *it's alright to hurt me you know*. The way he spread his saliva across your face with the palm of his hand. The way he stood in the doorway with his cock in his hand and said, *did you know really I'm fifteen, I'm just fifteen, my mother's out at work, we can go there, it'll be alright*; and then he's on his knees, this fucking fifteen-year-old, choking on you, he says, *why don't you come back tomorrow with your friend, you can both come, both of you, does he look like you?*

Boy could lie back on the white linen for you all night long, stretching his limbs into ravishing or rather ravished compositions, his arm thrown across his face so that when you looked up all you saw was his half-opened mouth. Or he could spend all night on his knees. He could do this, he could do that, because Boy did not know what to do, and so he did everything. I hope he never let anyone really hurt him; they said he would never let anyone play unsafe with him, Mother and Miss P had seen to that. And I hope that is true. He was still at risk, you see, I mean he was not in any way safe. Boy was still trying to get things right; he never thought that having met O meant that now he knew everything about what to do or about what he was supposed to do. Remember how young he was and how he had just arrived in the city and especially how he had no money. It should not be a surprise that he was grateful for everything, every request made of him, every meal, every lesson, every record played him, every story told him. The fact that he now had met O did not mean that he stopped needing all this from all those others.

When O found the marks of another man's teeth on his Boy, he would say nothing, but would always kiss the place. And in covering the bruise with a kiss would seem to say, for them both, that he trusted Boy; specifically, that he trusted Boy to be rich enough to be able to give away so much and still keep his capital. O understood, and Boy was learning, that there is such a thing as an economy of love.

*

And I suppose O also trusted him to not hurt himself
or get hurt because he knew that Mother was watching
over his Boy on the nights he was not there. I have said
I never saw her interfere, but one night I did see her
gently stopping Boy as he was about to leave The Bar
with someone. She often spoke to people just as they left,
being a good hostess, and would make a little pantomime
of kissing both the departing men goodnight, joking
about which one she ought to give a condom to from
the holy water stoup by the door. But on this occasion
she didn't just stop them for a brief goodnight chat; she
split them up, she must have said something to split them
up because the man left and Boy stayed (Mother bought
him another drink and sat him down with Stella) and
then half an hour later left on his own. Maybe the man
was too drunk or had a reputation for being careless, or
perhaps Mother just knew something about him that we
didn't know, because there were bad ones in the Bar, of
course there were.

When Boy left Mother kissed him and said, *Goodnight,
Boy,* and he said, *Goodnight, Mother,* but he still said it
very formally, as if she was still Madame, as if it was,
Goodnight, 'Mother', as if her care for him and his respect
for her were very formal things.

Boy thought all the time about men being together, and
he was troubled when he read about all the attacks.
    He was troubled when he read in the paper that a house
jointly owned by two of the regular customers at The Bar
had been set fire to in the night.
    He was troubled when, out walking just for the pleasure
of it on one night when he was not with O, he found
himself in the city's most beautiful park. The whole scene
was lit by a marvellous sunset, and by the floodlights

concealed in the islands of the lake, making the old trees and the fountains shine in the falling night. In the half dark, Boy saw a small child, he must have been about eleven, chasing after one of the pelicans that were a feature of the park—the first six birds had been given as a gift to the King, they said, and pelicans had been kept there ever since. When Boy saw the child chasing the bird across the darkening lawns, he laughed; the child was carrying a paper bag, and Boy assumed that the bag was full of stale bread, and that the child, enraged, was trying to get the ungrateful bird to feed from his hand. But this was not the reason,; the child was not shrieking with delight, but crying with hunger, screaming with rage and frustration, and in the bag was half a brick. The child, a boy, had come birding under cover of the dusk, and in his hunger had chosen the biggest bird in the park as his prey. He chased it though a sweet-smelling bed of wallflowers and peonies. Finally the boy threw his brick, but it was too heavy for him to throw accurately at the head of the dodging, clumsy bird, shining and squawking in the dusk, and he missed. He hit one of its great white wings; but the bird kept on running and dodging, apparently unhurt, crashing through the ornamental flowerbeds at the side of the lake. Then the bird made it to the water; there it regained its lost elegance; the white shell of its wake widened into a fan and then was lost as the bird went gliding into the now purple darkness of the lake, and the boy was left on the shore, crying, shouting at it, trampling and breaking the flowers in his frustration. Then he gave up and ran off into the lampless interior of the park. When Boy witnessed this scene, he wondered just exactly what kind of city it was that he was living in.

This same park was, that summer, made into one of the city's big tourist attractions. The idea was that on certain nights it was turned into a kind of historical theme park, a recreation of the way things had been one hundred years ago, and everybody was invited to turn up in fancy dress. Boy and O went one night to see it, and this too troubled Boy. This night too made Boy wonder what kind of city he was living in, exactly.

When they entered the park the gas lights were coming on under the trees, and you could hear the noise of the crowd when you were still streets away, music from Jim Crows, nigger melodies, shouting jew clothesmen over the top of everything, Italian Organ-boys, they'd got everything. The soldiers and the soldiers' girls were the noisiest and brightest part of the crowd, all done up for the evening, following the military band on its way to the restored pagoda-like bandstand; half the crowd seemed to be in scarlet, which Boy liked. Hansom cabs, with drivers in full period costumes, drove around the perimeter of the park taking people from attraction to attraction. You paid your fare with a real antique silver sixpence—you had to exchange your modern notes at special stalls which were conveniently placed throughout the park. Boy was enjoying himself; he felt that it was all a bit like one of their party nights at The Bar. He was used to this kind of dressing up in the night.

But then something went badly wrong. Something was wrong; the crowd thickened, word went round that someone had been arrested for a misdemeanour, some-one (some man, two men in fact) was being taken to the park police station (that ridiculous folly disguised as a thatched cottage). As a crowd rapidly gathered to see this new and unexpected attraction Boy thought he saw four men from The Bar, men he knew, although not well enough to speak to. They had dressed up for an elaborate evening picnic in period style, two of them in violently coloured 'fast' check jackets, one with excessively curled blonde hair and a low cut collar—this

one was wearing rouge and powder, and had a bracelet of
brilliants peeping from under his shirt cuff. As the crowd
grew, they got quickly up from their picnic cloth, sensing
that something was wrong. When they saw the two men
and the policemen, they turned quickly away and began
to gather up their picnic quickly and quietly; but they were
caught in the crowd. One of them turned white with fear,
dropped his cigarettes and just stood there. His friends
didn't dare to put an arm around his shoulder to hold
him up. As the crowd began to turn ugly the four men
separated without speaking, abandoned their picnic for
the crowd to trample, and walked quickly away, splitting
up into an inconspicuous pair and two singles and leaving
the park by different gates. O and Boy, who were not in
any kind of fancy dress, stayed in the crowd, or rather
mob, for that is what it felt like now as people began to
shout and push. They proceeded down the reconstruction
of what was known as The Birdcage Walk. This was lined
with flaring gaslamps and with gilded stakes, atop each
of which was a tethered parrot or macaw from the Royal
collection. The screams of the parrots began to mingle
with the screams of the crowd—one fell from its perch
and swung upside down on its chain with its wings open
and head up, screaming with laughter—when Boy saw
that he wanted to point it out to O, he wanted to tell
him about how he had imagined a bird exactly like
that as a sign of his own strange, unsettled feelings
when they were together sometimes; but this was not
the time for confidences, not in the middle of a crowd
like this. For the crowd was really getting into the period
spirit now; as the two men were escorted away, women
in the crowd began spitting at them, they kicked up their
skirts, they pulled the silver hatpins out of their elaborate
bonnets while all the men laughed their approval, one
woman screamed, *'E'll 'ave to get his 'air cut regular
now. . .*

O took hold of Boy's arm and firmly led him away from the scene. They stayed in the park until it was late, sitting on an elaborate reproduction cast-iron bench, smoking in silence. They had bought a packet of cigarettes which had been specially made for the theme park, nineteenth-century cigarettes, rich, cheap and unfiltered. They smoked steadily until they had finished the whole packet, as if they wanted to destroy or rather consume—not just throw away—their souvenir of this night, which was meant to have been a fantasy for everybody but for them had not been a fantasy at all.

When they went to go Boy said that he wanted to go back to his place alone that night, and when he got home he put the light on and got out his letters. Since meeting O he had begun to keep the letters which came every Tuesday in the shoe-box, with all the others. He began to re-read the last one he had received.

This letter featured the phrase 'those days' several times (*of course what I would really like is the kind of garden that they had in those days, almost a small park, with perhaps a pond or lake, and definitely with some birds and all the old roses . . . of course in those days they did this all very differently, they had a very different attitude, it was all more gracious then, less pushing . . .)* and when Boy read this, after what he had just seen, he suddenly found himself wanting to reply to one of these letters for the very first time. In fact he wanted to write two replies. The first would be full of kindness and would be carefully phrased, saying, *actually I am very happy just at the moment, things are going very well for me here, because I have met . . .* but the second letter would be so different that it would read as if written by a different person, it would say, *he does this to me, he does that to me, he does it so much it hurts, he hurts me, he hurts me and I love it, I love it when we do that.*

Boy planned sending both of these replies in the same envelope; both would be in the same handwriting; both would be signed, *Boy*, and they would both end with the same phrase.

They would both end, *Goodnight, Father.*

COURTSHIP (2)

That summer of their courtship they were, as we said, 'living together,' but with the accent on the first word, as in 'those two are certainly *living* together . . .' to indicate not that they were sharing the same premises (for they had not yet moved into the flat) but that they were indeed *living* together, living a fine life together, a life of quite scandalous promise and happiness. We talked about them all the time; we felt that their coupling was somehow different, that they were somehow, for the duration of that long summer, our mascots, our perfect pair, the sign of all our hopes. Each time they appeared in public we would note how well they looked, or how tired, and speculate on what made for such happiness, or what could be making a young man like Boy look so tired on a midweek evening, and especially we would speculate on when, oh when would O and his Boy declare themselves, and become a real couple and not just an affair, for we were all agreed that this was bound to happen. When, as Gary put it, would they be first heard or overheard to use the word 'we' in public when speaking of themselves.

We had no shortage of occasions for speculation; they appeared in public together several times a week that summer.

They had, as so many had at that time, a great hunger for entertainment.

Night after night they would dress at O's place, which is where Boy kept most of his clothes now, dress elaborately and late and then set out for that part of town where all the theatres were. They never paid for these visits, because O would always time their arrival to coincide with the first interval, and no manager or usher ever queried the right of such a handsome and proud-profiled couple to pass unhindered to their seats. Besides, they were so well dressed, and a lot of those ushers were gay boys themselves. There always seemed to be two empty stalls seats in whatever theatre they attended (O liked them to sit where they could see everything) and O would lead his Boy confidently to them and they would take their seats and then sit there surrounded by people who all looked much like each other, reasonably happy and well-dressed and well-coupled people, would sit there invisible in the particular, comfortable darkness of a theatre whose tickets are expensive, a darkness smelling of chocolates, hair and expensive fabrics, fans, the fresh gilt of restored cherubs, velvet, even furs, real leathers, the perfume of wives, the heavy breath of sleeping husbands.

They themselves never ate chocolate, or ordered drinks, since they came out with only their bus fares in O's pocket. Sometimes they felt that they had to go out every night of the week, sometimes O even wanted to see the same show three times in the same week, if work at the shop allowed him so many evenings off in one week. Boy always accompanied him, of course, and for days all day would be spent in bathing, resting and ironing so that even though they had few outfits in those days they would always be gorgeous, so handsome; as good to look at, in fact, as all those married people.

They never discussed what they saw. In fact they hardly
talked at all on those evenings; Boy was holding his breath
with the effort of being beautiful (Boy himself would have
said, *with the effort of being as handsome as he is*), and he
knew that O preferred him to be silent in public anyway,
very strange and well-bred; he wanted married women
to look at them as they passed and ask themselves the
question, *what is their story?*
    During these days of preparation and these evenings of
silence Boy felt in some way like an actor, saving himself
all day for his role; taking care to speak very quietly or
not at all so as to save his voice, rising late. Because he
was always waiting, always waiting for O, he felt like an
actor, or a lover.

The shows they saw never, of course, quite made sense,
since they had always missed the first hour of whatever
story there was. Boy guessed, and guessed correctly, that
it did not matter much to O what it was that they watched,
although he noticed that O avoided the family comedies
and preferred tragedies, operas and farces, any genre
in which the male characters are reduced or elevated
to tears. Boy himself wanted shows full of loud music,
expensive lighting, punishing dance routines executed by
desperate and expert boys and girls, astonishing stages
which rose and fell to reveal deep black spaces (Boy
thought, *that's how my heart works*) where moments
earlier metal walls had risen, or staircases of coloured
glass. But in every show they watched together their
desires did coincide exactly at one point; what they both
truly wanted (and they would sit together in silence,
would travel all the way there in silence just waiting for
this to happen) was for there to be a single moment, a very
special moment, in which a woman would be caught in a

spotlight, and would sing, well, would just sing her heart out, about what they never exactly cared, but they knew that it was for them, somehow, that she sang; for their condition. And they knew that it was for this moment that they had waited in silence each night, through the crowded streets, through the foyer and then silent amid the eager conversations before the second act curtain. It was this moment that they wanted, this moment when the woman turned and sang, sang for them, and they would sit there together in the dark and listen to her and let the tears come and let them roll down their faces and drip with no one to see them and no one to ask them why they needed this moment or what they were feeling.

Waiting for this moment, this moment whose arrival could never be guaranteed (because sometimes there was no song, or if there was, it was the wrong song, or the wrong singer), they would sit through as many as seven shows in a week. In the eighth week of their courtship and the tenth week of that especially hot summer—when all of the city, especially late at night and especially where we had gathered to flirt and sweat, seemed suspended in a state of strange anticipation—they watched many extraordinary things.

They watched shows in which a moaning chorus of giant gibbons took the curtain with their artificial and elongated limbs brushing the mirrored stage floor, each furred body topped by a tiny, human, sweating face. They watched women in cages hoisted aloft by bare-torsoed and grinning men; they watched shows in which entire cities slid mechanically to ruin, each yellow-lit skyscraper leaving a slick of blood in the snow as it went. On the Thursday night they watched the demolition of smoking barricades manned by child-actors (their small and exposed limbs making the fake timbers that fell on them seem larger than they really were)—the ruined

streets swung up on wires to reveal an inexplicable black
lake in which the reflections of artificial stars were made
to shimmer by the waving hands of white-gloved and
singing swimmers. On the hottest Friday of that year
they sat, surrounded by women, through a musical in
which sixty-year-old actresses sang the songs of forty
years ago, and were wildly applauded for exposing the
ruins of their voices. Their legs were still worth seeing,
if not for their elegance then for their strength, braced on
sequinned shoes, flashed from the sequinned sheaths or
spangled gauze ballgowns that they wore. The audience
seemed to know all the words of all the songs—Boy and
O knew them too, from Gary's repertoire at The Bar, but
they did not mouth them under their breath as the others
did, nor did they applaud at the end of each number. They
were waiting. They were waiting for the moment when,
at last, a single woman walked onto a stage suddenly
cleared and darkened and bared (the scenery took flight
in every direction), walked into a single light and stood
there alone, in a dress as black as O's eyes and with arms
as strong and white as Boy's. Just as Mother used to do
when she was singing her song, the woman turned her
exposed back to the audience for a moment, then with the
violins she turned again, she turned and looked right at
them and sang, sang her heart out, sang words no woman
in her right mind would say.

On the seventh night the show which O had chosen
did not give them what they wanted. On this, the final
night of a week of silent and elaborate revels, the tears
did not come. They sat and waited, as on the other
nights, but on this night they had to leave the theatre
unsatisfied. And it was on this night, Boy later told us,
it was on this night that O had finally, in his own way,
proposed. It was on this strange night that they declared

themselves to each other—although it was not until later, you understand, that the engagement was made public, and publicly celebrated.

The show that night was an historical epic entitled *By Night; or, The Dark Side of Our Great City.* Its final number was a famous spectacle at that time; a reconstructed Victorian pantomime, in whose Transformation Scene ludicrously-winged fairies hung on wires above the smouldering jewels of a lime-lit diamond mine. The touch of a wand, a swing of Harlequin's bat, and the jewels began to spit and sparkle in a display of synchronised fireworks. It was so beautiful that everyone, O and Boy as well, was jolted into applause. They stared and applauded as the sparks drifted upwards, applauded as one caught the gauze skirts of the fourteenth hanging fairy, applauded still as she hung there and burnt, twitching. They applauded out of simple shock as her hands tried to brush her skirt free of flames, as the glazed paper of her wings burnt especially brightly.

The reviews of the show reported (this was a clipping Boy long kept in his box of papers and would often read when O was out of the flat) that, in the original version of this scene, staged in a pantomime of 1867, thirteen women had burnt to death in front of an audience which included the Queen and four of the Royal Children. In fact, such incidents were common in those days. An eyewitness account of the deaths noted that the morning after Boxing Day there was already a queue of women at the stage door, frightened but hopeful. After all, all you had to do was hang on a wire and grin. It must have been terrible of course for those girls, and terrible for all the people watching, just sitting there watching, but it was a terrible job anyway. Terrible just having to hang there. Terrible. *Terrible money of course. The worst thing was if you were hanging up there and you felt a bit sick, and of course I did feel a bit sick, it was sickening, o dear*

*when Jenny was three months gone o fuck it was halfway
through the hellmouth scene and that bloody woman was
singing and up it all came, all down her dress and all over
the stage, bread and beer and all nicely warmed up and
all spilt all over Johnny in his devil outfit, but of course
you mustn't laugh because then the harness cuts into you
when you jiggle up and down, oh and the worst, Jenny,
the worst is when you come on, it's terrible, there you
are, hanging up there trying to keep still during the sea
ballet, and you can feel the blood trickling down your
sea-green, and you think, how are you going to get them
home to wash them, because he checks your baskets when
you leave because of course so many of the girls try and
sell their other tights and then wear the same pair for the
first three scenes, you can't really tell if they're yellow or red
anyway under those flower-girl outfits (I hate that fucking
scene, red cotton roses, red silk and red wax and you have
to kick the skirt forwards and up with every step, I don't
know how those poor girls managed in those days when
they had to do it all day for a living) and there you are
hanging up there dripping blood, it went all the way down
onto her shoe. The funny thing of course is having to grin
all the time no matter what's happening, that's all he ever
says, Smile Jenny, smile, and when you're having a break,
or after, you walk home, and it's not the feet, it's not the
shoulders, it's the face, your face hurts, your lips crack with
all that smiling, smiling all night, and I'm so embarrassed
about my teeth, it's awful, I don't mind showing my bits but
I do like to keep my lips closed if you know what I mean,
though of course the costumes don't half show off your legs
(of course, that's what they're paying for) I get so hysterical
if I see some Johnny I fancy, they think you can't see them,
there you are hanging on a wire with the footlights right
up your fucking frock and you get all hot and you see him
talking to his friends about you and you think O God don't
let there be a damp patch, he can see everything from down*

*there and all for fucking four and six, it's hysterical really,
but you mustn't start laughing of course because if one of
you kicks off that's it there you all are up there laughing
and jiggling and Jenny drops her wand and it just makes
me want to piss. I never have pissed up there, but I'd like
to. Imagine that, a bunch of fairies hanging up there,
Fairy of Piss, Fairy of Shite, Fairy of Bleeding, Fairy
Up-It-Comes, Fairy of Hysterical Laughter, Fairy Fairy,
Fairy Cunt, Fairy Fairy-Fucker, and as the centrepiece,
with tears of real crystal ladies and gentlemen, The Fairy
of Public Weeping, that would be something to see, imagine
us all up there in a row, each with her gimmick, that would
give them something to grin at. I'd like to see that on the
programme tonight. Tonight a Foreign Country with all
its Scenes and Features, and at the Grand Finale, the
Fairies will weep, Fairy of Come-Dripping-Out, Fairy of
Excuse-Me (that's the new girl, she must be desperate for
work!) and, on the lead wire, the Fairy of Dead Children,
an entirely new feature; glycerine tears, a headdress of India
Pearls and white Paris Sequins, her dress stitched entirely
with teardrops and the chiffon hand-dampened with Rose
Water by The Girls, and in her left hand the Tear Wand,
that drips when you squeeze, it doesn't half do your wrist,
and we all sing:*

> It only hurts me when I cry; I couldn't ever tell you
> why!
> My foot's got no shoe on it, I've lost me stockings
> too;
> I've sold me feather bonnet, And I don't know what
> to do—
> But my Boy he's a Butcher, He smiles and says to
> me;
> 'I'll give you good fresh meat, Girl—I gets it all for
> free!—

OH! That won't hurt you!
(That can't hurt me!)
This won't hurt you!
(Go on, hurt me!)
Does it hurt you?
(Does it hurt—ooooh!)
Does it hurt you,
Tell me please do!—

CHORUS:
Only when I cry, Johnny!
Only when I cry!
Only when I cry, Johnny!
Only when I cry!

Everybody off and change. Change Please!

SLEEPING TOGETHER

Boy had always slept like a child, exhausted from his walking or from his television or from being with some man. But now he found that he could not always sleep.

If he was at his own place, and suspected that he might wake, he would leave his photograph of the First World War soldier who looked like him out by his bed, as if it was a glass of water, something he might need in the night. He would place under it one or two pages torn from his favourite books, which he'd read immediately before sleeping, or even one of the letters from the box; if he woke he'd try to get back to sleep with his left arm outstretched and his left hand placed palm down on top of the small pile of paper. In the morning he would look to see if any of the print or images had been transferred to the palm of his hand. It was bit like going to sleep touching your lover, with your hand just touching his thigh or back because you want to be sure he's there.

If he was at O's place, Boy always woke in the night, or rather was woken. This was because of O's talking in his sleep. When this happened, Boy did not try to get back to sleep, but rather tried to stay awake, to listen.

When it first happened, Boy thought that his lover was having a recurring nightmare about being attacked or killed, because every night the dream seemed to end, in the same way, at four a.m., with O suddenly crying out, *I want to live, I want to live, I want to live.* Then Boy would hold him for a bit and he'd go quiet and sleep soundly.

But soon Boy realised that it could not be a single dream which was causing O to cry out. As O got used to having Boy there by his side, as if he felt that he knew him better and could talk to him more now, he began to talk more during the nights. Each night would still end with the same cry, but before it came Boy would lie awake and hear O's voice range through several dreams as if it was moving across the dial of the radio. A murmured speech would be interrupted by some song lyrics, then O would say, *please, release me, let me go,* or, *ev'ry night I dream just how good it used to be, ev'ry night imagine you are still here with me, every night it's you I surely lack, every night I cry, oh Baby come on back, I want, I want, I want to I want to live . . .*

As their courtship progressed, O's nocturnal speeches to his lover grew longer. They did not seem to distress him; he would not thrash and groan as he spoke, but lie quietly on his back and, once the night's main speech was in full flow, speak in a fast, level, calm voice. Sometimes he spoke in a way that reminded Boy of a programme he had once seen about spirit mediums; like a strange kind of ventriloquist. One night he spoke with a heavy Dutch or Belgian accent saying, *let's be honest yes the best is over. I think well you're thirty it's half your life and for us the best half too. When you're not twenty or twenty-five any more they keep on asking you where your wife is and that's hard sometimes, I want to live, I want to, I want to live by myself but they ask you questions they ask you all the time where is your wife because everybody has one*—then the speech just stopped, as if O was exhausted by the effort of his impersonation.

Sometimes these speeches were so long and so coherent that Boy could not believe that O was actually asleep. Then he thought that maybe O really did want to talk to him, confess something to him, but could not for some reason say it to his face, by daylight, and so had rehearsed this elaborate act of talking in his sleep. *He is saying what he really means*, Boy thought. *Declaring his true feelings*, Boy thought. He would look carefully to see if his lover's eyes were open in the dark (O kept a heavy drape over the window of his room, whereas Boy kept his window bare, he liked to see what kind of day it was as soon as he woke, and he liked especially to fall asleep looking at the stars or with the bright moon falling on his face.) But O's eyes were not open; they were squeezed tight shut. He was lying on his back with his arms down by his sides, staring at the ceiling with his eyes closed, saying, *I'll get a towel. You know, you're the first person I've had sex with since he left me. I don't mind for me so much of course because I'm older but if I think about him in the arms of another man I'll go crazy. I'll kill him. I know I could kill him if I saw it because I'm taller than he is, and stronger. I knew he wanted to go, and I woke up and I followed him downstairs, he was dressed, with his things in my bag which he'd taken, we were both screaming, and I was pulling him and holding him, he got the door open and we just stood on the doorstep at seven in the morning screaming at each other, hitting each other, I wasn't wearing any clothes. And there was a lot of blood. We woke everyone in the house and the landlady came in later and said please don't let it happen again. She was in her dressing gown. Everyone in the flats must have heard, I was screaming, but she came in her dressing gown, not her husband, he wouldn't come in the flat while we were living there and she said I do understand dear and I thought that was nice. I went up to the hotel where he works, he told me never to go up there because they didn't know, you see, and we just started crying*

*together and the manager came into the kitchen and saw us
and he lost his job. He told me he was at home but I called
up and he wasn't there, I called him where he lived and the
girl who answered the phone went down to his room and
said he wasn't there and then at eleven I called again and
he wasn't there, so I went down to the club and I walk in
and there he is with some friends and he won't talk to me,
everybody's watching, he knows I don't go to the club on a
Tuesday so he thought I wouldn't be there. He's only young,
he's nineteen, and I'm the only man who's had him since he
got down here. He never goes down to the club like that on
his own, never. Now I just want him back that's all, I just
want him back so we can live together, I want to live with
him and have him here, I want to live with him, I want to
live, I want to live, that's his picture there he's very cute with
nothing on, he's fabulous, what do you think?*

Then it stopped, and O rolled over very quickly and
wrapped Boy in his arms, very deeply asleep. His eyes
were still squeezed shut, but not tight enough to have
prevented the tears from coming out. His face shone
in the dark and the tears dripped onto Boy's cheeks
as he held him. Boy thought about O's cry, *I want to
live, I want to live, I want to live,* and wondered if this
time he should say something in the morning. Boy had
once, before he had met O, gone home with a man
who had cried like this all night. His lover had recently
died and he wanted to talk, not have sex. As Boy felt
O's tears on his face, he remembered this other man,
and wanted to see him again. As if O knew what he
was thinking, he quietly whispered to Boy, *I'm sorry for
getting all emotional.* Boy thought he was awake now,
and acknowledging that he had been talking in his sleep;
but then O said the line again, this time with a strong
Newcastle accent, *I'm sorry for getting all emotional. The
only other time that happened to me was with George.
I used to get all emotional with him, I remember one*

*time oh god it was when we were on holiday he made
me wait until it was sunset, he said I'll take you out
the night, and then we come into the square under this
arch, the mist was coming in knee deep, and there were
two boys singing under the arches and then we went
up the tower to see the sunset, and he asked me what
I thought, and I was blubbering, just standing there and
blubbering, and all I could say was oh god it's fab'lous, it's
fab'lous. Oh god it was fab'lous. People must have thought
I was off my face. I'm getting all teary tellin' you about it
now.*

And then later, in the same voice, but more urgently, O
whispered, *Kiss us, kiss us please.*

And then, later again,

Fuck us. Please fuck us. Please, I want to—

Then O had slept, and so had Boy too, eventually.

One night, having woken to find O lying silent asleep
beside him, Boy talked to him out loud, and said, *do you
really love me?* At once O replied: *I took them both out for
a walk and I made him walk behind, I said, you, behind,
your Father and I are going to talk business. And he says
well I don't want him getting hurt, you know, mixed up
with an older man. I said, look, the way I feel about your
son, I know how I feel, I'd fucking kill for him, and he said,
well if that's the way you feel, that's alright then, why didn't
you fucking say so, and I said less of the language Father;
and that's it, I've been part of the family ever since. I see
them most weekends. Every weekend really. And that's
how I want to live, I want to live—*Boy wanted to know
if this was an answer to his question. He wanted to know
if these stories were meant in some way to be about O and
himself. And he wanted to know whether O meant to tell
him all this, or would be angry if he knew that he had.

One morning, having talked that night for over an hour, O said, 'I want to . . . I dreamed that we lived together'; this was the only comment he ever made.

After one of these nights, by way of an explanation to himself of all this, Boy tore a page from one of his books and added it to the small pile by the bed. It was from the work of a writer who was known to have slept with men and so Boy thought that he must have written this passage after having similar trouble either with the nightmares of a partner (a boy he'd taken back to the expensive sheets of some grand hotel) or with his own nightmares and sleepless thoughts (when he knew it could only be days before they arrived at his door); *Oh that our eyelids might open some morning upon a world that had been fashioned anew in the darkness of our pleasure, a world in which the voices of the past would have little or no place, a world in which we might then live.*

Then came a night when O began to talk while still awake. It happened at four in the morning, which is when he usually talked; but they were still awake, having made love all night, since O did not have to work the next day. As they lay next to each other on the bed, each staring at the ceiling, with the semen drying on them, O said, awake, but with his sleepwalking voice, *I'm going to do up this apartment*

It was on a Friday night, when Boy had hoped that they might go out together to The Bar, for he wanted to parade his great happiness in front of all of us. But O had taken Boy to bed at six in the evening, not having said a world since he got home, and had been more violent, more lascivious than Boy had ever known him. I should say here that Boy never once wanted O to stop, and that he was used to sometimes being frightened by what O wanted to do, and by what he made Boy himself feel that he wanted to do, things he hadn't ever known that he wanted to do. Boy had never expected to be in love with or to be made love to by anyone like O without being frightened.

When it was over, Boy lay on his back, and in the silence he started to imagine that he was a piece of driftwood on a beach, his ribs and other bones bleached and pounded by careless waves, left high and dry for the sun to whiten, ready to be picked up for their curious shape and taken home as treasures by an eager child. He lay on the bed like this for a long time, and Boy found himself even listening carefully to see if he could hear the tide going out, the waters receding.

Boy was getting used to such silences; he never assumed that something was wrong when O didn't talk. It seemed to him that O only ever really talked in the night or when he was making love. That evening he had begun by slowly, clearly whispering more or less coherent plans for elaborate obscenities in Boy's ear, commanding his attention there, in his ear and in his mind, just as his fingers, later in the night, demanded all of Boy's concentration on the local sensation of a repeatedly stroked or shocked muscle or orifice (O had this way of making you forget everything except the part of you that he was working on, forget everything else, even which way up your body was, I remember feeling nothing except the instep of my foot at one point, and then, and I can remember this very distinctly still, the ring of muscle inside my arse opening very suddenly and sweetly, I know that's how it's always meant to happen or was meant to happen in those days, but it didn't always, but that night, the one night that I had with O, which is a long time ago now, we were both younger, that night I remember thinking, oh my god, this is perfect, perfect, perfect.) Later in their lovemaking O had raved, thrown sentences at Boy which were obscene in their tone of voice but not their sense, barked orders that only made sense as orders because the mouth that shaped them looked so handsome and cruel, breathed insults which were received by Boy as something like tenderness because he could hear the tears in O's voice at that point, *you fucker, you fucker, you fucker.* And so now when O, staring at the ceiling, said, *I'm going to do up this apartment.* Boy didn't expect him to continue and make a speech of it; he thought everything had been said for that night; he expected his unexplained statement to just hang there like cigarette smoke. But O said, *I want to live. I want to live, I want to live . . . I dreamed I lived with you, but it was somewhere grander than this. A prince should have a palace. I am fucking a prince and I want to fuck him in a palace.*

Boy's reaction to this was to turn to look to see if O was sleeping, talking in his sleep again. He saw O's eyes shining in the dark, so he knew that he was still awake.

Still expecting that O would go no further, that he would not in any way explain what he had said, Boy was already elaborating this fantasy in his own mind. He was already thinking, *he wants us to live here together, that's what he wants to tell me. That's why we didn't go out, I'll help him with the decorating . . . we'll work together and he'll make love to me on dustsheets, with paint splashes on his hands and in his hair.*

But O did go on to explain or at least expand on what he had said. And Boy was right to assume that, as O described it, the apartment was being done up as the scene of their future life together. That was what O was trying to talk to him about. As O made his fantastic proposals, Boy lay quietly there and listened, and incorporated himself into the fantasy. If not the naked centrepiece of this great room, sprawled open-legged on the warm and highly polished wood of the table which O described (he would gladly have taken that role), then Boy saw himself at least as a servant, dressed always to complement and complete the scheme of the room's decoration, its discreet finishing touch, a living ornament amidst its expensive menagerie of carved, gilded and frescoed bodies. Boy swiftly imagined the cut, cloth and gilt embroidery of a livery that would both suit the room and show off his own body (a highbacked jacket over tight breeches). He hung a pearl from his ear, and placed himself, silent and expectant, in the shadows which a shaded lamp threw low across the velvet-damasked wall; he equipped himself with a chased silver tray, covered it with a freshly starched linen napkin, and balanced on it a single miniature cut-crystal glass of an expensive, exotic and amber-coloured liqueur, served, bizarrely but correctly chilled, like vodka, so that the crystal was clouded with drops of condensation in the heat of the room, warmed as well as lit by the fire of scented cedarlogs. And there in the shadows in the corner of the room he waited, waited as long as he was required to, silently watching the bodies entwining by firelight (how many other seductions has he watched, this servant? How many other men has he seen stretched across these ebony chairs, these rare and costly rugs?), watching and waiting until his Lord and master's exertions over the sweating body of the amazed and intoxicated guest are temporarily over, when a single glance brings Boy swiftly to his place at his Master's elbow, offering his Master's guest, (panting and bathed in sweat, half stunned by the evening's rare wines and brutally passionate kisses) a reviving drink before their next bout of arduous lovemaking. Boy imagined his Master saying to him: *No verbal commands will be necessary ... A glance should suffice to tell you when I need you and for what. That is why I chose you for my household; you seem always to know what I want. Now retire to your place.*

*

While Boy was thinking all this, what O actually said was, *I'm going to do up this apartment. I'm going to sand the floor twice and bleach it and seal it. In the centre of the floor I shall have painted a copy of the mosaic panel from Hadrian's villa at Tivoli representing the Ascent of Ganymede, all properly done in the correct seven coloured marbles, and lapis for his eyes. I'll fix the bedroom window. The dado will be of seven different woods; and on the top of the dado will be a gilt rail, and on the rail will be perched a life-sized and perfectly realistic lion marmoset carved in white cherry wood; clutched in his left paw will be two stolen cherries carved in red mahogany; between his bared teeth of stained ivory the marmoset will be carrying a grape carved in ebony. Press this, and the staff will be summoned by a hidden electric bell. Above the dado I shall cover the walls with hammered and lacquered Spanish leather, and in the centre of each wall hang a grisaille panel depicting scenes from the lives of great men: Antinous drowned and perfect at the age of nineteen (I will commission the artist to make Antinous's body a copy of yours, and no one will know this but me); Will Hughes playing the gilded boy mentioned by Piers Gaveston in Marlowe's* Edward the Second; *Rimbaud in the house of glass which he built in Addis Ababa; Federico García Lorca on his first night in New York; Robbie Ross lifting his hat to the passing prisoner in the corridor of the Old Bailey. Pendant to each of these scenes will be a naked male figure representing each of the seven virtues: Charity, Promiscuity, Generosity, Dignity, Honesty, Beauty and Courage.*

The ceiling frieze, a painted plaster bas-relief, features imaginary portraits of all the twenty murderous lovers named in the eleventh chapter of The Picture of Dorian Gray; *their eyes are inlaid with all twenty-seven semi-precious stones listed in the same chapter. In the centre of the room are seven chairs, each carved from different wood. The seventh chair, the one by the window, is* always kept empty; on the back of this chair is painted, in a vermilion gothic script, the famous quotation from Hebrews, Chapter thirteen: Entertaining Angels Unawares. The chairs surround a unique table whose top is carved from a single slice of ebony, so polished that in its surface can be seen reflected every detail of the vaulted and frescoed ceiling. The dinner guests were thus afforded the satisfying sensation of touching the table's smooth, warm wood and seeming to touch the flesh of the ceiling's painted figures at the same time. On the ceiling is depicted an Allegory of Love Assaulting Mars, copied from Veronese; lying on his back on a bed of orange satin, his beard, naked chest and raised knees painted in expert foreshortening, Mars is shown with his white and muscular stomach straddled by a cheeky infant boy. His arms are raised in a gesture which can be interpreted as either a welcoming embrace or a halfhearted attempt to ward off the stinging slaps which the Cupid is delivering with his bow and arrow. From the centre of the ceiling hangs a recreation of the Pompeian lamp described by John Addington Symonds in his poem 'Midnight at Baiae', with the lascivious glare of a single bare bulb replacing the guttering, oil-fed flames of the original. On our left, the small stained-glass window, the only one that the artist ever designed, depicts the loves of David and Jonathan, Absalom and Saul, John and Christ, and the love of Eli for the Infant Samuel.

This room was designed by the second Duke, and was kept always for his exclusive use, in particular for his notorious all-male dinner parties, It is said to have been the scene of scandalous orgies. If, as you leave, you look beneath the beaten copper hood of the fireplace, you will see on the right the concealed figure of a naked and blindfolded boy, so placed that he is being scorched by the flames, but is unable to escape.

The original furnishing of the room included a set of seven Italian majolica plates depicting lost illustrations

*of Aretino's famous 'Positions'; these are now in a private
collection in Paris. We will now proceed to the Green or
'Summer' Drawing Room. Please do not touch the dining
room table as the surface marks very easily. Thank you.*

If, that summer, O dreamed of the kind of place they
might one day live in, Boy was happy to hear it, but he
himself had no real need to dream. Though sometimes
troubled, he was in a state of grace; he was O's dog, his
young prince, his slave and his Boy. He would go to sleep
with O's penis in his mouth if he could.

When I dream of a place where I might one day live,
I also dream about some kind of a palace. I would live
at one end of this great empty building and there would
be a man living at the other. Between us there would
be miles of derelict corridor and acres of grand, high-
ceiling, abandoned rooms, so many of them that I get
lost, so many that I am always finding new rooms . . .
and in these rooms I wander, and sometimes I meet
strangers, and sometimes him, and then I make love to
him in silence in the deserted ballroom with swallows
coming in through the glassless windows and frescoed
giants watching us from the ceiling, and we'd watch
ourselves in the clouded mirrors. And then I'd return
to my own rooms. At other times he would drive straight
to where I lived, to the one lighted window in that whole
ruined palace, and he'd stay for dinner and then he'd stay
for days.

And on one of these nights when O was raving, or talking anyway, in his sleep, maybe on a night when they were at the theatre, as that woman sang or seemed to sing to them, a hand came down on the face of Mr (I'll keep his name private), aged eighteen, who was at the time just travelling home on the bus with a man who he'd just met and who he was really looking forward to going to bed with (they had left The Bar at half past nine, so eager for each other were they). But although he was looking forward so much to seeing this man without anything on, he was also tired, for it was Saturday and he had worked all day; and in a moment of forgetfulness he had let his head fall and rest upon the other man's shoulder. And so even though it was only just days after another man we knew had been hurt (we all said, *oh no, not again*), the knife came down again, or rather not a knife this time, but a hand, and then spittle, and then a loud laugh.

I don't think that Boy knew that any of this was happening, not really. Despite all his nights staring out of the window, he was still in some ways very ignorant of life in the city.

*

And also in that same week there was this attack too, though people in The Bar couldn't see why I was so furious about it, they said, yes, but what has that got to do—

Bobby Sillock, aged forty, a power station worker from South Stifford, near Grays, Essex, was killed after telling five men to stop abusing the staff of The Night Palace Indian Restaurant with racial insults. The probable murder weapon, thrown from a car after the attack, has been recovered and is being examined by forensic scientists.

—but Mother knew why I was upset by that story. Mother dedicated her song that night to Bobby Sillock, even though she could see that half the boys had no idea who she was talking about, they probably thought that he was some dead writer or other whose obscure anniversary she was commemorating. You have to remember how strange it was for us, how unlikely we found it, even though it kept on happening, and right close to us and even to people we knew. One of the things about The Bar was that you felt so safe there, so strong, and it was difficult to talk about being frightened when you were in The Bar. You felt so strong there sometimes that you felt that not only could you take care of yourself but you could also take care of someone else if you had to.

And it was strange for us because at the same time as all this was happening we knew that in other countries it was not like this at all; some people I knew in The Bar used to go on holiday once or twice every year and when they came back they used to say they never knew how we could all stand it. I remember seeing a television programme at this time about another country where men could simply walk down the street holding hands. And this did not, they said on the programme, indicate an especial courage, or an especial pride; men will do it who have only known each other for a short while or indeed have only just met—and it does not occur on particular days of the

year, but irregularly, frequently, without carnival being
declared and without heads turning. It does not occur
on particular streets, but almost everywhere (I can't quite
believe that bit).

Boy saw this programme too; Mother recommended
that he watch it. He remembered quite vividly the camera
framing two hands clasped across a white plastic café
table-top, a circular table top, in the sun. And in a dream
these two hands reappeared, still clasped, but holding
each other by the wrists as if in a tug of war or an oath,
and they were severed just below the elbow. The two
stumps were bleeding, so that when the table tipped, as
it did in this dream, and the two clasped hands slid off
it and onto the cobbles of the street, they left two clear
pools and trails of blood on the table; a child's drawing
of two red flowers on a white ground. And in the dream
this picture was pinned up on a kitchen wall, as children's
first drawings are pinned up by proud parents. The thing
about these drawings is that you can't tell exactly what
they're supposed to be drawings of, unless the child
explains, or the parent explains, or unless the teacher
has written a title across the bottom of the picture in
emphatically legible handwriting. And in Boy's dream
this picture was entitled, not, TWO RED FLOWERS,
but DON'T EVER LEAVE ME.

ENGAGEMENT

They courted all that summer, and at the end of that
summer, at midnight on its longest and hottest night,
their courtship came to an end, or rather that phase of
it came to a fitting climax. On the night of the worst (or the
best, you might say, if you like to see the lightning coming
down over this city as I do) the worst thunderstorm
for twenty years, on a night when everyone else had
responded to the thick heat by taking everything off that
they reasonably could, O and Boy appeared at The Bar
in the most elaborate costumes in which we had yet seen
them.

Of course, we had already seen them make several
significant entrances, ones which had turned heads and
caused comment; had already noted the several changes
of costume which had marked the early stages of this
affair—the way O had apparently reduced his wardrobe
to just the one, stern outfit, a uniform really, which made
him seem even stronger, more serious and more grave
than we already thought him with that cropped black
hair; and the way Boy now usually wore just a plain
white cotton shirt with the sleeves rolled up to the top
of his arms, matching O's, whereas before he and O

had got serious it had been a different style of t shirt every night, as if he had been trying to get something right. As if he had been trying to find his character. And of course the particular (and popular) drama of O and Boy's affair aside, we were no strangers to these dramatic techniques, especially the techniques of costume drama. I mean, dramas happened all the time in The Bar: fights, kisses, seductions, all the things you usually have to go out to a theatre and pay to see. And not only were our embraces, dances and kisses rehearsed, performed repeatedly and always in public, each touch and gesture reviewed as soon as it was made (was this move to be considered an innovation, or a critical reworking of a classic theme?), but we all too often made a point of talking as if we were in some show, so that if someone had suddenly to leave a conversation in order to follow a handsome stranger who had just passed, he would simply announce, 'Excuse me, I'm on'; if the stranger who had passed had passed with a definite look of invitation, the announcement would be, 'Excuse me, I think this is my number.' If, later in the evening, two lovers who had spent the evening drinking and flirting apart had met up and had begun to argue because one of them wanted to wait just another ten minutes in case the man who had just turned his back turned again with a smile, the row would invariably end with the line, 'Honey, this is your five minute call . . . ', meaning, *listen you, you get any drunker and I'm hauling you out of here anyway*. And I remember that our favourite pick-up line that summer was always, *Buddy, will you take me home?* done just as she'd done it in the show (which we'd all seen twice) and the answer was always, or rather we always hoped it would be, *Sure I will . . .* everyone talked as if we were rehearsing some half-remembered but classic screenplay; as if we all knew what we should really say next. We could accept the most outrageous and unconvincing performances, provided that they accorded with the strict and publicly acknowledged rules of the genre. Whatever its apparent improbabilities, we still believed in the basic realism of the scene. We believed in theatre. And of course in The Bar we had coloured lights and mirrors every night anyway, and there was always at least someone in full makeup, even if it wasn't costume night (Oh those nights, the 'At Marble Arch I met a Serviceman' party, 'Night in Old Cairo', nights to remember, 'White Nights on the Nevsky Prospect', nights when you walked home with diamante ground into the soles of your boots, mornings when you woke late and found sequins glued to the skin of your stomach with sweat.) And we were used to people, regular customers, making their entrance in a conspicuously new outfit; when it happened someone who had seen them at the door would simply murmur, *places please*, and we would behave as if the party concerned had always dressed like that, had always looked like that for as long as we'd all known him. We had seen men arrive in our midst quiet and bitter in their office clothes, only to reappear two years later with muscles and an easy laugh and a boyfriend—and then reappear again, through the same door, with the same partner, but both of them older now, their makeup and hair considerably re-done, in suits again, with ties, not laughing so much now or kissing so much but still together and still coming out to The Bar sometimes. Sometimes these changes of costume would take years; sometimes the man who you thought was in character when soberly dressed, apparently for a minor part, the man you were sure would always dress like that, would change in the course of a single, riotous evening. Perhaps he became an animal, sweating and shirtless, down on his knees before a less than perfect stranger; perhaps a chorus girl, sweating in borrowed earrings and somebody else's wig, crying at the top of his voice, 'Confused? You won't be!'

And so you see The Bar always felt a bit like a theatre. I mean, nobody really arrived until it was dark, and nothing really happened until the lights had been dimmed and the music struck up. But still, the entrance they made and the way O and Boy were dressed that night did indeed make it a night to remember. And of course, that was the whole idea.

Two weeks previously, as The Bar was closing, after an evening in which these two had been playing The Couple even more conspicuously than usual, exchanging such kisses that even we had to avert our eyes and talk of something else, Mother had been heard to invite O and Boy up to her room above The Bar after closing time. Nobody went up there uninvited, and few received an invitation.

They climbed the steep wooden nineteenth-century stair-case—Boy I expect had no idea the building was so old. The stairs were so narrow that the flowered wallpaper was scarred and scratched all the way up; scratched and worn by the white sequins and crystal beading of Mother's frock, for it was down these stairs that she squeezed herself in that same frock every night that The Bar opened, every night for years now, down those stairs that she came unseen from her upper room, her hair and her face perfect, her mind composed for her entrance, her smile ready for her Boys.

The door was heavy (O knocked three times and Boy heard the wood ring solidly) and Boy saw that the room was small and ordinary (except for the red ceiling), and dark, with floral wallpaper, a single bed, several full-length mirrors, shelves of books (some in a glass-fronted case) and some old Turkish rugs. One wall was taken up entirely with a huge wardrobe, another with a dressing table, a huge ugly reproduction French piece with an oval mirror, bowed legs and gilt handles on the drawers. This was covered in papers, ledgers, cosmetics, glass scent bottles, two cut-glass candlesticks with unlit candles, and a heap of costume jewellery. The whole room smelt, but not of scent, for none of the bottles had been left unstoppered; a vase of dark purple night-scented stock stood on top of the wardrobe (next to a small bronze statuette) and Mother was drinking from her Waterford tumbler of neat gin, which was placed, with her cigarettes, on a small table next to her highbacked chair. This she had moved away from her bureau to the centre of the room.

When Boy entered the room for this, the first, time, he saw behind Mother's head one of the framed photographs, all of women, of which there were so many that they almost covered the walls. It was a copy of the famous van Vechten portrait of Bessie Smith in the ostrich and marabou hat. At the time, Boy thought that this was rather an error of taste, since cheap reproductions of this photograph were at that time available as part of a popular series marketed under the title 'Black and White'. Boy had doubtless expected Mother's room to be decorated with something stranger or at least more expensive.

Madame (in this scene she did look more like a Madame than a Mother) was sitting straightbacked in her chair; this was to be a formal audience. She indicated they should stand before her on the dull red Turkey rugs. She addressed them both, but seemed to be speaking mostly to O, as if Boy was expected to just listen and not be directly addressed even though he was being discussed; it was into O's eyes that she stared as she spoke, with that permanent half smile of hers that went so well with her phrasing, and he was half smiling too, as if they understood each other or had already discussed this matter and were now restaging their discussion, presumably for Boy's benefit.

'Boys,' Madame said, 'it is time that you took these painful amateur scenes to their logical conclusion. I think it is time that you decided to go professional, as it were; it is time for you to take the six steps up onto that stage of ours and publicly declare yourselves to be a double act. After all, Older, the fact that you, after all these years, should be finally, as they say, *settling down*, is already common knowledge, not to say a considerable public scandal. What's the secret? Is he spectacularly (she separated each syllable of the word, staring right into O's eyes, and O smiled) spec-tac-u-lar-ly good in bed?—No, please don't answer that.'

There was of course no question of speaking while Madame was speaking. She indicated two typewritten foolscap playscripts lying on the dressing table.

'I have decided to produce your debut personally. We will rehearse in The Bar during the day, Gary will play for you. It's all arranged; the premiere will be in one week's time and the invitations are already at the printers. Have you any questions?'

Boy, with a sudden access of courage, said:

'But Madame, what shall I wear?'

Madame was in the white beaded dress of course, having just finished work for the evening, *the* dress, and she said:

'As you know, Boy, I only ever appear in this one gown. I have, however, others in store. You may open my wardrobe and make your choice.'

Boy did as he was told. On the wardrobe rail were thirteen copies of the white beaded dress. Eight of them had been worn, and the beading was damaged, the satin was slightly yellowed, and some of these eight dresses were slightly smaller than the dress Madame wore now; these dresses were her past, each one worn until near destruction and then preserved. Five of the dresses were unworn, still hanging in thin plastic coverings on padded hangers. These dresses were the rest of Madame's life; she did not ever intend to change her dress, so to speak, and had commissioned these five copies from the only dressmaker in the city who still had a supply of the appropriate beads (not manufactured since the war), the only dressmaker who in her opinion still made finery well enough cut and stitched, strong enough to survive her nights at work, her nights in The Bar. As she put it on another occasion, 'I have no intention of ever coming apart at the seams.'

Also hanging on the wardrobe rail were twenty-four other gowns, all of them in different fabrics and colours, but all of them elaborate and heavy with feathers, silk flowers and embroidery. They seemed to be theatrical costumes of a kind; Boy found two whose silk was rotten, several whose necklines were stained with greasepaint and powder, and one whose generous but tightly fitted hips were covered in a lattice of fake pearl ropes decorated with red beading roses; to one rose was attached a small handwritten paper label reading *Mrs Cheveley, Act Two*.

Boy chose three dresses and laid them on the floor before Madame. All the time he had been working slowly through the dresses, Madame and O had been watching him intently; there was something very touching to both of them about the sight of a young man trying to make a choice. When he had lain the dresses down and then looked up at Madame for instructions she said, taking a well-timed sip from her glass:

'Try them on, Boy. I hope,' she said, 'now I hope you will not be embarrassed to strip naked.'

Boy paused, looked down at the carpet, looked up at O,

and then at Madame, and then he said, feeling somehow he could say anything:

'Oh no, Madame, I am used to stripping when I am told.'

And then Madame, said, very gently, looking not at Boy but at O, 'I am quite sure that you are';—and she smiled at O, and then she looked back at Boy—' and since you are, Boy, why don't you strip now. When a man is as lovely as you are it is not possible, as I am sure you realise, it is not possible to be naked too often.'

Boy took his clothes off slowly and carefully, laying them on the carpet. When he had done this he tried on each of the three dresses he had chosen. The first was in a heavy gold and black brocade, with a mandarin collar, and cut cripplingly tight in the Chinese style; the second was a plain scarlet taffeta ballgown from the famous April 1947 collection, with a satin sash and matching elbow-length gloves; the third was also in scarlet, but it was in silk, and was cut in the style of one hundred years earlier, leaving Boy's shoulders bare but his nipples covered by a boned, embroidered bodice decorated with antique lace, small silk and wax flowers, tartan ribbons and a cluster of jet beading. His back was left bare too, for he could not reach behind him to do up the forty hooks and eyes, so stiff was the boning. This dress he left on, and he looked again to Madame for her instructions, blushing slightly as he did so, for he was quite naked under the silk. She rose from her chair, and walked around him once. Then she walked to the dressing table, and opened a drawer. She took a gold and garnet necklace from a velvet-lined box and held it against Boy's bare shoulder. Unsatisfied, she went once more to the dressing table, returning with powder and a swansdown powder-duster. She powdered Boy's left shoulder with one movement of the swansdown, then held up the garnets for a second time, appraising the precise combination of colours; the blood of a blushing

skin beneath powder; the congealed blood of antique
garnets dulled by a bright gold setting; the scarlet,
brighter even than the freshest blood, of aniline-dyed
silk kept unworn in a wardrobe for a hundred years. She
returned to her chair.

'I think this last is the most appropriate. What do you
think, Boy?'

Boy looked at himself in the oval mirror and said,
'But Madame, how can I choose? How can I choose my
costume when I don't know what role I'm playing?'

And at this Madame just had to laugh, she laughed, she
looked straight at Boy and she said to him:

'Ah! How indeed!'

A week later, when the Bar was closed for the afternoon,
it being a Monday, Mother supervised the final rehearsal
herself, turning the spotlights on herself, sending the Boys
upstairs to change while she set out her best Turkey rug
and two valuable early nineteenth century dining chairs
as decor on the stage. She turned on all the coloured
lights and none of the white ones, so that the tiny stage
was striped and crossed by blue and yellow shadows. She
then sat and smoked for an hour; at the end of the hour
she knew that the boys were ready, for she heard Boy's
scarlet silks sweeping the walls of the staircase. He came
down first, followed by O in a wing collar and dress suit.

Mother was in her daytime working clothes; she had
poured herself a pint glass of cold water, pulled up a
stool and turned off all the lights except those on the
stage, so that all the semi-pornographic posters and the
ashtrays and the upturned chairs seemed not to be there
any more, and all she could see was the red of the carpet,
the blue and yellow shadows on the legs of the chairs,
and her two boys standing there in silence waiting for

her approval. O stood straightbacked in black and white behind one chair, his hair back and chin up, his hands clasped in the small of his back, already in the style of the period. Boy sat in the other chair in the chosen dress, to which he had now added all the accessories which Mother had selected to go with it and laid out beside it on the bed. His auburn wig had been freshly deepened with henna; his hands glittered with rings in which could be seen the distinct colours of several semi-precious stones; his powdered wrists (authentic *poudre de riz*) were circled with cameo bracelets, his neck and shoulders whitened to set off the garnets. When she saw them waiting on stage like this, Mother smiled, for she was very pleased by the way they wore their outfits; with such care, such accuracy and with such a promise of passion. She kept them waiting while she went behind the bar again and exchanged the pint of water for a glass of gin. She kept them waiting still; she lit another cigarette, looked up at her protegés and said:

'I am suitably impressed by your entrance. And yes, I have noticed that you are without your scripts and so are, I presume, word perfect. And perfect, as you know, is just how I want you. Imagine the music; begin.'

Boy at once stood, turned, clutched the back of his chair, turned again in an attitude of great fury and sank to his knees. O turned his back, one gloved hand still clasped in the small of his back, the other holding the back of his chair tightly enough to stretch the fine leather of his evening gloves, one knee bent, his perfect (*yes*, Mother noted, *perfect*) profile seemingly whitened and sharpened by anger, his nostrils flaring. Boy now let her hands (we may properly say *her* for he did, indeed, look like a lady) let her hands fall open to her sides in appeal or despair, her thin neck seeming to bend exhausted beneath the weight of her luxurious hair, her heavy embroidered dress rustling and glittering in a scarlet pool about her, flowing almost to the edges of the stage. The first line of the scene was O's. He said, in a voice thickened by rage:

'You are very hardhearted, my dear.'

and then Boy said, without looking up, said, in the stillest and strongest of voices:

'I hope not, Father.'

O turned his back; Mother took another drag of her cigarette, and Boy continued:

'I cannot ask you to understand, and I will not ask you to forgive me. My behaviour has indeed been perfectly disgraceful, but believe me, it has not hardened my heart. We live in such different worlds, do we not? Since nothing I do or say can shock you further, I will end this interview by asking you to lend me money. Please do not make the mistake of thinking that I leave this house because I have to. I rather choose to. I shall of course not make the mistake of thinking that you will acknowledge or even notice the difference between these two possible reasons for my departure. I need sixty-eight pounds to get to Paris, and I need it tonight.'

Boy's voice throughout this speech was level, quiet, astonishing in its intensity and quite perfect in its phrasing; he had practised it every night for seven nights. Every night for seven nights the woman who lived downstairs had heard the repeated thud first of the right knee and then of the left as he had experimented with the postures of 'supplication', 'entreaty', 'dignified rejection', 'end of

her tether' and finally 'penitence'. He had tied the two
heaviest blankets he could find in the flat around his waist
with an old belt to simulate the weight of the embroidered
gown, and had dragged them from room to room; the
paint on the back of his bedroom chair was now chipped
where for seven nights he had paced across the room,
turned and with one movement thrown his weight onto
both hands on the back of the chair, thrown back his head,
dug in his nails, made strange noises as of one choking
through clenched teeth and then turned again and slid to
his knees as he whispered again and again, 'I will not ask
you to forgive me, I *will* not ask you to forgive me, I will
not ask you to forgive me, I cannot bring myself to ask you
to forgive me, how can I ask you to forgive me, why should
I ask you to forgive me, Why? . . . '

His hours of rehearsal were well rewarded; his lines,
quiet as they were, came out with such force that O
couldn't remember his next line, even though he had
memorised his script. He turned, evidently alarmed by
the hushed violence of Boy's rendition. Mother too was
impressed; she stopped Boy with an abrupt gesture of
her hand, for she could see that, for all his self-control,
the young actor was breathing heavily, and appeared to
have forgotten where he was. She slipped off her stool
and came forward to the stage murmuring, *Boy, my
dear Boy*, and she offered him her glass of gin, which
he took without looking at her and drank in one fierce
gulp. And then he looked up and looked her full in the
face, which was the first time that he had really done
that, and his white-powdered female face and livid red
lips were suddenly split open by a masculine grin of
triumph. Mother climbed the six steps onto the stage and
she took hold of Boy's left hand and O took hold of his
right and they lifted him to his feet, and they stood there
for a moment and smiled at each other, all three of them,

O and Mother smiling with pleasure and pride in their young man, impressed, and Boy smiling because he had at last and so clearly and with such force said what he had wanted and waited so long to say. After a moment Mother cleared her throat, and the two men waited for her verdict.

'You are both good; very good. Splendid, in fact. I think we may assume that the rest of the piece will work without rehearsal. But splendid as it is, it is not enough. I want this performance to be remembered, discussed and imitated. Boy, I want you to go back upstairs now and to take off the dress and the wig, and to come back down here dressed as a man. You will find what you need in my wardrobe. Nothing else will need changing, except . . . '
    And here she took one of her famous and perfectly timed drags on her cigarette
    '. . . except that, of course, O, your first line will of course now read, "You are very hardhearted, *sir*."'

Mother had chosen for the night of their debut the anniversary of the death in prison of the famous writer who had once stayed in the building which was now The Bar; some of us even wore shirts which emblazoned the penultimate stanza of his most famous poem across our chests; they were discarded as the night grew hotter. The Bar opened late; so perhaps the dress rehearsal was after all a long one. The boys had been queueing outside, and they entered already sweating. They were hoping for great things, and they were not to be disappointed. The evening was indeed, as Mother had hoped, long remembered. Some of its most famous lines have since passed into common parlance. Indeed if you ask me now, even after all this time, if I am drunk again, or if you tell me that I'm looking tired, or if you come to me weeping to tell me that your affair is over, that your heart is this time for sure finally breaking, I am still likely to take a deep breath, summon all my conviction, look up at you and say, *I hope not, Father*. But the complete text of the evening has not survived, and though I will do my best to recall it really I can't do the whole scene like they did it, no one can, no one does it like that any more, we don't see shows like that any more. When Mother disappeared and finally left us, only one script could be found amongst the papers in her room; and the first three pages of the text, that famous and very terrible scene between the Father and his Son, had disappeared for some reason. O played the Father, of course, and Boy delivered the Son's famous solo. Then in this second scene O came back on as The Lover, speaking in the same voice and wearing exactly the same costume, only having changed his necktie for one of a different colour. We were not at all confused by this; things being as they were between the two of them, we all thought it quite proper that O should play both Father and Lover to Boy in a single evening.

And anyway, Mother had explained the whole scenario to us before the piece commenced, giving a synopsis and a brief oration in honour of the forgotten writer in front of the curtain: 'But don't you forget,' she said, 'don't any of you forget him,' with Gary playing Chopin or something like it on the piano the whole time she was speaking.

So here is the surviving text of that evening, and if you never saw Boy, not even when he was older, you'll just have to imagine the strongest, the most handsome, the most dark-eyed Boy you ever saw; you'll have to be nearly in love with him yourself, as we all were in those days, and leave it at that. And remember as you hear these lines that at this time they loved each other so much, and we had been waiting for their declaration for so long, and The Bar was full to screaming, and we all loved Mother so much, and our summer nights then

were to die, and that the storm was coming, and that on
this night of all nights we were all a little excited, a little
hopeful, a little drunk. And when they walked onstage
together with O in his clipped moustache and dogskin
gloves and evening dress with the wired gardenia in his
buttonhole, and Boy in black and white too, with Mother's
diamond on his finger which we hadn't seen for weeks
and all thought Mother must surely have sold, it was
worth so much; when they walked on I heard silence,
the only complete silence I ever heard in that bar. And
in that silence, the storm over the city began to break;
the thunder started, just quietly, but just loud enough
so that when Boy spoke he had to raise his voice just
a little, he lifted his perfect face up into the lights and
he raised his voice to meet the coming thunder, and he
said:

*(Lord Selby paces up and down the persian carpet, his
delicate features drawn and pale. His face is that of a
portrait by Van Dyck, while his hands have the nervous
pallor and energy of a Van Dyck copied by Whistler.
The ormolu clock strikes twelve.)*

SELBY: Oh, why is he not here! Why is he not here
to support me in my weakness?—to kindle in me
the flames of that passion which only he can ignite
and by whose flames alone I can warm these chilled
limbs of mine, this icy heart, this heart cooled first
by Shame and then by the fear of the death of
Love. He said he would he here—I heard him tell
Lord Derby he would be here—and yet it is gone
twelve. Oh, why should he be unfaithful on this
night of all the dark nights of my life? Why? For
it is tonight that I must choose, tonight that I must
accept him as my companion in flight, or leave him
for ever. I have heard it said that men are cruel,

that they don't know their strength; I have heard
it whispered that he is cruel, that he only plays
with me as a man may play with a woman—why
then do I wait here with such hope, such beatings
of the heart! It is madness to wait so, madness,
oh!

*(He places his hands against his temples in a gesture of
terror and pain. Claude Price has entered behind him,
unseen, as calm as ever. He carries a small valise, and
is wearing a magnificent fur. He has not forgotten that
it is better to travel well dressed than to arrive on time.
He stands for a moment watching Selby and listening
to his speech. Selby realises he is there, and turns with
a wild cry. Price takes his hand, kisses it, and then
releases it.)*

PRICE: And did you doubt me then? Was it so long
to wait? Did you think that I did not already know
your mind, that I had not already planned and paid
for our journey? Are you ready?
SELBY *(after a pause, solemnly)*: I may not be . . . but
take my hand again, and I will follow you.
PRICE: Come, then. I have arranged for a room to
be made ready for us in Paris. We shall be there
by dawn, and when we have rested I shall show
you all the pleasures of that great and sinful city.
I shall show you the life which you deserve; the
life of which I know you have often dreamt, young
as you are; a life lived far from your Father, far
from this house, far from the idle accusations of
this night. A life in which you need never feel fear
again, only that fear which is called excitement. A
life which we shall lead together; a life which now
begins.

(Price extends his hand; Lord Selby hesitates, then takes it. We do not see them kiss; Price stares into Selby's face, which brightens with courage as the curtain falls. Music.)

And as that curtain fell, the small curtain of fake red velvet with the appliquéd double crown which Gary had rigged up, the crowd was silent in The Bar—and I tell you, we were not often silent in that bar. And then under Gary's piano music (he was playing a Foster song now I think) there was a roll of thunder right over our heads, and then, from the back of the bar, came a piercing scream, from one of the girls, Stella probably, who had been standing on a chair so that she could see, and now could contain her delight no longer. And that scream did it to us all; we let go, and then it was screams, whistles, flowers of course, and such applause, a great roar of applause as the curtain went up again and Mother stood glittering in the footlights between her two men, her boys, wearing *the* dress of course, and then she took a step backward and ushered those two forward like the conductor does with his soloists at the ballet or at the opera, and then she took the step forward again, and without saying anything she lifted O's left hand and she lifted Boy's right hand high and then she did what we had all been waiting for her to do all night and what we had all come to see, she joined their hands together in public. And that got the loudest roar of all, I mean, that was it, they stared proudly out straight at their audience just as if we were all in some theatre or opera house for the evening, and then they turned and smiled at each other like they always do when they've just finished the greatest duet of the evening; chests heaving but pretending to be so calm; and they lifted their joined hands to the ceiling, and that was it, that was it, you couldn't hear the thunder for us shouting and clapping. And that was it; I had tears in my eyes, and they were engaged.

Then it was vodka cocktails and champagne all night for those of the congregation who stayed after the door was shut, and Gary was drunk too and played the duet from *Don Carlos* on the piano even when 'I only want to be with you' was playing over the loudspeakers at full volume, and I remember O with his moustache dripping with champagne and his bow tie undone but otherwise still looking the perfect gentleman (I fancied him so much in that outfit I had to stay at the other end of the bar and only look occasionally—have you never seen another man so handsome it makes you almost want to cry or leave the room? Haven't you? Why don't you get me a drink?) and I remember him later going down on Boy right here in the bar while we were all looking under a table for a lost pearl shirt-stud or something, and we were all kissing and laughing and almost falling over, and now I don't remember anything else about that famous night though I do remember that it was wild. And of course the thing was that none of us knew till the next morning, when those of us who had stayed all night opened the door and had to make our way home through empty streets littered with glass and fallen tree branches, none of us knew that around us in the darkness the city was being wrecked in the storm. We heard and saw nothing; we were too intent on our celebration.

And none of them knew that at the height of the storm, as Gary played that single note twelve times to indicate the striking of the ormolu clock, the city itself had celebrated O and Boy's engagement, but in the strangest fashion. There had been no assaults that night, but the storm had been strong enough to bring the streetlights down and fill the air with tiles coming down like slate knives; whole sheets of copper were torn from the domed roof of the court building and crashed down; parked cars rocked where they stood; the river turned black. The illuminated clock on the tower went dark for an hour, and above the deserted streets all the statues of the city were shaken and tested by the storm. They beckoned to each other, their arms upraised against the winds in benediction, exhortation, jubilation; and when the rain finally came, just before morning, the stone and metal of these limbs, which had become warm, almost as warm as flesh, in the heat of the long summer day and evening, seemed to take on a sort of life. Of course none of the statues was actually seen to move; that would have been a miracle; but as the rain fell they seemed, though immobile, to live. The Temple dragon in the Strand mewed a clear poison which dripped from under his forked tongue. The great, stupid, sleeping lions in the square drooled saliva and seemed about to rise and roar; a kind of clear blood ran down the blade of the uplifted scimitar with which the Allegory of Fortitude protected her naked child from the snake pinned beneath her foot at the Aldwych; there was so much blood it ran over the handle of the scimitar and down over her wrist. The wings of the Victory alighting atop the arch at Park Lane found a wind for once adequate to their size, weight and fury; her horses reared at the lightning and were lathered with sweat. On the parapet of the cathedral at Ludgate, St Agatha expressed a single drop of milk from the nipple of her stone breast. And on churches, tombstones, banks and derelict theatres, all the angels of London wept; tears dripped down their metal cheeks and trickled from under their stone eyelids. Since their faces did not move, their reasons for crying on this occasion remained hidden. There are, after all, times when people cry silently and without moving. One often cannot tell, at weddings or funerals or other festivals, whether people are crying for joy or in still, silent anger. The adolescent angel marking the vanished playground in which thirteen children had been killed by a bomb on the Commercial Road wept with downcast eyes; the gilt angel before the Palace wept and seemed to smile even as she held aloft her unextinguished flame; even Michael, Prince of all the city's angels, wept on the porch of St Peter, Cornhill. And above them all the great golden figure on the Old Bailey, Justice herself, blindfolded and armed just as Love is armed and blind, Justice herself was seen to move; she rocked and swayed in the storm.

. . . follow now the direction of her blinded gaze. On the other side of the city, lost in a park, two war memorials stand facing each other, and here too a male couple hold hands before their peers. On one memorial six identical men stand silently at attention. The rain drips from their heavy capes—sodden canvas turned cold as metal, and as heavy—and it drips from the brims of the metal helmets that hide their faces. And down those darkened faces the tears also run. On the other, older memorial, overlooked by their weeping comrades, two men, both moustachioed and wild-eyed, hold onto each other and gaze away from the city to some far horizon, and they too are crying tonight. The younger has fallen to his knees, but is supported and steadied by the hand of the other, who, older, is still able to stand. His shirt is open, and the rain makes his perfect and heroic chest sweat.

These two memorials stand in an avenue of plane trees, and a single branch of one tree endlessly, silently, brushes the standing soldier's shoulder, endlessly tapping, as if endlessly trying to make him turn again, turn again. And in this night's storm the branch begins to slash at and break itself on the standing man's broad and unfeeling back; the wind makes the tree desperate, a hoyden, breaking its nails and bruising its fingers, pulling tirelessly at the metal buckle on his shoulder; and the soldier is crying, and he holds his dear Friend's hand, holding on for dear life; and the tree is crying out into the night wind, saying to him all night, turn, turn, turn, turn, turn.

Sunday

Dear Boy,
I expect you will have seen on the news how terrible
it has been down here. We have been hit worse than
anyone I think.

You know that I have always liked to think of
this small part of the world as something which I'll
be handing down to future generations, something of
value which I can leave behind me having done a
good job. I'm more of a custodian or guardian than
an owner is how I see it. It is, in a very special
way and without being sentimental about it, my life's
work; but it also represents the lives of all the other
men who have lived and laboured here.

I often think about the men who planted the or-
chard, and I have done so many times in the last
week while surveying the damage. They must have
known they would never have seen the trees
mature themselves, but must have hoped that their
children and indeed children's children might one
day pick the fruit on summer evenings, and think of
them as they did so. It makes me sad to think of
all the children who have climbed in those trees,

*and indeed all the times when ordinary decent men
and women have walked under them, holding hands
when their work was done—you know how sweet the
evenings can be here—I expect those trees have seen
some lovemaking and even children conceived in the
grass beneath them in their time. Well it's all gone
now, the whole lot, and the copper beech too, down
right across the road it is. All destroyed in one night.*

*Of course they'll never be replanted, that's the sad
thing, not that you could replant that orchard now
anyway, fifteen different varieties there were, and you
can't get those old varieties any more, just can't find
them. They'll bulldoze the trees I expect and sell the
field for housing. It make me sad just to think about
it, tiny houses, cheap houses I expect, all crammed
together, and such apples they were, sweetest straight
off the tree.*

*The rest of the garden is unrecognisable. The
quince was torn right off the wall; the big bed
of roses, which as you know holds such special
memories for me, is all but gone.*

*It's a sad day for all of us I think,
goodnight, Father.*

PUBLISHING THE BANNS

That was a strange couple of days then, with the city
picking itself up, and you noticed how much was gone
or fallen in the storm, and you wondered who wasn't in
to work; despite hearing the word frequently on the news,
we were all surprised that there could be 'devastation' in
our time and in our city. People told each other stories,
went to bed at night listening out for the sound of the wind
rising.

In the aftermath of the storm everything was precarious
and strange. Even though the wind had died down, for
days afterwards loosened slates would still slide down
onto the streets. The injuries the storm caused were
frightening; especially because we associated knives and
fists coming down with darkness, with shouting, whereas
these 'assaults' came in daylight; one slate sliced open the
astonished face of a four-year-old child walking across
a school playground. A man walking on the Charing
Cross Road was brought to his knees by a great sheet
of hardboard which fell silently and suddenly from a
boarded-up façade high above him. It rained on the stage
of the opera house; beneath the stage, unseen, a lake was
said to be spreading. In the National Gallery a plank
came through a glass roof and smashed the face from a

valuable terracotta bust; and that night rainwater worked
its way down the walls towards the surface of a great and
priceless painting. The next morning they rescued the
painting and polished the stained gallery floor; an elderly
woman, staring intently at the masterpiece, slipped on the
over-polished floor, sat there dazed and badly hurt, not
knowing why or how she had fallen.

And also there was another assault, the day after
the storm, but it went unremarked amongst all these
incidents. The knife came down on a man of about
thirty-four that time I think. It was a strange couple of
days.

That was when Boy received the next letter, which
I have included above.

They were strange days, and difficult ones for Boy and
O. We worried about them. Mother said:

'What does happen next, Gary? I mean, I know I've
seen this film before. Is this the scene where he . . . '

And there she petered out, and Gary didn't answer, he
just began to pick out her song on the piano, as if that was
some kind of answer to her question.

And Boy said to Older, 'You know what's happening,
don't you, you know all about it?'

and O replied:

'No. She's never done this before. I mean, I don't know
why she's doing this to us in particular; God knows, there
are enough of us about.'

O took Boy in his arms and said:

'It would be a great mistake for you to ever assume that
I know that much more about what we're doing than you
do.'

The truth was, Mother had taken back the diamond, after
lending it to them for their engagement night, but she was
giving them money. One man that she had chosen mostly

for his looks and one man she had hardly ever spoken to, yet here she was spending considerable money and more time on turning these two into a couple, a prize pair. There was a fierceness about the way she did it; as if this was the last chance for her, for all of us, not just for them. Sometimes she seemed to be staring at them all night, watching every single move they made and you did sometimes wonder why she was doing it, cultivating them like this. I suppose somebody had to be perfect, that was it. She kept no diary, so there is no record of her thoughts on this matter, and nothing was found in her papers to explain it (though what we did find was a meticulous record of every penny she had spent on them, not just the furniture and the flat but also every drink which she had bought them since the very first day of Boy's life in The Bar). There was one note which I think is something of an explanation:

'I have never minded before but the buildings are torn down so fast these days, and I don't mean the storm. Every time you go back something's gone. Never sure that the schools and public buildings won't just go too. I think we're getting used to having things taken away, a few speeches on the nine o'clock news, and everyone will get used to walking from Stepney to the Haymarket again, or from Camden to Covent Garden, at four in the morning like they used to, the cold fingers, and hiring a van once a year to take all the children in the building—'

When O was working every day of the week, Boy missed him, and wanted to ask him if he would come home for lunch. It was as if he worried about him whenever he couldn't actually see him. This was the first time he had ever felt this; it was a new feeling. A new phase. Then O suddenly told Boy that he wasn't going to see him for two days. He said he needed to sleep on his own for two days, needed to rest, needed to eat, needed to go to the pool and do his face and hair. He said *meet me in two days time OK, give me forty-eight hours*. What he wanted to say was, *I need to think*. What he really wanted to say was, *I need to decide*.

They had arranged to meet somewhere else for a change, because O had said he didn't want to be watched by everyone. *You'd think*, he said, *they were waiting for the next instalment of their favourite soap opera. I want you to myself for once. What's happening between us is private*. Boy hadn't replied to this observation, but had agreed nonetheless to meet O in a cheap restaurant in a different part of town in two days' time.

Boy had spent the two days waiting, and then finally on the Tuesday night specified he had laid his clothes out, and bathed, and shaved without cutting himself, and did his hair and dressed without changing his mind, which was unusual, and had set out exactly on time. He was looking especially handsome, having chosen a white t shirt which looked ordinary but in fact had cost him four weeks of economy; it fitted his chest and his stomach with an elegant indecency which, in another age, had expressed itself in a made-to-measure glove, a white evening glove in which one young man's hand reached out to cup another young man's chin.

Boy thought he had got used to waiting for O, since now all he did (or so he thought) was wait; especially since O had phoned him that time, because now even when he was alone in his room there was the possibility that not only was O thinking about him but he might actually pick up the phone and call. But evidently he had not got used to the waiting, because now he found that as he was sitting on the bus riding to his appointment with O he was actually holding his breath. He thought, *by now, surely, surely by now I should be sure that everything is going to*

*be all right. Surely now I don't need to worry about what
is going to happen next.*

He knew at first glance that O was not there. He drank
two glasses of wine, which he pretended to enjoy, and
even at one point managed to concentrate on the music
which was playing. By nine thirty he knew that O was not
coming, and of course he also knew where to find him.

It didn't occur to him to be angry, since he thought of
everything that O did to him as some sort of deliberate
test which he must pass. This was another. He walked
from the restaurant to The Bar, which was an hour away,
and when he arrived he was tired and calm and ready
to sit down. Everybody saw Boy come in and of course
everybody was thinking, *well, here he is at last, we were
wondering what had happened.* Boy had a beer, feeling
the need to act casually, and then casually he asked if
anyone had seen O that evening, and he guessed why
they were all half-smiling, and he half-guessed what they
would say, and indeed Gary said it, without even pausing
in his rendition of 'Only You' on the piano, (because it was
a Tuesday night, which was show-song night); Gary said,
he's upstairs with Mother. Gary said it as if it was quite
an ordinary thing to say, as if this happened all the time,
and although Boy knew that everyone said no one, but
no one, went up to Mother's room, he thought to himself
that perhaps this did happen all the time, perhaps O was
often upstairs with Mother, perhaps they went upstairs
and planned their next move. Perhaps they were talking
about him now.

Boy had the wit not to make for the door behind the
bar immediately. He did not especially want everyone
to watch him. He finished his beer slowly, knowing
somehow that it would be considered tactless to move
too fast. He even looked around The Bar, as if to say,
is there anyone else here tonight who would do, is there

anyone else I could spend time with instead? And then, *well no, perhaps not, OK, I'll finish my drink now, yes, there it is, finished, and I'm climbing down off my stool* (he had sat on the stool which O usually occupied), *and here I go, I'm walking behind the bar which only the most important customers are allowed to do, here is the door, which no one opens except by invitation, and here are the stairs, I'm closing the door behind me, here are the stairs, all I have to do now is climb them.*

Let us imagine the scene; we'll have to, since Boy shut the door behind him, and left us to speculate as to what happened. Boy very much wanted to go upstairs, to interrupt Mother and O while they were talking. Or rather what he really wanted to do was to overhear, to hear them talking about him, to know what they really thought about him. But in fact, he only got half way up the stairs, and then sat there in the dark, his chin in his hands. And I think that is where O found him when he came down; I think O just picked him up, explained that Mother had wanted to talk to him about money, and that it was all arranged, that they were indeed going to live together, that he'd decided, that she was going to provide the money for somewhere suitable for them to live together, and that they should go downstairs now and have a drink and then go quietly home and talk about what sort of place they would need and if they could get it on the rent Mother was proposing. Because when they came down it was very much together, and Boy looked very quiet and happy and had lost that lost-dog expression he had had when he went upstairs. Clearly they had come to some agreement.

But while Boy was sitting there in the dark, waiting, he must have been thinking, and this may have been what he was thinking or imagining. Since he wanted so much to go upstairs, he may have imagined himself doing it, pushing open the heavy door in silence, and watching the two of them.

The first thing he saw was a hundred candles, some guttering and colouring the atmosphere of the room with a layered blue haze, but most of them burning brightly, so that he felt a wave of heat as if he had opened the door onto a ballroom and its blazing chandeliers.

In fact what he actually saw were the two candles in the cut-glass candlesticks on Mother's bureau, one extinguished and smoking, the steady flame of the other reflected and multiplied in the shining surfaces of the room, the mirrors, the polished wood of the wardrobe, the glass and the gilt frames of all the pictures, the burnished bronze. Each mitred pane on the bookcase held the reflection of a flame; behind the glass the gold lettering on the red leather spines of Mother's library shone. The desktop itself shone as if newly French-polished; the light of the single flame also made the thighs and uplifted arm of the small bronze statue on top of the wardrobe (which Boy had not noticed before) shine as if the miniature athlete had just oiled himself. Above, what Boy had thought before was just red paint on the ceiling now seemed to be some kind of rich lacquer or gilding, and the glow of the multiplied candle flames was caught in that too; and the wallpaper which he had thought was just paper had become, by candlelight, a cut velvet brocade with a gold thread in it; and the curtains, which had been drawn back on the only other occasion on which he had seen this room, were now drawn across the window, and they were scarlet brocade, a deep thicket of scarlet foliage in which golden birds stalked, preened and courted. On the desk itself glittered Mother's gilt-and-crystal scent bottles and her scattered jewellery, including the gold-set garnets; there was a single glass of wine which had been poured from a Bohemian ruby glass decanter. One bottle

of scent was unstoppered, and the room was heavy with
musk.

To Boy's dazed eyes, the whole room was scarlet
and gold—the curtain, the damasked walls, the Turkey
rugs—and, in the midst of it, Mother herself seemed to
be in scarlet too, wearing an extraordinary scarlet copy
of her usually white and silver dress. Then Boy realised
that it was the red room and the candlelight that made her
scarlet; the crystal and sequin work of the dress reflected
the colours around her.

O was sitting in Mother's chair, with Mother standing
behind him, so that Boy could see them both reflected
in and framed by the oval mirror over the desk. They
were watching themselves. O was naked, and shirtless,
and his jeans and underpants were pulled down like
hobbles around his ankles. His body was the only white
thing in the room. His head was tipped back and was
resting between Mother's great breasts, and his throat
was working like a baby's when it is suckling; he was
gasping for air. His face was half hidden; Mother had let
down her hair and it had fallen and covered him. This was
something which her public never saw; Mother's great
treasury of raven hair released from its silver pins one
by one and let down, as heavy as a theatre curtain and
as luxurious as a coat with a collar of lynx or wolf.

In the centre of a red room, then, Boy saw an oval
mirror, and in the centre of the mirror, a white body,
and in the centre of the white body the black target of
O's black-haired belly, groin and thighs; and in the centre
of this blackness, O's cock, and around it, the white and
scarlet of Mother's red-nailed left hand; for Mother has
one hand cupped under O's chin and with the other, the
hand on which her diamond is shining, she has reached
down to his erect penis and is slowly, slowly masturbating
him. O's genitals too are shining in the light; there is a
small cut-glass jar of some ointment open on Mother's

desk and with this she has covered her hand and O's cock, and his cock and all the black hair around it is shining and glistening as her hand moves steadily up and down.

Boy is not horrified to see this but fascinated. The way that Mother is touching O is so firm and so intimate that Boy guesses that this is the kind of lovemaking that old friends indulge in, or people who have been together for years; the kind of expert touch that evokes the memories of all the sex that has happened before. As Mother continues her firm strokes, going right from the head of his cock to the balls, Boy sees O's stomach begin to tense and heave slightly, and hears him begin to whimper. Then he sees him reach up and pull a handful of Mother's black hair into his mouth to stop himself from crying out, or perhaps to smell and feel it more fully, or perhaps without thinking but just because he wants something in his mouth. Knowing that he is nearly there, Mother moves her hand not faster but slower and slower, and slower, and O slowly arches back in the chair, and then he comes and his come splashes over Mother's hand and flows down over her rings.

All this is done in silence, with only Mother's hand moving, and the reflections of the candle flame wavering slightly.

And Boy wants to break the silence, he wants to let them know that he is there, he wants to just quietly say, *I do that, I do that too.*

Now Boy sees Mother slowly looking up from her task; as she looks up her hair is pulled out of O's mouth and away from his face, and in fact both of them are now looking at Boy standing there in the mirror; from the way they look it seems that both of them knew all along that he was watching. The crystals of Mother's dress crackle slightly in the candlelight as she shifts her weight and pushes her hair back with one hand; Boy can see now

that the scarlet lipstick is wiped half across her face, and
that there is scarlet on O's face and around his nipples;
and that his shoulders and neck are red where they have
been rubbed and scratched by the beading of Mother's
dress. And he sees that the black of O's eyes, the black of
Mother's eyes, and the black of O's hair, and the black of
Mother's hair, is exactly the same black. O's chest is still
heaving from his orgasm. Mother places herself squarely
behind him and puts her hands on his shoulders—a bit
like the move that a barber makes when he has finished
your hair and checks that the cut is perfect, or like that of
an angel displaying the corpse of a saint. She seems to be
displaying O or rather O's body to Boy, and she smiles and
she says, *I know you do, I know you do that too Boy. Take
him, he's all yours. No, really, he is all yours, but remember,
I taught him everything he knows.*

And Boy understands what Mother means, in the way that
one does understand people in dreams, because he knows
that what she says is true, that every trick and skill of O's
body, every sound he makes and position that he knows
has been shaped by the advice and admiration of other
men, and that Mother feels herself to be responsible for
all the men who have ever slept with O, all the men he has
ever met in her bar, that she has witnessed or imagined
them all; that every phrase of his confessions, both filthy
and tender, has been learnt or adapted from someone else
under her jurisdiction or on her premises, and that now he
has brought all of this history of his body, has brought it
to Mother and confessed it to her, asking her permission
to now give it over into the care of another. And that now
Mother has indeed given her permission.

Boy was not sure, as Mother lifted O up out of his
chair, and held him there with his semen splashed all
over his stomach and thighs, if she was leading him, or
pushing him, or giving him away; but he knew that she

was somehow saying, *this is what you get, here he is, take him off my hands. He's yours now. He's decided.*

She bent forward, and gave Boy O's hand. Did Boy imagine that she also gave him a big fat roll of money? Did she do that? Did he remember that right?

The other thing that Boy noticed in this scene and tried to remember later was the photographs. He looked again at the set of six portraits of famous women which he had thought were reproductions; and he saw that the paper was not the thin paper of a modern reproduction, but a thick matt paper with a look as rich as powdered skin. And he saw, written across Bessie Smith's half-exposed left breast in fat brown ink, the words *Missie, Miss, Mother, Mama—what the hell—Bessie.* And he saw, written right across the silk draperies behind Billie's beautiful face *All of me—why not?—take all of me.* And these words seemed to him to be a kind of confirmation or permission granted; specifically, the autographs on the portraits looked to him like the signatures of witnesses, signatures on the contract which he felt had been made in that scarlet room.

So anyway they came back downstairs, with Boy's arm around O's shoulders, which was the first time that we'd seen that particular gesture. They'd made their agreement, they'd confirmed their decision, they'd decided to live together, and they looked more ordinary somehow. A regular couple, just like an ordinary couple, as if they were going to start talking about a mortgage and furnishings.

We all said, *will it last?* (And do you doubt it? Do you doubt this whole story? Do you find it strange that two men should come together like this and then stay

together? Do you find it strange that we should have
wanted so much for them to stay together? Do you?)

Mother said, *it will last.* She practised speeches about
them under her breath while she sat there on her stool.
Never had she seen (and she had seen so many in her
years on that stool), never had she seen such a matching
pair of beauties; never had she seen a pair so deserving
of being a couple. *My Boys* she called them, *my dogs,
my matching carriage pair; bitch and daughter is always
the best pairing they say, and that's you two, my boys.
Why don't you two get married?*, she says in jest as she
passes, *why don't you two get married?* she says. *Fall in
love, get married, have a baby*, she says, *you're so fucking
gorgeous I can't stand it. I'd pay good money to watch you
two doing it*, she says. *You two walk hand in hand down
the promenade and I'll think the revolution's come*, she
says. *You two walk down the street holding hands and no
one's going to bring the knife down on you*, Mother says.

Mother says: *for this cause shall a man leave his Mother
and his Father.*

ROBING THE BRIDE

I do not want to give the impression that this whole
betrothal of theirs was strangeness and difficulty. Some
nights they were so happy. I can remember watching
them when Stella II was on one night, doing her 'That Was
Then But This Is Now' selection, and Boy was mouthing
the lyrics at O, *signed, sealed, delivered, I'm yours*, and
they both laughed, O laughing longest until his laugh
was stopped by Boy's sweet kiss. They were always about
to kiss, like actors in an Indian film, always about to kiss
and making you want to see them do it. Of course they
kissed all the time, in public, indeed they were notorious
for it, they could even make me turn aside and not look,
so passionate and personal were their kisses. And again
when one time I was sitting near them and when O came
back from the toilet he had an erection, I could see it, and
Boy saw it too and smiled a dirty smile and O just stood
in front of him and cupped his balls and his stiff cock in
his hand, grabbing himself down there, and said to Boy,
that's how strong my love is, using the exact intonation
that Otis Redding used in 1964. Oh they were so happy,
so very happy, I wish you could have seen them. It would
do you good to see them. You know, sometimes you see
two men, and you think, *oh, oh yes—*

It would not have surprised me to have seen them at that time walk naked and hand in hand down the street, so proud were they of each other; or at least bare-chested and barefoot and sweeping the pavements with some extraordinary gowns, like saints, that was the way they walked when they were out together. They were so very much in love; I used to just stand and watch them. I had not seen so many men be that way, and I still could not quite believe that it could be that way. In fact these days I still cannot quite believe it, I cannot believe that an affair like that is either legal or possible.

You just can't believe that these things happen.

This period was the height of their fame. We normally used the phrase *the crown jewels* to refer to the packet on somebody; but now the phrase began to be used of O and Boy when they were out together; you'd look round to see if they were in, and if they were, you'd say, *I see the Crown Jewels are on display again tonight*, which was mocking, but it was heartfelt too. We were so proud of them that year. We were glad to have them in our midst. Of course every year or so there is a new reigning couple, a new pair of heroes that the young men arriving look at and think, *oh, I want it to be me, I want it to be me, I want it to be me*; and that is why men like them are fabulous, in the true sense of the word. Because we need them to be. When people say, *was it really like that?* you want to say, *yes*, and you want to say, *and it still is*.

They had made their choice, they'd made their decision, they'd had their decision approved; they even had the money. Now what they had to do was name the day for the actual ceremony.

It happened at a very famous party, one of our best. The title for the evening was 'It Was Twenty Years Ago Today', and it took us weeks to get ready.

Mother had fake hardboard walls put up which made The Bar much smaller, even though she was expecting a capacity crowd. In the event, it was a real crush, which was correct, I mean it was historically correct, because you see everywhere was much smaller in those days, everywhere was upstairs or down the stairs, well hidden. Those places—you went in on a Friday night, and you'd come out on Sunday morning with no clothes left. The music was period (not that you noticed, because we had never really stopped playing the old music anyway), and the pictures were of curly-haired Californian boys in shorts, sitting astride logs in cut-off shorts, smiling. (You never see men smiling in these pictures nowadays.) And of course the costumes were period; things we never thought we would see again. I wondered how O and Boy were going to come, because I was thinking, I don't remember there being affairs like theirs twenty years ago, you couldn't do it in the same way. In the end they came as Banker and Rent, O in a velvet collared overcoat and Boy taking pills in the toilet, it was quite an act.

The costume of the evening, predictably, was Stella's. It had taken her weeks. She came as Mother, or, more precisely, as Miss, which is who Mother had been twenty years ago. The dress was relatively easy, since they'd persuaded Mother's own dressmaker to make a copy for them. The wig too, because they'd found a photograph which showed the correct style. Mother was a blonde then. They even faked the diamond. The face was the hard part; Stella and Stella II had devoted a week of experimentation to recreating the effect of the period combination of panstick, powder and thick eyebrow pencil.

When I saw her come in, I was shocked. It was perfect. Mother herself paled slightly, and the cigarette she had

been moving to her lips stopped in mid gesture. Everyone
turned to watch the confrontation. Stella, she who always
looked everyone straight in the eye, as if to say, *you got
a problem darling?*, even Stella had to look down and
could not meet Mother's eyes; she felt like she was at
a presentation at court, and had to resist the temptation
to drop into a full curtsey. Mother looked at Stella, then
opened her handbag and took out a small photograph,
which was in fact a snapshot of herself in those days.
She was checking the accuracy of Stella's impersonation.
Then she lifted Stella's face up by taking her under the
chin, very regal, and said, said to herself as it were:

'How lovely it is to see you again after all these years.'

And then she took Stella to the bar and bought her eight
pints of bitter which is what she told Stella she used to
drink of an evening.

She said to Stella, installing her on the stool next to her
own, the seat of honour for the evening:

'I think you know almost as much about all this as I do,
girl.'

There were two Mothers in The Bar that evening; they
spent the whole night talking. At the end of the party, O
and Boy were summoned. Stella said:

'Shall I be Mother?'

and Mother gave her permission, saying:

'Be my guest.'

'Well,' said Stella, clearly relishing the role, 'what we
want to know is, just when exactly when are you going
to make an honest woman of him, O? We need to know.
After all, there will be sewing to do and suchlike. Name
the Day.'

And of course, put like that, well, he just had to. He
named the day, they got their flat and they went ahead
and got married.

*

Immediately prior to the wedding there was the period of final preparation, which we referred to as The Robing of the Bride.

We all said this must have been very hard for Boy, no matter how much he wanted it, and some of us thought that O was going too far now, there were things he did in this period of the affair that we didn't know whether to believe or not. And I for one at this point did wonder just why he and Madame were working so hard, so very hard, what it was they had to prove which meant they had to make such extravagant efforts, why they couldn't make it just a little easier, especially on Boy.

The charades began in the living room of O's flat, and they took a whole week.

The first costume was that of a drag queen, which in a way was the easiest to do. Stella told Boy sisterly stories of harassment and insult while ruthlessly criticising his appearance, rubbing foundation into the cuts on his hastily-shaved neck, working at speed, not deigning to comment on the half erection he got when he put on the high heels.

When he was ready, Stella called O into the room to see the finished transformation.

Stella said:

'He looks terrible. Quite frankly, the whole thing is ridiculous.'

A week earlier Stella had asked Boy for a photograph of himself at school, and Boy had found one in his box of papers and had handed it over. This was in preparation for the second night, when, having gone to great trouble to find exactly the correct school uniform in a theatrical hire agency and having had it copied in larger size, Stella made Boy look fourteen again. When she had done this she was so excited, she wanted to stay and watch the scene; but O sent her home. Then O pretended to be Boy's teacher, and asked him questions that would have mortified Boy at fourteen; at nineteen, they made him realise how little he still knew, how easily he still blushed, how hard he found it to look in a man's eyes, how he still didn't have a way of talking about these things.

O behaved as if he had just caught Boy doing something filthy, but was also clearly using the interview as an excuse to excite himself.

To all of his questions, Boy answered only *Yes Sir* or *No*; but O continued with the questions as if he had given full answers.

'Now Boy, (he said it as if the master addressed all the boys in the school this way, not as if it was an especial or personal name) I want to talk to you about the Facts of Life. Do you know about all this?

'Do you know what two people do when they go to bed together? They fuck, Boy, that's what they do, there's no need to be embarrassed about that word is there, Boy?

'Did you know that men go to bed with each other too, Boy?

'And do you know what those men actually do to each other in bed?'

Boy kept on answering just *Yes* or *No*. O handed him a photograph.

'Have you ever kissed a man like that Boy?

'How many men do you know like that? You do know men like that don't you?

'Are you like that? Are you sure you're like that? How do you know? What are you going to do about it?'

Boy thought, but didn't say, *surely I've got through that stage? Surely I've grown out of that?*

This interview ended in Boy and O having sex on the living room floor.

The third charade featured Boy in the role of a straight soldier out looking for trade. They needed a woman to make sense of this scenario, so Stella sat on his knee in a skirt and made him drink lager and smoke Benson and Hedges until he felt sick, saying, *you come home with me love, I'll get you something to eat, you look as though you need something nice and warm inside you.* Stella played it like some terrible old queen, in a terrible fake Lancashire accent, but Boy was very moved anyway. At the end of this evening, having seen him in uniform, O cut off all of Boy's hair, clipped it right short except for the handful at the front, and that is how Boy wore his hair from then on.

Boy knew, while he was being taught all this, that he was very lucky. He would say to himself out loud, so as to reassure himself that it was worth being this frightened this much of the time, *I'm so lucky, so lucky, so lucky.* And he knew that the wedding was due once he'd got through this week.

On the fourth night Boy had to play at being what Stella referred to as a small town queen ('And God, I should know,' she said). This time they smoked Marlboro and drank milky instant coffee; Stella had the television on all evening too. She put cushions covered in green dralon with cat hairs on them on the sofa, and put a copy of *Dance with a Stranger* on the coffee table. She said:

'Have you read that book? I've read it twice. It's really brilliant that book.'

For this charade she streaked Boy's new hairstyle with ash-blonde highlights, and dressed him in tight ice-blue jeans, two thin gold chains and a gold bracelet. She also asked O to bite Boy's neck so that he had two conspicuous bruises. The costume was easy; but it took two hours to practise the correct eye movements; the blatant but also frightened stare across the living room at O. Stella also made Boy practise the lines, 'What do you do then?' and 'Where are you from then?' over and over again. Referring to O, who was sitting watching the television, she said:

'Don't mind him, that's my friend Tom, he's a bit stoned. Been working all day haven't you love? Tom's a chef at the club.'

Then she said confidentially to Boy:

'He says he's straight, but it's alright, he won't mind. He's used to it.'

Then, having arranged this previously with O, Stella made love to Boy on the sofa with O watching. All the time they were doing it Stella kept on whispering in Boy's ear, keeping up a constant flow of comment, *oh yes, yes*, saying, *that's wonderful, that feels wonderful, ooh, kiss me, kiss me*, moaning, *oh darling, darling*.

When they'd finished Stella said to Boy:

'You know, you should never laugh. In this game you have to respect either everyone or no one and it had better be everyone. D'you want another coffee?'

For the fifth night O had written an actual script, and had typed it out. Despite Stella's help—she kept on suggesting different characters off the television that Boy could try doing—Boy could not get the voice right. This was the script:

Of course in those days we actually were rich. We used to buy the flowers first, and then think about who to give them to. I remember you used to arrive late, and there'd be so many flowers already you didn't even ask anybody to put them in water, you just left them right there on the hall table and went up. One boy I knew, he had this marvellous place right on Eaton Square, he always had to have white flowers, anything else and he wouldn't have it in the house, and everyone would vie to bring the strangest white flowers you'd ever seen, things you didn't even know existed, I mean I wasn't about to turn up with twenty white roses was I, anyway, you'd walk in, there'd be so many flowers, flowers for ever, and I said, Darling, did somebody die? It was flowers for days, and the drink, and the boys, darling, Guardsmen on duty in every room . . .

Boy could not do this voice, because he did not know what to think of this man.

On Thursday, they dressed Boy up as a black man. Stella made him up down to the bottom of the neck and up to the wrists and even made up his calves where they showed between the socks and suit trousers when he sat down. The costume was a shiny grey silk-mixture double-breasted suit, a seventy-two-pound cream silk shirt and a midnight-blue silk tie. A lizard skin strap on the watch; leather shoes and blue silk socks matching the tie. They made him take the trousers down; Stella made up his buttocks and his cock, and pushed it back into the pair of silk boxer shorts. She put three gold rings on each hand and gave him a bag of records bearing the label of a newly fashionable record store.

Of course Boy did not look like a black man at all. And neither O nor Stella had any precise ideas about how he should act or what he should say; but they took a polaroid of him anyway as they did with all these outfits.

All of these scenes were very private and we never knew about them until Stella spilt it all later ('After all I did for that Boy,' she said.) I think O knew that Stella would tell us all about it sooner or later; you see that way he made sure that we were all party to Boy's trials and humiliations, to his preparation for life in the city, their life. Boy knew as well, I think; he knew that when he next walked into The Bar we would all know, from Stella, just exactly what he had been through and what a fool he had made of himself for love (well that's how Stella put it anyway). But you see O fixed it very nicely; Boy did it in private, but what he did in private was public knowledge.

As I said this week of charades took place in O's living room. The seventh night however did involve Boy in going out.

This last and hardest transformation required that Boy become a woman. Stella explained that she wasn't quite sure what image to go for (she was lying; she knew exactly what she was doing, but was making Boy wait), but that she did know that she wanted to see Boy in a pair of sheer black tights, and perhaps her favourite silver charm bracelet. He took off all his clothes except his underwear and pulled on the tights, and put on the bracelet. 'Terrible,' said Stella.

'"No, No, No," they cried in unison,' said Stella, '"Off with his hair!"'

Stella asked if he knew how to do it, and Boy badly wanted to say *yes, I can do it by myself*, but what he said instead was *no*, so O and Stella put Boy in the bath of hot water they'd run for him, and Stella showed him how to use the razor properly, and then they sat on the side and talked, ignoring Boy, and Boy scraped and scraped until everything was smooth and the water was all red from where he'd cut himself on the backs of his knees and over the joints of his ankles and wrists. O sent Stella out of the bathroom. Boy stood up out of the bath of red water—he caught a glimpse of himself in the bathroom mirror, looking like a child again, hairless—and then like a child he stepped out of the bath and into the large white towel that O was holding up for him, and he let himself be wrapped and patted and powdered, and then and only then did O make him stand in front of the mirror and look at himself properly, a grown man with his lover standing behind him but looking just like a little boy, the forearms bare and pale, his belly, groin and thighs pure white again. O smiled at him in the mirror and lifted his hand and kissed it—Boy had even removed the hair from the backs of his hands and fingers.

Then O led Boy back into the living room where Stella had already smoked eight cigarettes and was listening, impatiently, to the Georgia Brown version of 'As Long As He Needs Me' for the fourth time in a row.

Stella did not consult Boy about what he wanted to wear; she's already emptied her black binliner of drag out in a heap on the living room floor, and now she began to work fast, holding dresses up against Boy's body, digging through the pile to find the right earrings, sticking pins into him in her haste (*fast, and furious*, thought Boy), saying, *turn round, lift your arms, keep them up, breathe in, bend over.*

Stella knew what she was doing. The dressing up was in fact the easy bit; she made the best of Boy's colouring and figure with expensive, fine black stockings and a cheap, short, tight, backless black dress from an Oxford Street store. High black shoes, red nails, red lips, pale powder, hair gelled right back like a shining skullcap, Stella's best earrings and a quilted clutch bag for the cigarettes.

Then came the hard part. Stella explained that it was one thing to drag up on stage and another to walk down the street as a woman. Stella made Boy walk up and down the living room carpet for eighty minutes while she worked on his walk. In fact Boy was very good at this; but Stella insisted that he was doing it wrong, that he was trying too hard, that if he walked like that they'd spot him the minute he walked out of the door. After eighty minutes she said she'd had enough and put Boy to the test. She told him to sit on the sofa, and then took his handbag and put it on the mantelpiece over the gas fire. She took her Silk Cut and her lighter from her own bag, sat down opposite Boy and very elaborately went to light a cigarette. At the climax of her gesture, she very deliberately dropped her lighter. She stopped herself (a held arabesque of wrist, lips, raised cigarette and raised eyebrow) and looked at Boy. Boy got up from the sofa, walked calmly over to Stella and picked up the lighter, remembering to bend at the knees with his knees together. Then he murmured quietly, *can I help?*, and flicked the lighter. It did not work, of course; Stella had earlier secreted a dud copy of her usual lighter in her bag specifically for the purpose of playing out this scene with props. Stella continued to hold her arabesque with the cigarette, leaning forward and still expecting a flame. Boy kept his nerve; he smiled again, rose, turned, walked across the room, got his bag, opened his bag, got out a book of matches from a fashionable restaurant which Stella had put in there earlier, tore off a match, lit it (none of these things are easily done with red-painted nails, with a short skirt and with a permanent yet natural smile), crossed the room with the lighted match, bent down and finally lit Stella's cigarette. She inhaled gratefully and thanked him sweetly. Then Boy rose, turned one last time and walked back across the room to the sofa, conspicuously displaying his back in the low cut of the dress. That was, after all, why Stella had chosen it.

'Impressive,' said Stella. 'One last thing; sit down.'

Boy did as he was told.

Stella sent O out of the room and closed the door, and then very quietly, and with great bitterness, and at great length, she described being on a night bus with a friend and seeing a man pull out a screwdriver and use it like a knife, bringing it down and pushing it in for no apparent reason, just with pure crude hatred, saying, while he did so, *you cunt, you cunt.* Then she filled her lungs with a single deep, sudden breath and in that one breath she called Boy all the names she herself had ever been called, beginning *you cunt, you bitch, you stupid fucking bitch, you stupid queen, do you know what I would like to do to you, you stupid fucking queen?* She repeated all the foulest and most humiliating insults that men and women had ever thrown at her. When this was done Stella was white faced and exhausted. She said, *I've taught you everything I know.* Then she kissed Boy on both cheeks like a sister and invited O back into the room. He had dressed up too; he was wearing black tie, and a fake diamond earstud which he would never have worn normally, and aftershave too. Stella called them a cab and O took Boy to a nightclub in the West End, which was much too expensive for them to have attended normally. No one in the club said anything, not because they could not see that Boy was in fact a man and not a woman, but because this strange couple looked so glamorous and so apparently unafraid (this was of course not true) that no one challenged them. Boy remembered all of Stella's patiently recited and rehearsed etiquette. *Smile at everyone and anyone, drink very slowly but steadily, spirits only or champagne, accept gestures such as a hand placed on the naked small of your back as compliments even if they are meant as questions. If someone asks you, are you on your own, you do not say 'Actually I'm with my boyfriend,' you say 'I am hoping to meet someone later,' and smile, and then look at the floor.*

All night, Boy could feel every inch of his body. The air on the small of his back—the unzipped, plunging back of the dress was so low that he could feel the air just touching the cleft at the top of his buttocks. He could feel the clasp of his string of pearls (Stella's parting gift as they had got into the mini-cab) resting just above his atlas vertebra.

When they got home, Older got undressed quickly and went to bed; he said to Boy, curtly, *clean yourself up and come to bed.* It took Boy half an hour to get his make up off, rubbing the mascara into a big grey ring around his eyes, having to use both grease and soap till his skin was raw. He felt all the particular pains that you feel after a night in drag; the calves of his legs ached, his face aching too from all the smiling, the cuts on his legs hurt, his feet were almost numb with pain from the shoes.

When he crawled into bed O was asleep with his back turned, like a husband or a man who has worked all week. It was four in the morning, and Boy understood that this was the end of this particular charade.

The next night there was no costume, and so Boy thought that his trials were over. Only later in the night did he understand that on this night, as an epilogue to the week of lessons, the costume was to be nakedness. When they were both undressed, O took Boy in his arms and laid him down on the bed, and deliberately laid him so that Boy was lying on his back. Then O lay down beside him and laid his head on Boy's chest as if it was wide, and warm and furry—he snuggled up to him; he did, in fact, what Boy usually did. And then Boy heard him say, as if O's deeper voice was somehow coming out of his own

body, for O was copying exactly the posture in which
Boy liked to lie on O's chest after Boy had come and
before they went to sleep, heard him say, 'Take care of
me now, you take care of me.' And Boy understood then
that their courtship was nearly concluded, that they were
almost there now.

And after all this dressing up was truly over, the next time
they went out to The Bar, O said to Boy, *which outfit do
you prefer? Or would you rather go just as yourself tonight?*

When they did come back to The Bar, when they finally
returned to the stage after this strange week in the
dressing room, I asked Stella how it had gone. I wondered
why they had been so private about it. *Oh*, she said,
the bride mustn't be seen in her dress, it's unlucky. And
I wondered why she'd given Boy such a hard time.
      'Oh I'm not sorry for that one. Not sorry at all darling.'
Stella pulled excessively hard on her Silk Cut. 'She makes
me cross sometimes that one.'
      I waited for the explanation of this remark; when Stella
got cross you knew it was going to come out anyway.
Stella was not someone to whom you said, *how are you
feeling?* When Stella was feeling, she told you about it.
This was the explanation:
      'You remember that boy I was seeing last year. That's
what I mean. It was the same with him. Firstly he was the
best thing since sliced bread and he knew it. Secondly . . .'
      Stella stubbed out her Silk Cut unnecessarily and
angrily and lit another one straight away.
      'Secondly, you know when it was cabaret night and
he did "Strangers in the Night" with Gary, I said to
myself, wouldn't you fucking know it, he can sing too.
The body of Death and he can sing too. The body of
Death. Montgomery Fucking Clift in a white fucking

dinner jacket. And he's clever. I thought to myself, that one won't stay long; he'll be off with someone with money. You'll see. He won't stay long in a place like this. You see someone with arms and a chest like that, and thighs, he was built like a fucking footballer, and you think—oh . . .'

Stella took a deep drag on her cigarette.

'. . . oh he was so good in bed, girl. D'you know he used to make me think he was a sailor.'

I asked Stella, why a sailor in particular?

'Oh, you know . . . girl in every port. No really, it was his eyes that got me. Eyes as blue as the ocean and there was I all ready to take a cruise, a proper sea queen, packed my frocks for that one I did, ticket booked, first class, all ready to strip off and dive in the pool I was. Eyes like a fucking swimming pool. It wasn't just sex with him and me you know. You know what I mean?'

Of course I knew what Stella meant.

'Still makes me mad,' said Stella.

'*Mad about the Boy*, listen to me,' said Stella.

But what about these two, Stella, do you think these two will last?

'I don't want to think about it.'

Well you should think about it, you should, it does happen you know.

'Always the bridesmaid and never the fucking bride,' said Stella.

Story of my fucking life, girl.

And if you, hearing the details, if you also are wondering why she had given Boy such a hard time, and why O had let her or even apparently paid her to (after all, you may ask, did Boy really need such a testing or strengthening time? He was after all nineteen and it was not as if he had just left home the week before . . .) well you have to remember how strange the times were. Dangerous, looking back, although I don't remember anyone using that word at the time. You have to remember that we lived in a city in which, according to the latest figures, 63 per cent of the population did not think that people like us should exist. (These figures were of course all disputed.) 72 per cent of the population did not think that we should be allowed to express affection in public, although there was some disagreement amongst the researchers as to whether the word 'express' referred to the holding of hands, the exchange of glances, the exchanging of rings, the falling of tired head on a less tired shoulder, the shouted words 'I love you, I love you, My heart is a rose!' (once heard echoing along a subway platform late at night), oral sex up against the railings, or simply one man standing on the doorstep and saying, 'Goodbye, take care and I'll see you on Tuesday then,' while the other man walks away into the uncrowded (at 8.20 a.m.) suburban street. 82 per cent did not think that the names of men like us, or rather, 'men like that' should be read out at school assemblies, especially those involving younger children. 42 per cent didn't even want to think about it. 32 per cent did not know what techniques they used when they were in bed together, but would have liked to watch if it could be arranged. 51 per cent said that honestly they would prefer it if they could simply vanish, just not be there. 27 per cent said they would have brought the knife down themselves, even on friends, colleagues and sons, but I have to say that I myself don't really believe that this question was asked, or if it was asked they just made up these responses, I do not believe it, I think that's just a way of selling papers to include that sort of detail in a story. You, of course, living in a rather different time or in different countries, will find all this hard to credit now, everything they went through, it all seems so elaborate, but anyway you get the point which is that O only had Boy's best interest at heart when he was training him like this. I've always loved those adverts that say, *strict tuition given.*

Anyway when it was all over they announced the wedding, Mother printed the invitations, and we were all invited although that party was not, I can tell you, a simple pleasure.

*Dear Boy, It is just another day of course though
I cannot help but remember such a special day,
the proudest of my life in fact, I remember it still
standing there in church so smart and proud. I so
hope that one day you will be able to come to me
and tell me that you too have found someone with
whom to share your life, it is the greatest thing life
has to offer and it would mean so much to me to be
able to think of you in that way even if I cannot be
there to watch just to know. Father.*

MARRIAGE

The day of the wedding is confused in my mind with another event and I am not now sure if the two things did in fact happen on the same day or were in fact in any way related. I remember the man crying but I cannot remember exactly what he was crying for is what I mean.

What I remember is seeing a grown man lean against a wall and cry. As I remember it the wall was in the hallway of O and Boy's new flat and the man was one of the guests at the wedding, a big handsome man of about sixty, and he went pale and put his hand up to his face as he started to cry and then quite unselfconsciously leant against the wall, because he had to hold himself up. And he said, over and over again, as he was crying, *oh I miss him, oh I wish he was here, Oh I miss him, oh, I wish he was here.*

Now as I say this may not in fact have been at the wedding, it might have been at some other ceremony of ours and sometimes I think I have seen men crying so often now (whoever was it said that men don't cry? Who made that one up and why?) that I confuse the different reasons and occasions they might have for crying. It seems to me, you just cry, that's all. This one was crying almost silently, but crying so deeply and so alone that it was impossible to approach or comfort him, his misery was too deep and solitary for that. Maybe he was crying because he had been hurt, throughout this story I have been trying to remind you of how often we got hurt those days, how often it was about people you knew being assaulted or badly insulted at least. But I think he was crying because someone else had been hurt, someone else, not him. Thinking of it now it's like one of those scenes where there is a war and then the letter comes and the mother of the young soldier has to give her daughter-in-law the letter telling her that her husband of six weeks is dead and even though it is some stupid old black and white film that you are watching in the middle of the afternoon you just cry, well I cry anyway, not for the woman in the film really and not for any particular reason, you just cry for all the lost men, and the ones who went away, the ones you lost, the ones we all lost. And I don't try and stop myself, I just let the pain well up (I feel it quite precisely under and around where my heart is), and then I just let the tears drip down my face.

And that's how I remember this man doing it, just leaning there and letting the tears drip down his face, as if he had some grief or anger that was impossible to contain or forgive, some pain that just spilled over he was so full of it. As if his lover had been hurt to death or had been left to die, as if a dear friend or a lover had been lost to him.

As I say he's the one I remember crying, if indeed it was at the wedding that he was crying, but there were lots of us who were close to tears I think.

Mother came in the dress of course, and the ring, and some very special feathers, actual paradise. Mother was wonderful. She took the service, of course; *Dearly beloved*, she said, *we are gathered together here, in the sight of God and in the face of considerable opposition* . . .

everyone else was in their very best clothes, with almost
everyone having had their hair cut for the occasion, and
a lot of us were looking uncomfortable in white shirts and
ties just like at a real wedding, and of course O and Boy
looking like they would bring the dead back to life, I just
wanted to bite him in that outfit, though Boy was not in
drag as Mother had told us there would be no priest and
no frock, this being an actual ceremony and not some
party or parody. Lord knows we would all have helped to
make it, especially Stella. Our two black queens, Missy-
Missy and Sapphire, made their own protest against this
lack of outrage by arriving in perfect and matching outfits;
cheap veiled and feathered hats, lace gloves, handbags
to match their high-heeled, strappy shoes, eyeshadow to
match their corsages of orange roses with maidenhair
fern in silver foil, two beautiful brand new dresses which
they had bought from Petticoat Lane the Sunday before
for just seventeen pounds each, they looked wonderful,
just wonderful. And those two refused to behave, they
sighed and applauded when Boy said *Yes I do* and again
when O said *yes*, and then at the end opened up their bags
and threw rice at them and kissed them on both cheeks.

It was complicated though. Some people were not
comfortable with the ceremony and half left, ending up
in the kitchen while they exchanged the rings and made
the actual vows, which was all done in the living room.

The vows were read very slowly, as if there could be
time enough in those long pauses for us all to think
about what those famous and infamous words might
really mean on this particular occasion, and how you
could make them mean what you wanted them to mean
with regard to this person who you wished to spend time
with and honour in some way, to cherish, to care for in
some real way for whatever time. I do understand why
they said all that out loud, and I do love that bit where
it says, *for the mutual society, help and comfort, that the*

one ought to have the other. I believe we should in some sense *have* each other, for whatever length of time, *have each other in* that sense maybe, and *with my body I thee worship,* yes I can understand that bit certainly, but still it was so hard to hear those words spoken in that room:

to have and

to hold

honour

and obey

And though I thought I knew what O was trying to say by arranging things this way, all I could think of when they made the vows was, *Oh my mother said that. My grandmother said that, I don't know what this means any more.* It wasn't that I was jealous, or wished it was me (although Missy-Missy and Sapphire were to be heard at this point singing 'It Should Have Been Me' in the kitchen, very drunk). It was just that a lot of us there at the wedding had slept with O or with Boy at some point, and so inevitably we were thinking a bit about what it would be like to be standing there in their place, and though some of the boys were shocked by what was said, there was no laughter, they were so serious about it, standing there together, O *on the right hand* and Boy *on the left hand* just like it says in the prayerbook, and their voices were so sweet and serious, and the flowers were so beautiful, it was almost too much.

And of course we all wanted to bless them and have a party and wish them luck, but as you watched that ceremony you couldn't help thinking to yourself, *I no longer know what love means; I cannot show any good reason why they should not lawfully be joined together,*

*but if this is the answer then why did my Mother live like
she did, and why did my Father talk like he did.* You do
think all of these things at a wedding. Perhaps that's what
weddings are for.

And so amidst everything, they had made their choice,
they had made their vows and they were finally married
now. Photographs to prove it. And everyone was there,
everyone.

And then after the wedding there was the reception
which was in their new flat too.

O and Boy lived on the fifth floor of a post-war block, not
far from Boy's estate. The fifth floor was the top floor;
Mother had got this flat in particular because, as she put
it, she did not want anyone walking over their heads.

It was six rooms, including the hall, kitchen and
bathroom, but we all fitted in.

Some party; but they always were.

Then Mother announced that everyone had to go, just
as if it was closing time at The Bar, and she even stood
at the door with O and Boy shaking hands and saying
goodbye to everyone, *Mother of the Bride*, said Gary. And
we all went home like we were told, for now there was
nothing more we could do to make them happy or bless
their union except leave them alone together to get on
with it; and as we left, we left slowly, and wondering,
most of us, half wishing that it was us left behind and
not doing the leaving, imagining the night to come and
then the days to come.

And when we'd all gone, when she'd got us all out,
Mother didn't stay to help them clear up or talk to them,
she kissed them once each, and said:

'Goodnight, Boys' (it was five in the afternoon)

and they said:

'Goodnight Mother, we won't . . .'

'. . . do anything you wouldn't want your Mother to hear about, yes, I know,' she said, and turned, and left quickly and quietly, and closed their front door behind her and got a taxi straight to work.

When the door, their front door, was finally shut, they were finally, finally—after all the plans and rehearsal and new outfits and best wishes—finally left alone at five o'clock on the last real summer's day that year, left alone with the cigarette ends and the plastic cups everywhere and nowhere to sit, no chairs, not a stick of furniture in the whole flat except the bed and the stacks of books and records everywhere, for they were real newlyweds in that way. All they had on that first afternoon alone together as a properly married couple in their flat was a bed and plenty to drink; and everywhere the great big bunches of flowers, dying already, some of them wild flowers, seeding and smelling of fields; and the early evening sun coming in and turning the bare walls yellow.

When everyone was gone they didn't want to talk much or even move much, they just wanted to be alone and taste this novel sensation of being left alone as a couple in their new flat, to be quiet; but they were both so happy that every now and then they had to say something to each other or touch each other, so O would come up to Boy for a kiss and Boy would pull away and smile and say, *do you really want to hurt me, do you really want to see me cry?*, and then O would play looking very serious and say, *Babe, I'm going to show you that a woman can be tough, so come on, come on*—and then he would pull Boy to his feet and into his arms and say—*take it, take another little piece of my heart now baby, break it,* and they'd slow dance in the middle of the empty room for a while with no one to watch them and no music playing except what they imagined they could hear. Then O left Boy leaning

against a bare wall in the sun, watching him, and he lit
a cigarette and opened another beer and he sat in the
middle of the floor and he wired up the stereo which had
been our collective wedding present to the happy couple.
This was the first truly domestic act of their married life,
prior to making a cup of tea or making the bed. And then
O opened one of the big cardboard boxes and took out a
set of records from the pile that was in there. Boy watched
him all the time, smiling; watched him while he took the
second record in the set out of its sleeve and carefully
selected the right place on the second side for the needle
to go down, but before he put the needle down O went
over to the window and threw it full open, and Boy knew
as he watched him that this was not just to let in the sun,
which was now turning to real solid gold along the walls,
making the flowers, even the dead ones, shine in strange
high-summer colours, but also because he wanted all the
neighbours to hear this song. Then O turned the volume
up and he put the needle down and it started to play.

It was a man singing in Italian, a man now forty
years dead, singing the aria called 'Dalla Sua Pace'
from Mozart's opera of *Don Giovanni*, although Boy did
not know these details until much later, when they had
been living together for some time, and O had explained
to him where all his records had come from and why. All
Boy knew for now was that the voice was high and strong
and beautiful, and as he listened to it he knew that this
song was for him and for all the neighbours, knew that it
was O's public and very special gift to him on the occasion
of their wedding, more precious than the ring and more
personal somehow. O looked up at Boy from where he
was crouched by the record player in the middle of the
floor, and then he came back to where Boy was standing
and leaning against the wall in the sun, and he reached
out and he ran his fingers through the lock of hair on
Boy's brow, and pushed him hard back against the wall,

and pushed one knee between Boy's legs and brought his
face right up close to Boy's. Boy thought he was going to
get kissed. Instead what happened first was that O just
filled his hands with his beloved's hair like it was a breast,
or a bird, then took hold of it harder, as if the bird was
struggling, and then he began gently knocking Boy's head
back against the wall, staring all the time right into his
eyes. Boy put his hands up on O's shoulders and returned
his gaze and let him do what he was doing, seeing that
O wanted to speak, but couldn't, and that he was biting
his lip and that his eyes were beginning to fill with tears.
Then Boy did get kissed; O drew his left hand out of the
black hair and let his fingers go down over Boy's temple
and then his cheek, and then he brought his face even
closer and kissed him, kissed him gently under the eye.
Then he bit him over the cheekbone, and Boy was crying
now too, silently, and his cheek was wet and his head
swam from all the drink and the promises and the kisses
there had been that afternoon, and from the hairpulling
which was beginning to hurt, and his face was sore from
O's stubble and from his teeth, and O's knee was hurting
him between his legs, and the music was playing, and his
heart was so full that his ribs heaved and ached on the
left side and he couldn't speak at all but he was thinking,
this is love, this is love, this is love, this is my lover; and
O didn't think that he could speak either what with the
music and the sunlight and holding his Boy so loving
and handsome in his hands, but after a time he did find
a voice; the music on the record dipped to a sweet hush for
a moment and looking Boy right in the eyes, still with his
right hand full of hair and with his voice brought low and
gentle and broken by his feelings he said:
    'Do you know what this means?'
meaning, the music, meaning the words that the man was
singing, since he was singing in Italian, and Boy said, he
wanted to say, *yes*, but instead he said:

'No'
and at that point the voice on the record soared up again
and all the neighbours could hear and even see through
the open window, and O put his mouth close to Boy's ear
and sang the lyrics to Boy, or rather half sang them, for he
did them in English so that Boy could understand every
word of what he was saying. By way of introducing his
translation he said, in a voice close to breaking, as the
voice on the record rose again:
    'Let me tell you the meaning of this.'
and then he did the aria itself, and what he said was:

> *Upon your peace of mind, mine depends.*
> *When you sigh, I feel my own chest heave.*
> *Your joy is my joy; you know that when you come that*
>   *makes me come too.*
> *I can't see you weep except through tears of my own,*
> *And when I can't see you, I worry about you; take*
>   *good care of yourself.*
> *If you're not free, I'm not free;*
> *If you can't walk the streets in safety, then I can't walk*
>   *either.*

Boy had never had a man sing to him before. He had
always assumed that all the songs he had ever loved
were sung to him, or at least sung for him, but it had
always been the women's voices that he'd heard that had
really moved him. But this was very different; he had
never heard a man's voice this beautiful. He had never
had a man sing like this to him before, and, for all his
journeys and wanderings, he had never heard one man
telling another man that he loved him before. It did not
occur to him that this was at all a strange way of doing it.

There was another attack on their wedding night, another face cut open, another knife. But I don't want to tell you about that now, though I know that I should. I want everything to be perfect just for a while, because that was how we all felt that night. That night, going home from The Bar (which is where we had all gone on to) I felt different. I kept on saying to myself, *go on look at me, I dare you to look at me, why don't you, just try it and see where it gets you.* I think I even forgot that people might look at me. It was a special night.

HONEYMOON

It was of course a special night for them, that first night. It was, Boy said, different. The sex was different. It felt new; it meant something else. We certainly knew what he meant by that, even if we couldn't quite believe him, couldn't quite believe that it made that much of a difference.

That first night, that honeymoon night of all nights, O gave his boy a real hard time. He gave him real dirt. He talked real dirty to him. He didn't touch him too much at first. He made him bend over and spread his buttocks with both hands. He made him display the marks on his back, display his armpits, the soles of his feet and the roots of his hair; as if Boy was an animal and O was deciding whether to buy that animal or not. O made Boy pull back his eyelids, his lips and his foreskin. And all the time O kept on talking, talking very low so that Boy had to listen very hard even when he didn't want to, didn't quite want to hear what he was in fact hearing his lover say. It made him feel like they'd just met, like he was a boy again. He had to listen so hard, Boy found that he couldn't think any longer about what he himself was doing, couldn't keep up, couldn't keep his balance, couldn't keep his feet

on the floor, could answer O's quiet, incessant, persistent
questions, questions in which he demanded to know the
most humiliating details, questions about Boy's body,
about what he wanted, where he hurt, what he was
thinking, what he really wanted to do next, couldn't
even think about which way up he was because O talked
so low to him, talked so bad, said things you never heard
one man say to another before, said, *baby you hold onto
yourself, baby don't give yourself away, don't give it away,
don't give up the ghost, don't give me that shit,* and then
without stopping talking he took hold of Boy right down
there real hard with both hands, one hand round his balls
and three fingers up his arse and he pushed so hard that
the two sets of fingers almost met through Boy's skin and
then he said, and this was the worst of all, he got so close
to Boy's ear that it was more like biting than whispering
and he said, *do you like it like that, do you, do you want
me to get you like that, do you want me to hold you like
that, do you, do you want me to hold you, do you want
me to take care of you then, will you let me put you in the
bath? Can I give you the bottle, do you need the toilet, do
you want me to do that, can I watch, can I watch you do
it, can you do it for me, can I stand over you, can I stand
by you, can I stand up for you, can I promise you I won't
die because you see you're my Boy. You're my boy, you're
my body, you're my woman, you're my pussy; you're my
dog with a bone, you're my bruised and broken darling,
you're the song in my heart, you're my sky at night, you're
my little brother, you're my river through the city, you're
the bird in the bush, you're my lover in my arms, you're my
daddy home from work. You're my fucker, fucker, fucker,
fucker what are you?*

Boy had got used to the idea that O's mouth could do just
what it wanted, could lick, open or bite him anywhere.

Since he had been covered in spittle, he didn't see why
he shouldn't be covered in words as well.

When all that, the violence, was over, O and his Boy
made love just like a married couple for the very first time.
They did it with a tender concentration and a complete
lack of fear that surprised them both given the way they
had courted, the way they lived. They felt like they were
doing it for the very first time, which they weren't. They
felt that it was extraordinary; but I would say myself that
they looked just like several other hundreds of men in
similar beds in that city and at that particular time.

Each was so eager to mark and use every muscle and
joint of the other that neither looked up from the bed
during their lovemaking. Neither of them looked up and
saw, hovering over that white and isolated bed, or rather
not hovering but crowding, pressing, stretching up on
their toes some of them so that they could see, a crowd
of fifty or sixty men. All of them were whiteskinned and
darkeyed, like the lovers; and all of them, like the lovers,
were naked. These were the ones who had come before,
the men whom O and Boy never knew or had never even
heard about, their witnesses and peers, the attendants
and guests of honour at this ceremony, this great labour
of love; the ones we forgot to invite. All of these men
were quite still, and all them smiled; all of them cast
down their eyes to behold the slow-moving wonder on
the bed.

Some were frankly fascinated, watching two handsome
men engage in sexual practices which had not been
current in their own century; their eyes opened wide.
One older man's eyes wrinkled in a great grin and then
slowly brimmed over with two fat tears of admiration.
The room was so full that those at the front of the
crowd were pressed against the bed, and some even
knelt at the edge of it; they appeared to have dropped
to their knees like attendants in a painted Adoration.

One even held up both hands open-palmed, and his face, open-mouthed with delight at the beauty of what he saw, was lit gently from below by the single candle that O had placed in a saucer by the bed to light the scene.

Some of the men held hands, or seemed to be lovers themselves, for they stood pressing themselves against a thigh or the small of another man's back, or just constantly, idly touched another's hair or shoulders with the tenderness of habit.

Some were themselves sexually excited, perhaps by being in such a crowd, or perhaps by what they were watching. One young cock was upright, beating slowly against a black-furred stomach, until the four fingers and thumb of an older hand closed round it and held it still. The young man did not turn round to see whose hand it was; indeed no one looked round, looked away or talked; apart from these few, small, occasional, emblematic gestures of contact and love, the crowd was quite still, as still as the Kings and the Shepherds always are in such scenes, as still even as the angels whose very draperies hang quiet and immobile in the night air for sheer wonder.

Had O or Boy looked up, they would have seen that some faces appeared in the crowd several times. Each time the face appeared, it appeared with a different body (a different physique or the same physique at a different age), the nakedness of the limbs set off by the hairstyles and accessories of different centuries—a seventeenth-century betrothal ring in which two chased silver hands clasped a chipped and crowned garnet heart; a badly-hennaed auburn wig, burnt by the curling tongs; a regulation moustache clipped by a Forces barber. One man, a sixty-year-old with white hair on his fat stomach and across his shoulders, was holding, wrapped in his

huge arms, a smiling butcher's assistant whose neck
and chest were red and sore and covered with bites
and bruises. The young man's features were strangely
like those of the older man, as if they were related—their
hands were the same, too. The young man's stomach
was flat, and his eyes were not red and clouded like
the ones that gazed over his shoulder. The whitehaired
man was in fact holding his younger self in his arms,
holding him tight; and the young man looked glad to be
held.

When O and Boy had both come, and curled up
together, and drifted apart and fallen asleep with no
sheet to cover them, the candle was not extinguished,
and seemed not to burn low or even gutter, but to
burn for several hours more; and the crowd of men
stayed quite still and silent around it, quite still; and
all of them, all of them, smiling. In time a few, at the
back of the crowd, seeing the sky beginning to lighten
through the window and finding that they were not able
to see the tableaux the sleeping bodies made, did turn
away and began to look around them, leafing through
O's unpacked collection of books just like you do when
you're alone in a strange apartment for the first time.
The rest remained watching the lovers, watching them
and watching over them on this, the first night of their
marriage, so that anyone walking home late that night
could have looked up at the bedroom window at four a.m.,
and seen an inexplicable sight: framed by a bedroom
window on the fifth floor, lit by a single candle flame, a
silent crowd of fifty or sixty smiling, naked men, pressed
close together, fifty or sixty of them together in a single
council flat bedroom.

In the morning the lovers did not notice that the clothes
that they had left lying on the bedroom floor had been
walked on, rearranged, or that their jeans were slightly
damp with dew. They were too busy clearing up after the

party, too busy setting up their new home, too busy for such details. They knew nothing, nothing, nothing.

Years later they found a single baroque pearl which had dropped that night from a white-leaded ear, but they assumed it was a fake, and they put it in the dressing-up box with the rest of their spare jewellery.

SETTING UP HOME

Sunday

Dear Boy,
I'm happy to hear that you have found somewhere
to live. I think it's always a relief to know that you've
got that kind of security. Have you considered buying
the flat? You know I expect that everyone is entitled
to purchase their own flat now, you should try and
get the details. I've certainly never regretted taking
out the mortgage when I did.

Life here continues much the same. I have just
finished reading the book that you sent me, with
much pleasure. What an extraordinary life the man
had. I remember when I was a boy my own Father
had a picture of him up in his study I think. He
was very strict about his study, Mother was never
allowed in there not even to dust, he used to do it
himself. Of course he was quite capable of cleaning
for himself what with having been in the army.
I remember the picture quite well, very dark but with
a handsome scarlet jacket. Very handsome he was too
when young.

Do you remember me ever telling you about my
sister's husband Geoff? I had a very sad letter two

*days ago telling me that he was dying of cancer.
I don't think I shall go to the funeral as I haven't
seen that side of the family for years. It will be so
terrible for her to be on her own.*

*I am trying to cook for myself more as you suggested
and am quite happily 'looking after myself a bit
more' as you put it. The nights are drawing in now
down here, and this will be the first frost tonight
I think. There are still a lot of roses by the back
door, 'Ena Harkness'.*
I am glad everything is going so well for you.
Goodnight, Father

Sunday

Are you lonely? You say that you're not of course
and I hope that it's true. I certainly hope you're not
lonely, I hope you have people to look after you and
to be close to you, as you get older you'll understand
this better though I expect you think it will never
happen to you; I think it is a source of great sadness
to see people grow old on their own. Sad and lonely.
I bought one small tin of fish, a packet of bread and
some milk and that cost me one pound thirty pence.
I had an apple in the basket but I had to leave it,
it was so embarrassing. I am not sure you realise just
how difficult it is to manage on your own. I am on
my own a lot of the time now.

Dear Boy,
There was a wonderful gardening programme last
night (Saturday), did you see it I wonder. I thought of
you of course.
    There was an orchard of fifteen or seventeen of the
old varieties, all different, quince and roses together
all round the door, and a marvellous copper beech
at least one hundred and fifty years old they said.
There was a guided tour where they explained it all
for you. Those were the days for that kind of thing;
of course there aren't the men with those kinds of
skills now, nor the plants, you just can't find them.
Still it was lovely to see it and to be allowed to share
in it, marvellous really that it's still there for us all
to share. I often wish I had more of a garden of my
own. Something at least to look out on not just the
television when I am here on my own so much.
'Father'

(In all of these letters this man never asked Boy to visit
him or suggested that he come and stay with Boy, not
even at Christmas.)

They quickly got the flat furnished. The wedding was the last time that Mother was seen wearing the diamond; she got them a washing machine, a good bed, a fridge, a good television, the phone put in and a cooker. Her wedding gift to them, besides all these practical things, was a bedspread, a great scarlet and gold bedspread in real antique nineteenth-century Venetian-style velvet brocade. *Jewels need a setting*, she said. *You two stretched out on that will look, well . . . perfect.* She set them up; I don't know how she managed to get them into a flat so quickly, it wasn't easy to do that then. And it was quite big too. Mother said, *you need several rooms to love someone properly.*

They painted everything white, so that the flat just had white walls and all these expensive appliances (Mother had bought stuff that was the best quality and would last. I wonder now, looking back, if she was already planning to leave, to leave all this behind in good running order, knowing they were provided for), it really did look like a show flat or a flat in an advert, or as if they were playing house. The model couple in the model flat, Boy at home all day with the appliances and O out to work.

They would come into The Bar splashed with paint from the decorating, grinning. Mother would say, *we're all here* (she indicated her well-populated kingdom with a small, ritualised gesture of her beringed right hand, a gesture which indicated 'I am waving'), *any time you need our help, just call, we're all here.*

And again when they were leaving she placed her hand on O's arm and looked at him and quietly said, *remember, Mother's here, pick up the phone.*

But they never called us for help with the decorating or indeed with anything.

O had mostly books, records and his own collection of films on video, and Boy had just his shoebox and his packing case full of letters; that was all they brought to their new home from their respective old ones.

Boy had told O about the letters, but it was only now that they lived together that O realised just how often they came; they started arriving at the new address the morning after the wedding. Sometimes they would come every day for a week; quite often there would be two or three letters in the same post. The envelopes were all re-used ones that had been torn open, readdressed and sealed with sellotape. When a letter arrived Boy would read it at once, and O noticed that he was always quiet for a bit then.

O had already talked to Mother about them, upstairs in her room, while she'd been putting her hair up in the oval mirror, with Billie and Bessie staring over her shoulder.

'What do you think I should do then?'

'You're asking me for advice on how to keep a young man?'

'I was wondering if I should try and stop them. I was thinking I could just stop them. Boy would probably be glad and not even talk about it. I could get up first and get them off the postman, or I could write to this Father and tell him to stop them.'

'Darling,' said Mother, twisting the last coil of hair up onto her head and taking a silver pin from the cut-glass vanity tray on the dressing table, 'this so-called "Father" sounds like he would be quite capable of wrapping his next letter around a brick and delivering it personally. So long as he stays several postal districts or, better still, several counties away, so much the better. Listen to Mother; these Fathers are low-down and miserable fuckers to a man.'

There was a pause, and then O said what he had really wanted to say:

'I don't think he really can be his father.'

Mother did her lips. Then her eyebrows. When she was perfect, she looked at O in the mirror and said to him:

'So if you want it to stop then fight him over it. All you have to do is imagine that the man who's writing your Boy these letters is twenty-eight and gorgeous and I'm sure you'll know exactly what to do about it. Get drunk again if you have to . . . After all,' she said, as she adjusted the final silver pin, pushing it further in, 'you've got everything to lose.'

Dear Boy,
I am as comfortable as I can be I suppose under the
circumstances but sometimes I wonder if it wouldn't
be better if I was gone. I don't mean the pain—Lord
knows I am used to that by now and well able to
stand it. But every time I turn on the television, all
those men, well it seems to me that I understand you
people less and less, though as you know I do try.
It seems to me there is no respect and no attempt
to look after anything properly. Litter, divorce, strike,
strike, divorce, litter; litter all over the lawns as I look
out of my window and blowing into the flowerbeds,
that's all there is, and you know how much I like to
still try and keep the garden in good shape.
    Careless, that's what I think when I see it all
carrying on. Why don't people care any more? After
the war we all had such a clear sense that we were
all working for something, trying to build something
if you like, and when people got married then or got
jobs it was for ever, you just tried to make a go of it.
That's it, people tried, *they made a go of things, they*
stuck to it. Why can't you do that? Why can't you?
Take a little pride in your own life. People used to

really look after each other then you know.

I do try as you know to understand but it does upset me when I see people living how they do these days. It upsets me to think of you living like that. Forgive me for going on like this but I am your 'Father'

P.S. It is still very warm down here, the bean flowers are still out which is extraordinary for this time of year. Sweet pea and honeysuckle, lovely.

This letter made Boy so angry that he stayed silent all day after reading it. Since Boy never replied to these letters, he had no real reason to expect that they would ever refer to O or congratulate him on his new life with O, or even mention it, how could they; the man who wrote them knew nothing of all that, nothing. But still Boy was angry, white with anger.

It was a mid-week evening, and when O got home Boy didn't speak all the way through the dinner which he had prepared for them. At nine o'clock he got up and went to his cupboard in the bedroom and got out his shoebox and packing case and two binliners (for the packing case had been full for some time now and Boy had started to keep the letters just in binliners, there were so many of them). He brought them into the living room and he emptied them in a heap on the living room floor in front of O and turned off the television. It was as if he was setting O a herculean version of the task which he set himself on the nights when he used to lay out his letters in a circle around his bed; to sort the papers into some sort of order, some sort of sense, some story. Except that now the collection of letters had grown from a small, precious, personal collection into what looked more like a heap of wastepaper, a litter, a waste and confusion of paper.

'I am going out to The Bar,' Boy said. 'I think you'd better stay in and read these.'

When Boy got back, at three in the morning, O was still sitting in the middle of the living room floor, surrounded by the letters. He had spread them into a circle right round him, and was still trying to sort them into some kind of order or sequence, but looked as if he had given up, had been overwhelmed by the sheer number of them. He started talking as soon as Boy walked in the door:
     'This "Father" as you call him . . . '
But Boy had obviously been thinking too, Boy too was right ready with something he had to say, and he cut O off with
     'That's my secret and don't you ever ask me. I never asked you to explain all the things you said during the night.'

Boy went into the kitchen to put on the kettle, then came and stood in the doorway while it was boiling, and said to O:
     'I love him in my own kind of way.'
     'You can't love a man who talks like that.'
     'You've never met him.'
     'You can't love a man who writes letters like he writes letters.'
     Boy was silent; O tried again:
     'What does he think about me? He never mentions me. Haven't you told him?'
     'I never told him anything. I never write back you know. He makes it all up, all of it. All of it.'
     Boy went to make the tea.
     And while he was in the kitchen he must have changed his mind about something, because he came into the living room with the pot of tea and two mugs and sat

down with O in the midst of the papers, and started to
explain as best he could:

'I think you ought to know about him if we're going to
live together. For a start, I just call him Father from habit.
I mean we all call Madame "Mother", don't we . . . '

O interrupted him and said, 'What did he do to you?'

and Boy paused, and then said, very quietly, not looking
at O:

'I don't know exactly. I've been trying to forget for so
long . . . and now I can't remember.'

By way of continuing his explanation or account, Boy
picked out two particular letters from the pile and read
them out loud to O. They were not picked out at random;
he spent nearly ten minutes looking for the right ones.
It seemed that he almost knew them off by heart. O
wondered if this was what Boy had been doing in the
long, angry silences that always came just after he had
received the letters; memorising them. He read them in
a voice which could have been either close to tears or
choked with rage; O couldn't tell.

> *I feel like a Father to you, you know. You know that.*
> *I would have died for you. You know I would have*
> *laid down my life for you if anybody had ever asked*
> *me to.*

and then (this was a paragraph from a long letter, ten
pages at least, on blue paper; this seemed harder to
read than the first, because Boy kept on stopping and
re-starting when he read it):

> *We went through a lot of things together at that time,*
> *as a lot of men did, and I still cannot forget those*
> *times, and the promise that I made him to look after*
> *you as if my own is one that I have not forgotten*

either and is one that I intend to keep.

From the way that Boy read these two extracts it seemed that they were very important to him, almost as if they were the two vital clues to an interpretation or reading of the whole pile and as if he now expected O to understand everything, to have worked out the whole story. But O said:

'I still don't understand'

and Boy said:

'Don't interrupt me, and I'll tell you everything I know.'

Then he paused and said, quietly again:

'I have never told anyone else about this.'

And when he said that, O wanted to take him in his arms, or at least hold his hand, for he thought of all the other men, young men often, who had said that to him, *I never told anyone about this before*, or, *I never said this to a man before*, or, *I have something I want to tell you.*

Then Boy began his explanation; he illustrated it with further readings from the letters, and it took him the rest of the night, until dawn in fact. But as he explained the story of the letters and the man who sent them he sounded like someone who was explaining a dream, trying to explain it while still half asleep. The more he explained, the more his explanation seemed unconvincing. You wake from a dream that overwhelms you with its power, but then you say, *I dreamt about a horse, that must mean I was thinking about your body; and I dreamt about a river, because I'm getting older; and I dreamt about riding a white horse through a river, and that means that I'll love you forever*; and as you hear yourself making this explanation you know that it sounds ridiculous.

Of course O knew that the idea behind the story was not impossible; and he knew that it was not that unlikely that a man like this should know nothing of Boy's life but still fill his letters with references to well-built young men,

young men working in the garden, neighbour's children
growing up to be fine young men. And he had heard
from Mother several variations on this story of being
some man's 'Best friend' during the War, and then not
knowing how to live once the war was over. He'd heard
stories about couples she'd given her bed to for the night
because one of them was leaving in the morning and they
had nowhere else to go; stories about the ones who got
through the whole thing safely and kept in touch, the
ones whose mates never said anything, but then when
the letter came and he went white and almost wept in
front of all of them they took him to his bunk and sat
with him and didn't ask too many questions and didn't
laugh, not even when he called out a man's name in the
night and they all heard. But this story he was hearing
now O did not believe. The meeting on the emergency
stairs of a tube station on a Saturday afternoon; the
desperate pledge made in darkness at the height of an
air-raid; it was all too like a film. The explanation that
this 'Father' was no parent at all, but had assumed that
name in honour of a pledge made to a stranger. And
this story of a lonely childhood, a boy brought up by
an incompetent and often absent man, or rather not
brought up by him but placed in care. And then the
weekly letters, every week for years, and every single
letter claiming that he *felt like a Father to him*. It was
unconvincing; something was missing. O had heard many
different stories about fathers; this was not the strangest.
But it did not make any sense. As he listened to Boy, O
rewrote the story for himself, deciding that the real parent
and this so-called 'Father' had been lovers, and that the
whole story had been invented to excuse the dumping of
an unwanted child, the two men abandoning the child
of a mistaken marriage so that they could pursue their
own affair more freely. Certainly the wartime setting of
the story was false, O knew that, since Boy not only said

he was, but clearly was, nineteen, and so could not have been a helpless infant in 1945.

Or was the story something Boy had made up? Was the fear in his voice fear of a real father? Were the letters an extraordinary, obsessive act of forgery?

This last explanation began to seriously frighten O as he thought of it; then he remembered that this could not possibly be the case, since the letters were not in Boy's handwriting or anything like it. This 'Father', whoever he was, was a real person; and whatever the actual history of their relationship, the man clearly was in every respect a father figure to Boy, and had been for a long time and since an early age; and that is what mattered to O. He knew that the clumsiness with which you explain your dreams doesn't make them go away or mean that you never had them.

It was dawn now, and Boy was still talking, still explaining.

'First he signed himself "Father",' he said, 'and now he signs himself Father. And he isn't. And he doesn't live in a small town with neighbours and roses, and he doesn't live on his own. He's old, he's badly ill and he's in a home. And it isn't in the country, it's here in the city, it's right here, it's only an hour away on the bus, an hour away, and he has no house, and he has no garden, and he never has. And all this talk of things being wrecked in the storm and the big trees being down is just talk. Talk. I never answer the letters, I never have, but I had to give them my address so that they can notify me in an emergency. They said, *one day he might need you.*'

In the end, when there was indeed an emergency, and Father did indeed need a son (which does happen eventually, although you always do think it's boys who need fathers and not the other way round), it finally came out that this man definitely wasn't the real Father, and so in the end we knew nothing about where Boy came from. But that wasn't unusual. It's like all the men in The Bar; you see them all the time and you think you know everything about them, but you know nothing about all that part of their lives; you see them go home for Christmas and that's all you see, or you hear about Hugh Hapsley, that awful Hugh, who had to sell the pearls and go and live in the country, returning seven years later after his mother's death, older and quieter and chastened. You remember Gary's story about sleeping in his childhood bedroom and lying sleepless all night and then not knowing what to say at breakfast. Sometimes I think we're all parentless, and that The Bar is just one big orphans' home anyway, and that's why we use all those words all the time to each other, Mother, Daddy, Baby, Sister.

And what about all those father and son fantasies that no one ever admits to but that everybody has, though some people do get as far as dressing up and calling him 'Daddy' for the night, or for the darkest part of the night anyway.

But I know of course that it's not always like that. I am letting my own bitterness get to this part of the story I know. There was once a couple who regularly brought their mother into The Bar in the early evening—they both called her Mother, although of course she was really only a Mother-in-law to Terry. Mother, our Mother, would always come over and greet her very formally, which she liked, and then she would sit at her regular table slowly drinking her single half pint of what she used to call milk stout, always making the same decision about what to have every time they brought her. One by one almost all the regulars in The Bar would come up and ask her how she was and say it was nice to see her; and she never remembered anyone's name, but was so happy that her

sons (or rather I should say her son and her son-in-law)
had so many friends. And she would smile at everyone.
She'd talk about the television (which of course we were
good at talking about) and how she was keeping; and at
seven, her half pint sipped away, they would take her
home. And then often they'd be back at midnight, rather
differently dressed I must say. When the affair was over,
she used to come in with just Terry. I wanted to tell you
this because the point was that everyone was very happy
to have her there, there was no mystery or oddity to it,
but at the same time I was always a bit shocked by her, a
bit shocked by seeing her there. I found it extraordinary,
even though I was watching it happen, and always used
to go up and say good evening to her along with everyone
else. What I mean is that for me I could never imagine this
happening though I often wanted it to somehow.

I have tried to imagine how I could have made the
invitation.

   I have watched Terry and Bobby and Bobby's mother
together and I have thought, well times are changing, but
then when I think of my own situation I cannot think that
times have changed at all or if they have then it's too late
for me. Not for you maybe, but for me. And then also
I think of everything that Boy went through, and people
said he should just have refused to get involved, that he
owed the man nothing, but I always said I understood.
I understood that you can't choose whether you owe them
anything.

   Listen to me, excuse me, I know, I do try not to be
bitter, and so does everyone I know. You spend a long
time feeling that you are gradually leaving, leaving home,
gradually distancing yourself, getting to a distance. A
distance from which you can see the view properly. A
point from which you can now write a letter home, make
a call home, send them a photograph of the way you look

now, tell them about just as much of your life as you want them to know about (I think this is why Boy kept all of those letters; he was trying to measure the distance, to see how far he'd come, laying them out on the bedroom floor as if they were signposts or as if they somehow made up a map. Every deliberately-unanswered letter a crumb laid on the forest floor, like in the story, a way of finding your path back home should you ever need to; but also each one a milestone, another step taken on the journey, something that you put behind you). And then there comes a time, years later, when you realise that you do finally live another kind of life and that you are, finally, living it in quite another city, a very different place from the one that you were born in. That you have, finally, left home.

But still, even though it's taken you so long, you still feel like you ran away at night taking only what you needed, only what you could carry in the one small bag. And now you know that that one small bag is all you have with you, and now here you are in the cold morning at a railway station, a bus station maybe, and you realise that all your skills and your memories and your phone numbers are all in that one bag, and of course there is the one address, and that one photo of you, with them, always there at the bottom of the bag; they are all that you have in a way, your bag and your jacket that you wear everywhere and your shoes that you wear everywhere. And sometimes then you want to cry, cry, cry, you wish they'd have you back, you wish there was somewhere to go back to or some home to go back to, a way back or more exactly a way that you need never have left . . . and at other times well you pick up that bag, you pick up that bag smiling to yourself and you get on that train.

I don't know exactly when in the period of their setting up home this happened, but sometime between their becoming a couple and their becoming a family there was another attack, another face cut open.

I know there's not always blood, it's just that each time I hear this, that's what I see, a knife coming down. Sometimes it's not that at all, but a metal bar across the legs. Or a single word thrown out of a car window, tossed at you like a bottle, so like a bottle that you even involuntarily duck to avoid it, or look down to see the broken glass at your feet. Listen to me, what am I saying.

LIVING TOGETHER

Although this is a short chapter, this was in fact the longest chapter in the period of their lives that I'm telling you about. The reason for its brevity is that this part of their story, which I call The Domestic Life, had no public climaxes, no emblematic scenes, nothing much really for us to talk about.

Of course we still saw them, in The Bar, but they were now one couple amongst many. And we did see O carrying the shopping, working his way through the supermarket with a list, but this was not considered an heroic or an erotic activity. It was not worthy of dramatisation or comment. Every week the list was the same. On the top of the trolley were six bottles of water, because O liked to drink this particular brand of water which came in plastic bottles, but also came, way back, from the mountains of ice shown on the labels. This was water that had never been through a city, that had been filtered only through icc and glacial gravel, water that (O explained one night) had come straight to them, almost, from the pure and driven snow.

And, if we were passing, we saw O at work. He was happy to go out and work in the video shop, because it gave him time to think. When he was in the same room or the same building as Boy (or even if he was ten tube stops away, on his way to him) he found it hard to think about anything else. This had not yet worn off.

I expect you want to know how they managed. Shall I describe the arrangements of their home life at this time? What do you want to know—what they ate, whether the sex remained the same or changed now they were living together? I often wonder about that. Passion without novelty. If it is true that sex always changes, does it change every night? And are those changes dramatic (*no, let me do it . . .*) or gradual, so slight that an observer would miss them, so slight that the actors themselves don't notice that the script is changing from performance to performance, from night to night. Small gestures can be great pleasures, they can mean a great deal, when you get to know somebody else's body and its reactions as well as your own.

Do you think that ever really actually happens?

Do you think this whole thing that I am describing ever really happens?

Do you want to see their bank statements? Shall I keep O working at the video shop, or shall I give him a new job now, something better paid, or shall I lie to you and say they got lucky, shall I have them find a newspaper parcel of used notes in the street? Shall I document for you just how cheaply two men can live if they really try, because then that way you will be able to believe me when I tell you that yes, they did manage to live on the one income, with Mother paying half their rent. And that they were not hurt by it and did not hurt each other, never hit each other. Not even when the cigarette packet was empty by eight o'clock in the evening.

Do you believe me? Do you?

Shall I tell you what they were wearing then?

*

It was the autumn by now, which is relevant, because it marks the passing of time, and also it reminds us that this year is like last year and will be like next year. You see what O and Boy had to do now was not start, but continue. They had to make their happiness routine.

Part of the routine was their nights in The Bar; they were still a feature. They held hands and stayed together all night: they would especially hold hands during Mother's song. Once I saw them slowdancing in the middle of an uptempo number, everyone else was sweating, but they were just holding tight and dancing slowly, ignoring the music, O had his head on Boy's shoulder, and Boy was singing quietly into his ear, inaudible with all that noise but I could read his lips, shaping the words, *all of me, why not take all of me, can't you see . . .*

One night when they were in, just a routine night, Mother made a point of refusing to sing for them (that's right; it did seem to me that it was their song now, not just hers). She put on a whole new act, which was so elaborate that she must have rehearsed it for some time. I mention it because I think it was for O and Boy's benefit that she did it. It seemed to me she was saying, *you've done that, all of yourself, you've given all of yourself, your lips, your arms, now think about the problem this way.*

That night she came down the stairs slowly, a step at a time, swearing as if her feet hurt her, muttering, *all of me, I'll give you bleeding all of me*, looking at least twenty years older. It was quite an entrance.

She had streaked her hair a dull grey; then she'd caked her skin with too much powder, and rubbed under her eyes until they were bagged and swollen. She had on one of the old dresses, one from the wardrobe. The sequin work was dulled and some of the beading worn away; the whole dress was too tight for comfort and made Mother look uncomfortable, and fatter than she was.

She couldn't get on and off her stool without assistance. I even think she must have sat with her feet right over an electric fire or something because you could see that her feet were swollen and hurting in the silver shoes that she had had made for her and which had always fitted perfectly, usually she could work in them all night and not feel the heels at all.

She played the role with alarming perfection, all night. She even practised not being able to read the till chits, holding them up close and squinting and then passing them to one of the barmen and saying, *I'm sorry, I'm sorry, dear, but could you just read that for me please, I've left my glasses in my other bag. Now, did I give you a five pound note or a ten pound note*—Mother, who had never made a mistake at a till in her life. We were shocked. She said, *it's alright, Boys, I'm practising. I want you all to see me like this. I want to get used to seeing myself like this in the mirrors.*

When Boy and O came to say goodnight to her she said, still in character, *you know, it happens to us all, dear. And who's going to look after us, that's what I'd like to know. Who's going to take care of us? Spent my whole bleeding life caring for people I have and now look at me.*

Sunday

Dear Son,
Not so good I'm afraid. The weather has not been too
good either. It's been rain all day since Thursday and
I've been out to stake what's left of the dahlias twice,
I think I'm going to lose them. Do you remember,
the dark red ones. I don't want to catch a chill either,
that's not so funny at my age, it's not so funny sitting
here crouched over the one bar. Which is what I've
been doing son because the bill last quarter was
forty-six pounds and I've only budgeted for forty
pounds this time. Also there's no one to cook for me
just now so it's tins. I don't want to burden you with
all this as I'm keeping quite cheery really. I have been
watching the television a lot, and sorting out the old
photos again. I've been burning most of them. I was
handsome then, wasn't I? All that black hair I had.
yours,
'Father'

P.S. there was a thing on the television about the
trouble in the park. I hope you aren't mixed up in any
of that.

Dear Son,
Not so good again I'm afraid. I have not been out
since I last wrote, no gardening for me. They tell me
I shouldn't be doing it at my age and it does increase
the pains which were very bad yesterday evening.
It's not as if I'm still one of those strong young men.
I can't do the garden at all, that's what they're trying
to tell me, even when it gets to the spring.
   There was a programme about the Olympic swim-
ming team I turned it off, all those young men, it's
alright for them. Here comes my tea now. Hope you
are well.
Father.

Sunday afternoon

Dear Son,

The pain has been getting worse and now they come out and tell me it's angina. I have to keep warm all the time they say. The bloody food here doesn't help it's cold by the time you get it.

I would like to be out in the garden, just a walk round to see what the damage is. Also I should tread down where the new bulbs are.

They gave me a bath yesterday. All the nurses here are men, male nurses they call them. And I had my injections. The young man that I have always hurts me when he sticks it in, he's clumsy, he just sticks it right in me and I sometimes think he does it deliberately I'm that sore.

I hope you are well, as ever,

Father

The letters always seemed to have been written on a
Sunday. They often seemed to be about things his father
did or thought about on that day. The best way to make
any kind of sense of them was to read them as a fantasy
on the themes of the adverts in the Sunday papers. A day
devoted to food and the garden and sitting by the fire and
thinking about your family and being very, very content.
And if they were not about all that, then they were about
all the other things that appear in full-page photographs
in the colour supplements alongside the adverts: misery,
poverty, violence, foreign countries, all the frightening
things. The things outside the garden.

Then there was a two-week gap in the sequence of letters.
And then a single letter arrived, except it was more like a
parcel than a letter. It seemed to have been opened and
resealed several times, with sellotape, before it had been
sent. This letter came on a Saturday. O was at home.
  Boy spread the contents of the envelope out on the living
room table, where O was finishing breakfast, and started
to sort them out. It didn't seem to matter in what order
you read the pages of these letters, since the catalogue of
events and feelings was always more or less the same, but
this time there was just so much of it that Boy had to sort
it out; at first it looked as though the envelope had just
been filled with the contents of a waste-paper basket. O
helped him do it.
  The pages of the letter itself were mixed up with pieces
of newspapers, some neatly clipped and folded, some just
torn out and stuffed in. These cuttings were mostly brief
accounts of petty crimes and domestic burglaries such
as appear on the inside pages of the free local papers
from the suburbs. Seven cases of assault against elderly
women living on their own had been included. When
they were from the national papers and from the *Radio*
and *TV Times* the clippings were not whole stories, but

just words or headlines, *rape, windows smashed every weekend, the continuing dilemma, knife.* There was also a full-page editorial from a popular newspaper describing the face of a black man being like the face of *a monkey in a cage fat with bananas.* It wasn't clear if this had been kept because the accompanying story of a burnt housing estate was frightening, or because the face of the black man was frightening, or because the fact that a newspaper should sell itself by putting that picture and those words on its front page was frightening.

When he'd sorted out the pages of the letter itself from all this newspaper (there were over seventy cuttings) Boy read the last page first. This was the last sentence: *I should never have written all this down as I don't want to worry you about me and I probably shan't send it anyway, my love as ever, I'm fine* and there was the usual signature, *Father.*

When finally assembled, the letter was seventeen pages long. It catalogued all the bruises, burns, insults, terrors, sweats, nightmares and long hours of simple grief (*I get this hard pain in my throat and under my stomach and then I'm suddenly doubled up in the chair, that's how it gets me . . .*) to which the old man claimed his body had recently been subjected. It listed forty-two separate incidents involving physical injury; it claimed that burning rags had been pushed through his letter box onto the hall carpet; that a twelve-year-old boy had sung an obscene rhyme to him while he was at the bus stop and that for fifteen minutes afterwards he, a grown man, had leant against a wall and then had had to sit down and had missed the bus; that four men he knew had been abused on the telephone; six not invited home for Christmas and one turned away from Church, refused communion; that another had walked past the house late at night with blood running down his chin; that he himself had, two nights ago, bitten his lip so hard while watching the television news that the blood had run down his chin and he had not been able to get the blood out of his shirt even with soaking and now his lip would not heal and was bleeding in the night, and he didn't like to dirty the bed.

It was not clear from the letter whether these incidents were being described from experience, or were copied from the papers, or had been invented, or had been dreamt, or if he'd just seen them on the television somewhere. One or two of the anecdotes were rendered incomprehensible by the way the sentences were written (*Wednesday a stiff neck again, Thursday ducked to avoid the blow and pulled neck*). Several were made improbable, despite the inclusion of realistic details, by the fact that the incidents were described at least four times with the details slightly rearranged. In one case a list of wounds inflicted in the course of an assault and burglary were transferred from the hands and face of a pensioner living alone to the arms, legs and chest of a handsome, single young man in the prime of his life.

One entire page was blotted by tears and illegible.

In all this catalogue of injuries and fears, surface wounds, bruises and deeper cuts, not one of the recent attacks on customers at The Bar was mentioned.

Boy was holding the tear-stained page, and O was reading the editorial about the man in the cage, when Boy said:
'I'm going to get him.'

He said it again (in the voice he had once used to say the line *I will not ask you to forgive me, I cannot ask you to forgive me*), 'I'm going to get him. I'll take care of him. And I can fight him better when I've got him where I can see him all the time.'

FAMILY

They redecorated the small spare room for him.

Boy had started reading up medical textbooks and books about how to care for the sick, and one of these explained how to get the room ready. They made sure that there was a large ashtray that would not spill easily; and this was the only room in the flat that they carpeted, because the book explained that a carpet made it less likely that an unsteady patient will trip or slip, also that *splinters from a wooden floor are dangerous when the child is crawling.* They bought an electric fire, because heating is essential; the old or newborn may become severely chilled if the temperature drops at night. They decorated the room with framed pictures of famous gardens; even the calendar had a different brightly coloured picture of a garden for every month. Boy thought the old man would like that.

The books Boy read up were full of good advice. They also had the most beautiful diagrams, usually of a single man embracing an older man, which at first sight looked like diagrams of sexual positions; in fact they were accompanied by instructions about how to sit the patient up, how to bathe him, how to lift him out of a low bed by yourself. These books also contained texts of great beauty:

*Healthy people are usually able to choose their envi-
ronment. If anything makes it uncomfortable or dangerous, they are free to make adjustments or to move
away. This man, however, is dependent upon those
who care for him, and who care about him, to see
that his surroundings are safe.*

Had O ever looked closely at the envelopes of Boy's letters
he would have seen their postmarks, and would have
known, even before Boy explained the whole thing, that
they didn't come from far away but from a part of the city
busy with traffic and adjacent to the black city trees of a
common that had not been real country for a hundred and
fifty years. But he never had; even now, he could not get
used to the idea that they did not come from somewhere
distant, another country almost. So when Boy announced
his decision to go and get this man, O was still somehow
expecting a train journey into the country.

Instead they went on a bus which went straight there and
only took just over an hour.

When they got there they saw Father already standing
there in the reception area in his coat, with his two
black binliners ready at his feet. He was standing right
up against the plate-glass window, looking out for them,
like an angry, shortsighted puppy in a shop window,
watching every person that went past or came in. He
had a walking stick; evidently furious that he'd had to
wait for so long (the nurse said he'd been standing there
since seven that morning), he let his stick fall, shouted,
I shan't be needing that now, and reached for Boy. Boy
didn't know whether to kiss him, or take his hand, or
to shake his hand formally. As it was, he had no time
to greet him; the old man grabbed hold of Boy's upper

arm, almost fell onto it, clutched it so hard that he made
the first of many marks on Boy's body with his strong and
bony fingers. The left hand had a gold wedding ring, it
was the same design as Boy's; the right hand, O saw (for
O was staring at him), was stained yellow with nicotine.
The man's hair was dead white, and he was small, shorter
than Boy, shrivelled looking.

He did not say much, just expected to be taken home
straight away. *Let's go*, he kept on saying, *let's go*. He
certainly didn't say anything to O, didn't even really
look at him, and when Boy introduced them (Boy said,
carefully, *Hello father, this is my friend*), all that the old
man said was *Yes*.

As they walked to the bus O carried the bags and Father
made a great show of using Boy to support himself,
walking by pushing each of his feet forward in turn,
demonstrating the peculiar walk of those long used to
shuffling down parquet-floored corridors in their slippers.
He had his slippers on still, with his suit. He was talking
vigorously all the time, but under his breath, saying
let's go, thank you, let's go, yes. O thought that for all his
exaggerated frailty he actually looked as though he could
walk quite well by himself if he had wanted to.

On the whole of the journey home, walking or sitting
on the bus, the old man seemed to be leaning slightly
forward, pushing Boy as much as leaning on him (for he
never let go of Boy on the journey, not once). He seemed
to have an urgent need to get somewhere, almost as if he
had to get to the toilet. On the bus, he made Boy sit next
to him so that O had to sit on the seat behind. Sitting in
the front of the bus (*Let me see*, he shouted, *I want to see*),
he leant forward and watched everything as it went past,
the people and streets. Boy wondered if he was watching
out for how things had changed, and wondered how many
years it was since this man had last been out on a bus.

It was as if he was watching for something, or as if he wanted to memorise the route. And the first time the bus stopped at some lights, which was only three minutes after they'd got on it, he said to Boy, *is this it?*

This happened every time the bus stopped on the whole journey, and every time Boy would patiently say, *No this isn't it, not yet.*

And when they got him home everything was immediately different. Who did what in which room, the hours of the day, the food, the television programmes, everything.

They climbed the five flights of stairs with grim slowness; Boy remembered a sentence from one of the books of advice, *gripping the hand or the arm is often a sign of fear*.

As soon as they were inside Boy installed Father in the armchair, got him an ashtray, put the gas fire on full, turned on the television and produced tea and a fruit cake, which is something they never normally had, with cups and saucers and cake plates, which they never usually got out. The three of them ate in silence, except when Father said *thankyou*. He ate pieces of cake until the whole thing was gone, as if to prove that he hadn't been well fed or looked after, and all during the tea he watched the television intently. Boy knew that he couldn't be watching it for the novelty, because they had had the television on at the home all the time.

Boy cleared away the tea things, and washed up, and still no one talked; he left O and Father sitting in the living room in silence. At four o'clock Boy came in and said to the old man, *it's time for you to lie down* (he always addressed him like that, he never said 'It's time to lie down, Father,' he never said, 'Goodnight, Father,' when the old man left the room to go to bed); he helped him up from his chair and, letting himself be used as a support, walked the old man to his room, sat him on the edge of the bed and shut the door and left him.

O had not seen Boy talk or behave like this before; his voice was not unkind, but it was firm; parental, almost. He never asked Father whether he wanted to do anything; for instance, he simply filled his plate with cake each time it became empty. O thought this was probably the right way to do things, the way recommended by the books; after all, you don't ever ask a baby what it wants, you just give it what you think it needs. You decide on its behalf. You don't ask a child why it's unhappy, you just hold it, don't you.

Also it seemed right because Father was so deeply withdrawn, as if shocked or tranquillised. It didn't seem right to ask him questions. And he always did what he was told.

Father did not change his routine when he came to live with them; he expected Boy and O to conform to his hours and needs, like a baby does. Their mealtimes and even their cups of tea (seven, eleven, three, seven, ten) duplicated the hours of the home—Boy had got all this information from the nurses. The flat even smelt like the home, because Father more or less chainsmoked, Benson and Hedges. It was hot like the home, too; the heating was always kept turned up now. And the television was always on. Sometimes Father would behave exactly as if he was still there; he would come into a room and sit there as if the other people in it (O and Boy) were strangers, fellow patients or inmates, not people he knew or should acknowledge in any way. When they fed him or bathed him, he did not thank them or make conversation; they were his new nurses as far as he was concerned.

If O and Boy were shocked or offended by this behaviour they didn't show it. Boy seemed very determined not to be thrown by anything the old man did; he very much wanted to prove himself capable of satisfying any demand or eccentricity.

Why he had to prove himself like this wasn't entirely clear. Sometimes his eagerness to do everything properly, to get it right, was so constant that it seemed fierce; his way of caring for the old man seemed as close to anger as it was to care somehow, and the silences in the flat seemed almost like the intervals in a long and violent argument. As if something Boy felt but could not bring himself to say was having to be expressed through this constant service and petty attention. Each correctly timed or arbitrarily refused cup of tea, every visit to the toilet seemed like a point scored. And all O could think of doing was to support Boy in this task or effort.

It was not made any easier by the fact that Father never went out. The stairs would not have been easy for him, and he had no need to go out, since Boy did all the shopping. But he didn't even seem to want to go out; he didn't even stare out of the windows. He would sit in the living room most of the day, occasionally coming and standing in the kitchen if Boy was there preparing food.

When he sat in the big armchair in the living room he looked very small; one of the effects that senility had on him was to gradually shrink him. In the last weeks of his illness he seemed so small that Boy even suggested to O that he might come into their bed and sleep between them like a child.

After two weeks Father did begin to talk. He wouldn't really make conversation—he never answered questions; but if either O or Boy was there in the living room with him he would start to talk. His anecdotes were often about the War, although he never really talked about the past in the sense of giving an explanation of who he was or what his real relationship with Boy was. When he talked about friends it was always in the past tense; he was always very insistent that everybody he knew was dead now, *that was the third suicide of people I'd known since the war,* he'd say; then, *I met this serviceman at Marble Arch, he only had an hour. I never saw him again but I know he's dead now.* He often told the same anecdotes over and over, as if their lack of credibility could be disguised by repetition. Sometimes he would sit there and simply recite *Marble Arch, Coventry Street, Regent Street, Piccadilly, the platform at Chancery Lane Station.* Sometimes Boy thought that if he heard the phrase *of course in those days* again he would have to leave the room. But he was determined never to be defeated by this man, O could see that.

Oddly enough Father never talked about his imaginary or remembered garden; in fact he never talked about the things he had talked about in the final sequence of letters at all, as if all that had never happened, as if he had never said any of those things.

Often he talked about a lost partner *(of course I never did that for myself),* about distant and now dead family relations, obscure cousins who had invited him to their weddings but whom he had never seen. He was always at pains to emphasise that he had never seen them and couldn't even remember most of their names.

When he heard all of this it seemed to Boy that this man's fantasy of his own life was failing him, just at the time when Boy's fantasy of his own life was beginning to seem real, like a real thing. *He's losing, and we're winning,* Boy thought.

One ending, and one beginning, it's often like that, Boy thought.

And he's the one who always said I'd be lonely.

Boy continued to read up on the subject of senility and the medical problems of old age; in particular, he became an expert on the possible causes and forms of angina.

One obvious cause was the constant smoking. The other causes listed in the books were stranger; these he read out loud to O one night when Father was in his room, speaking quietly so he wouldn't be heard. *How about this as a good explanation of the whole thing,* he said. *Poor adjustment of people to their environment, for example discrepancy between expectation and reality,* he said. *Over exertion resulting from conflicting roles or violent role changes,* he said.

Problems due to lack of life fulfilment.

Changes in social norms (marriage, partnership, authority and emancipation).

As well as accustoming himself to the old man's silence and his aimless, uncommunicative talking, Boy also had to get used to his crying. Like some babies do, Father would regularly cry between his dinner at six and his drink at ten. He had developed the knack of crying silently: Boy would come into the living room (O and he had developed the habit of spending much of the evenings in their bedroom) to ask him if he wanted more tea, and would find him sitting there all wet. The first few times, Boy asked him what was the matter; but he soon realised that Father found this as humiliating as if Boy had come into the living room and found him with not just his shirtfront and cardigan wet but with his trousers wet too, the chair seat a cold puddle. Once when Father did cry out loud, and then had managed to stop crying when Boy had come into the room to see what it was, he had said, *I'm sorry, I couldn't hold it in any longer.* Boy learned to just quietly fetch the towel, and Father either learned not to be embarrassed by crying in front of a young man, or he just stopped caring, because he would sit there and cry anyway. He could smoke and cry at the same time.

After three weeks, without asking, Father began one afternoon to play O's records on the stereo. Boy guessed that there must have been a record player in the home, because he seemed very confident about using it. Listening from the kitchen or from the bedroom, Boy and O couldn't work out any sense to Father's choice of music; he listened to disco, then to a torch song, then to a collection of Italian tenor arias; they could not imagine how or why he was making the choice of what to put on next. Then they realised that Father was simply working through the whole of O's collection of records from the left of the shelf to the right, playing every single one until he got to the end. This took him almost four days of listening.

His other main occupation was the television. In the afternoons Boy would sit with him while he watched.

As with the records, it seemed at first that Father just accepted one thing and then the next thing, without choosing; but Boy soon realised that there was an elaborate system of justification underlying his choice of programme, because he would complain quickly and bitterly if the wrong programme was on. Boy bought him the *Radio Times* and the *TV Times* each week, and by the end of the day on which he had received them he would appear to have memorised the schedules for the whole week. He would say, in the middle of an otherwise silent meal, that he was looking forward to seeing a particular film, a particular actress. He would say, *you know she was in* Flame in the Streets, *that was in 1961 too, she marries that black man. It's on at half past one on Tuesday afternoon.*

He liked all films in black and white, and seemed to have seen them all before and to know what happened in all of them. He could go to sleep during a film and then wake up during the final credits and still say, *I enjoyed that one, it's the one where,* and then proceed to give a correct and detailed summary of the plot. He would watch with close and unembarrassed attention any programme with nakedness or sex in it, and also all sports programmes in which there were partially-clothed male athletes, especially swimming, gymnastics and boxing. Boy never saw him watch golf, cricket, motor racing or horse racing.

Boy would watch the old films with him, and found that he too recognised some of them, from his days of constant television before he had met O. He watched them very differently from how he had watched them then; now he identified with completely different characters.

On Sunday evenings Boy and Father would sit together and watch the nature programmes. In the living room of a flat which Boy shared with another man, in the room next to the room in which O and Boy slept and made violent love together, Boy and Father saw all the dark secrets of sex and violence exposed and explained in glorious colour. They watched all the most intricate rituals of courtship, pairing and reproduction, filmed in shocking closeup. Boy saw tigers mating, saw everything of which he had once been ignorant, all the things he'd had to come to the city and especially to The Bar to find. And as he watched, with Father beside him, Boy gradually persuaded himself that he could in fact remember something of the childhood from which he thought all such things had been absent, and which he thought he had completely forgotten.

It was the nature programmes that brought it back. He felt sure he could remember having lived at some time with this man, presumably as a small boy, at some time and in some home all other details of which were now forgotten or deliberately forgotten, except for this one scene. He had the overwhelming sense that he had sat beside this man before, watching these programmes. And if that was the case, then it wasn't true that he had never seen these things, sex, courtship, marriage, before;

it wasn't true that as a child images such as these had been banned from his sight. He must have remembered it wrong for some reason

The exact combination of sensations that Boy thought he could remember was that of *watching* with *silence*. A silence which this man was, as Boy remembered it, somehow enforcing and which Boy knew (I mean, knew *then*), knew he could never break. He had only ever been allowed to watch these things in the dark, just before bedtime; he had known that there was something vaguely wrong about witnessing these secrets, that the other man felt that the pleasure they took in these programmes was wrong too; but he had never been allowed to talk about them, he had been expected to sit there in rapt and embarrassed silence while the images lit up the darkened living room carpet. He had seen the tigers mating, the societies of the birds, the families of fish, the different pairings of albatross and lovebird, hawk and dove. He had known it was there, this world. His father had shown him this world, but had never spoken of it. Or that was what Boy thought he remembered. Watching in silence on a Sunday evening. But not talking. And that was why he felt that all this had been taken away, or denied him, or just denied.

That was the feeling he remembered.

That was what it felt like.

That was it. It must have been.

Boy never watched these programmes with O; but when O was out he sat with Father and he watched, as he had done before he met O, as he had done when he was a child, as he had done when he was really a boy.

O was often out of the house; he was working every day, including Saturday usually, and also he would deliberately 'get out of the house' even when he wasn't working. He sensed that Boy needed a lot of time to be alone with this new man in his life, and he himself also needed to escape from the silence, the television, the atmosphere of sudden and complete emotional tension that now filled the flat. Boy coped by working as hard as a professional nurse; O coped by diving every morning into the cool water of an empty swimming pool. He would get there early so that he would have the first ticket, and would strip naked quickly, before anyone else did, for he liked best of all to dive into a completely still and empty pool. Sometimes he wouldn't dive, but would lower himself into the water extremely slowly, taking care not to disturb the silent, perfect mirror of its surface, and then he would watch the pattern of ripples spreading across it from the first sure strokes of his arms and legs. When he swam, he swam hard, very hard; O sensed that in some way he was not now just keeping himself strong, which he had always done, but keeping himself strong against the arrival of some particular crisis. Some night or day when he might have to actually rescue someone, keep them afloat, catch them in his arms and keep them from drowning. This is what he felt when he was in the flat with Boy: *I'm here if you need me.*

Boy almost never went out; as long as Father stayed in, he stayed in, except to shop. O asked Boy why he had to stay in all day, and Boy said, *I have to watch him. I have to watch him. I have to keep an eye on him all the time.*

This was true, but it was not as if Father was so infirm or crazy that he was in constant danger of falling and hurting himself, or scalding himself if he made his own tea; he didn't have to be watched in that sense. It was more as if Boy had to watch him for clues, was watching in the hope of finding out who this man really was. Or watching him so that he didn't steal anything. Watching him so that eventually under the pressure of being watched he might one afternoon give way and be civil and perhaps even start to talk, to really talk, to hold a conversation. To answer questions.

If Boy could have expressed it, maybe that is what he would have said. He wanted this man to answer his questions, to be answerable for this situation. He wanted him to tell him what had happened. He wanted him to be responsible for the whole thing. He wanted him to admit that he was responsible. That he was to blame. If only he would have admitted that he was to blame, then Boy could have started to punish him adequately.

There was no break in Boy's scrutiny of this man. Even if he was in another room, Boy would be listening, in case he said anything or admitted anything; let anything slip. Boy would even lie awake at night, listening; and Father would lie awake too. It was as if each day was a bout in a fight which neither of them could end, in case ending meant giving in first.

Sometimes in the night Boy would hear a scratching sound, he would hear Father scratching, and would wonder if perhaps he had started writing the letters again.

Sometimes in the night Father would hear sounds like sobbing coming from the other bedroom, and he must have wondered if this was in fact someone crying, or someone making love. Perhaps he would try and picture it; an athlete crying on another's shoulder . . . two grooms in a stable, two soldiers in uniform, two soldiers on a statue, one supporting the other, they're crying, he thinks he's seen that somewhere before, he thinks he can picture that.

They found it hard to make love; Boy said he found it hard to make love with the old man just eight inches away on the other side of the bedroom wall. He suspected that he stayed awake to listen.

They found it hard to even talk about him; Boy said he found it hard to talk about the old man when he knew he could hear in the other room. Even if they watched TV or one of O's video's together, they would do it very quietly, with the sound barely on, waiting until twenty minutes after the old man had gone to bed before they had it on at all. Father himself would always turn the television off when he went to bed, even if it was in the middle of a programme that he had been watching with O and Boy; at a quarter past ten, when he'd had his ten o'clock cup of tea, he would get up, turn it off and leave the room without saying anything to them, just muttering under his breath, *Radio off, TV out, Goodnight Mother.*

They found it hard.

Boy kept on reading his books of medical advice, asking O to get him new ones from the library, and after the old man had been with them for five weeks, he found a paragraph that inspired him to make the next decisive move against his father or so-called father. The book said, *a meal should be as enjoyable an occasion as possible. It is all the more pleasurable if eaten in agreeable surroundings, at a well-appointed table. This applies to a sick person no less than it does to a healthy one.*

O woke up at six o'clock in the morning to the sound of someone moving around the flat. He listened to them working, washing up or sweeping or something, doing housework of some kind. He was about to get up to make sure that Boy was all right when Boy came back into the bedroom, fully clothed. He said nothing, but took O's face in both hands and kissed him so hard he hurt him; then he took off his clothes and made love to O, which he had not done for ten days, made love to him urgently and in ferocious silence, his hands cold and smelling of detergent. Then Boy got up, and dressed again, and took

Father his seven o'clock cup of tea. At seven-thirty, when
O got up too, the gas fire was on full and the table in
the living room was set with a full breakfast; a linen
tablecloth (O didn't know that they had one), cutlery, a
toastrack; there was cereal in the bowls, milk in a jug
and sugar in a bowl, napkins, butter in a dish and the
marmalade jar already opened. The orange juice was
already poured. The smell of bacon grilling came from
the kitchen, telling the breakfasters that they only had a
few minutes before the cooked part of the meal arrived.
It was as if the living room had become the guest room of
a bed and breakfast; it was nothing like the way Boy and
O usually breakfasted.

On his way to the bathroom O saw Father already sitting
at the breakfast table, dressed and smoking, waiting. Only
two places were laid; and clearly Boy was staying in the
kitchen, serving, not eating. O wondered what he should
wear for this apparently formal meal. He had been used to
having breakfast with Boy with one or both of them naked,
indeed they had often used to wander round the flat naked
at all hours of the day before Father had arrived. Now
he knew, without being told, not to do this, even when
Father was asleep or in his room. His first thought was
just to put on his bathrobe; but this was made of scarlet
towelling, and O knew the red robe had too often been
worn before, during or after sex, to be appropriate to this
new occasion; its colour and cut were designed to make
a splendid setting for his body, not to cover it. Then he
thought that perhaps he should wear Boy's robe, which
was white, but he thought that to wear his lover's clothes
(which he would usually have done without thinking,
they were always wearing each other's underwear and
t shirts) to have breakfast with his lover's Father would
be too ostentatious, too obvious a declaration of their
relationship. And should he wear underpants under the
robe in case it fell open, which he never did, usually,

because he wanted Boy to see him naked, wanted Boy to be suddenly struck by the sight of him, wanted Boy to unknot the robe and sink to his knees? Would he have to take care how he sat so that his genitals should not ever be exposed to this other man's sight . . . O got tired of thinking and went to breakfast in jeans and a shirt though he hated getting fully dressed that early.

The breakfast was eaten in silence; Boy cleared away the cereal, brought in the tea with the bacon and fried eggs, cleared that away, brought in the toast, then refilled the teapot. They heard him already washing up, as if he was a woman working in a guest house hurrying to get upstairs to get the guests' beds done. Then they heard the front door; then six minutes later they heard it again, and Boy came into the living room and in front of O he put a copy of his usual newspaper, and in front of Father he put a copy of the *Radio Times*. As he put the paper down he said, *I want you to meet my Father*, and as he put the *Radio Times* down he said, *Father, this is my lover*. And then he left. He left them to it; he went out for two hours.

They finished the toast, all of it, and drank the tea until it was cold. All this in silence. When they finally talked, both O and Father could barely conceal their anger. The older man's bitterness was inarticulate, general; he smelt of bitterness almost as he did of cigarette smoke. It was always in the room with him. O's was very specific. Left alone with him like this, he realised he was furious at not being able to love and make love to his Boy, not being able to fuck him on the floor just because this man was here. Furious that he had to play this scene, entitled 'I want to take you home to meet my parents'. Furious because if this man was not actually Boy's Father, then why should they worry what he thought about noises in the night, why should they even have him here?

Father said:

'What's it like that paper then?'

'Do you want to read it?'

'Why don't you read me a bit. Read me a good interesting bit.'

O hunted through the paper, making a point of being seen to be choosing something 'suitable' (he might even have said, *I could read this story, but you wouldn't understand it*). Then he began to read a piece about Gardening Tasks for the Winter Months, about how the more delicate plants can be helped to endure the frost and the killing winds of winter. He wanted to say, *you'll be interested in this bit*, meaning, *you'll have to pretend to be interested in this, won't you? I know about you and your famous garden. I know all about you. I know what you like. I know what you want.*

When he got to the bit about how to ensure that your Christmas roses, perfect and unrotted, flower in the middle of the darkest week of the year, Father interrupted him. While O was still reading, without looking at him, grinding out his cigarette on the tablecloth (though of course Boy had put out a clean ashtray for him), he said,

'You make enough noise you two don't you? I've heard you. I've heard you. And I've seen you. I've seen you.'

Now he did look up at O, to see what effect he was having, still grinding out his cigarette stub, burning the tablecloth.

'I get up in the night and look through your door. Is he good in bed that Boy of mine then? Is he?'

O didn't reply. He thought the old man was going to go on and describe what he'd seen; he was smiling, as if to prove that he had stood in the dark and watched them fucking, as if he'd scored a point by catching them at it, more of a dirty, contemptuous grin than a smile. But he didn't describe them fucking. What he said was:

'I've seen you lying there all hours of the night looking at him while he's sleeping. I've seen you pulling up the cover over his left shoulder like you was his mother or something.'

The old man's voice broke and he stood up in his chair and O could see he was shaking, his hands were white where he was gripping the sides of the chair. He was shouting now. 'I suppose you love him. I suppose you think you love him more than I do. I'm going to my room now.'

He spent all of that day in his room, O could hear him crying with rage. When Boy got home, O told him about the scene, and Boy said, almost with triumph:

'You know he always told me that it would be me who would be lonely.'

In the second month, Father got older and he got sicker. Now he slept during the day as well as during the night, never more than for a couple of hours at a time, but at least eleven hours out of the twenty-four, and sometimes as many as eighteen, which is as much as a baby sleeps in the first few weeks of its life. Like a baby, Father did not now seem to distinguish between night and day.

Often O would wake up in the night to find himself alone in the bed. He'd get up, go into Father's room, and there he'd find Boy standing over the bed. He'd stand there with a pillow; the first time that O saw him standing there like that, he thought Boy was going to do something awful, thought he was going to kill the old man, smother him, for he was hugging a pillow to his chest with clenched fists as if trying to restrain himself from attacking the sleeping body . . . then Boy expertly lifted the old man's head up without waking him and put the extra pillow under his head; he said to O, whispering, *he'll sleep better now.* O said, whispering too, *why are you doing this?* and Boy said, innocently misunderstanding the question and thinking that O had just asked him why he was up again at four a.m., *I can hear it when his breathing changes, and I just needed to check if he was alright. Listen, it's different now, I can tell when he's rolled over onto his back just by listening to him. That's what makes him breathe like that.*

Fear undoubtedly keeps people awake, the text book said.

It is pointless to pretend that it does not exist, the textbook said.

When Father whimpered in the night, or cried in his sleep, for he cried both when sleeping and when awake now, Boy would sit by him and gently read out loud to him even if he thought Father was asleep. He read passages from the books he had kept by him in his first days in the city; also from the books that Mother had given him. If they were passages that were especially dear to him, or passages describing sexual activity, Boy would wait until he was sure the old man was asleep. He wanted to say these things to him, but he did not want him to hear them.

Shall I still be attractive to my boyfriend or husband? Am I becoming a burden as I become older? Who will look after me when I cannot cope any longer? Shall I be able to bear the pain? Am I going to die? All these are very real anxieties, some without solution, the book said.

Boy also tried whispering to him, as a sort of lullaby, *Goodnight, Father; Goodnight, Father*, over and over again; but again he only said this when he thought the old man could not hear him, sat there in the dark and said it very quietly, *goodnight, father; goodnight, father; goodnight, father.*

Late one night, in a desperate effort to calm him, for he was making so much noise that neither O nor Boy could sleep, Boy climbed onto the bed beside Father and pulled

the covers off him. It looked as if he was going to hit him,
drag him across his knee and hit him. What he in fact did
was haul him, sweating and still asleep (he was on pills
now) in to his lap. This was quite easy, for Father was
getting smaller and smaller and lighter and lighter.

Boy had looked up the correct posture in his book.
He was wearing a shirt; he unbuttoned the shirt and,
guiding Father's head by placing his hand on the back
of his neck, he brought Father's lips to his left nipple.
The old man remained half asleep, and kept on crying;
but he let his face be pushed into Boy's chest, and then
he began, quite involuntarily, to suckle, half biting, half
sucking at the nipple. Boy put his other arm round him
and rocked him and crooned to him, with one hand still
supporting his head and the other arm right round him.
It seemed to work; they stayed there for a long time like
that, with Father gradually getting calmer and calmer,
sucking steadily on the nipple now. Boy didn't look down
at his Father, but stared calmly ahead, at the picture of a
moonlit garden which was the picture for December on
Father's calendar.

At four in the morning, Boy felt a wetness on his chest;
but no miracle had occurred. No miraculous milk of
charity had begun to flow; it was Father's tears that were
trickling down from his nipple and wetting his chest. Boy
stayed like that till dawn, his arms aching and his chest
wet, while Father gently cried himself into a deep, true
sleep.

When Boy went to lay him down on the bed, Father
whimpered slightly and threatened to wake; Boy put a
finger in his mouth to calm him.

And that is how he finally slept and that is how Boy
stayed with him. His Father went to sleep with Boy's
finger in his mouth, just as Boy had once loved to go to
sleep with O's penis in his mouth. Father went to sleep
with Boy watching over him, just as O had watched over

Boy with tears of love in his eyes, just as Boy had watched over O on the nights of his dreaming. And all the time Boy was whispering, *Goodnight, Goodnight, Father.*

With their days and nights taken up like this, of course they never went out much, though I think O used to phone Mother regularly so that she knew what was happening and that they were basically all right.

So that she knew what she was getting for her money.

The two times I did see them out, Boy just wanted to talk about his Father (the way people want to talk about their children when they're very young. *It's not just because he's old,* he'd say, *I think it's because he's unhappy, and because he's unhappy—well, you don't ask a child why it's unhappy, you just hold it, don't you?*). The period of their absence from The Bar wasn't very long however; this whole episode with the sick Father was over in less than three months.

And if I can't talk about them kissing or standing in The Bar, at this period of their lives, I hope you notice how I still want to tell you everything about them, how they coped, the food that they ate, their housework and who did it. I want you to know, you see. I want you to believe me.

Goodnight, father; goodnight, father; goodnight, father.

The book said: *A sagging posture suggests weariness, dejection or unhappiness. The outstretched arms of a mother promise love and security. From earliest childhood we are taught to recognise these signs, and others.*

Boy hardly ever left Father now that he was visibly getting worse. He watched him all the time, looking for physical signs of how he felt. It seemed to Boy that it was important to try and determine if his pain and misery came from an illness, or from some deeper unhappiness. He looked in his books at the diagrams of internal organs, as if that might provide a clue to or reason for this man's condition.

Father, for his part, gave no explanation. He hardly ever spoke, and kept his face turned away, mostly. When he did this Boy wondered if his refusal to talk was a symptom too; if the old man wanted to throw himself on their mercy, to throw himself helplessly at them as the last thing he could do to hurt them or take them away from each other. Boy had never said to him, *do you know that you're dying.* All three of them knew it though.

Because there was nothing he could do to get through to him, as he got sicker and sicker, Boy made more and

more work for himself in the flat. All the hours and all the
energy that he had previously expended on the elaborate
and time-consuming rituals of sexual contact which had
characterised his life with O were now dedicated to
elaborate rituals of housework. The ridiculous breakfast
became a permanent feature of their life, and the other
meals of the day grew to match it. He began to serve high
teas of tinned grapefruit segments, sliced ham with lettuce
and salad cream, fruit cake—food which seemed to carry
some memory of another place and another time, as if he
had learnt to do all this somewhere else, in another house,
run by someone from another generation. On Sunday he
did a roast—and every Sunday, as a matter of course,
not as a joke or a celebration. He even went out and
bought a table for the kitchen, which they had never
had before, and now he made them do things really
properly; breakfast in the kitchen, lunch on a tray and
supper on the living room table, with different china
and a different tablecloth. He would be up at seven
every morning, working in his dressing gown, laying
the table with milk, cereal, the toastrack, even napkins,
a formal cruet and both brown and tomato sauce bottles;
and then when O appeared from the bedroom he would
serve (in silence) fried eggs and fried bread, and often
tea and coffee at the same time. Then he would take
Father his tea in bed. And then when O had left for
work (taking the sandwiches that Boy now made for
him the night before) he would wash up immediately
after the meal, which he had never done before. He
made himself so busy that he had no time to complain.
Sometimes he made himself so busy that he apparently
completely forgot the usual reason for eating (hunger,
propriety, variety); so intense was his dedication to his
domestic role that he would serve four meals a day instead
of three, or serve exactly the same meal for dinner three
nights running.

Boy now did all the shopping and cleaning, whereas before O and Boy had shared these jobs without even talking about it, except during one of their rare rows. Now when O came home the fridge would already be full, dinner would be on and the bathroom smelling of Ajax and Flash. O said nothing, but let Boy do it, and ate as much of the food as he could. He swam every day now, because Boy's new diet of meat, potatoes and vegetables for every evening meal, plus the breakfast, was making him put on weight. He did not complain, even when he began to notice that Boy was buying much more food than they needed, going shopping every single day, so that often there would be perfectly good food, especially bread and milk, thrown into the bin just to make space in the fridge so that Boy could go shopping again. O didn't complain because he understood that all this domestic labour, this labour of love, now had nothing to do with being practical. He never told Boy what he should or shouldn't do. This took considerable nerve; he even let Boy hurt himself, but only slightly; if Boy had ever fallen, I know that O would have been right there to catch him, and that his arms would have been strong enough to lift him up again. He watched in silence as Boy's body began to be marked with various small wounds. He cut his knuckles under the taps while scouring the bath. He got splinters under his nails from scrubbing the kitchen worktop so hard. His eyes were bruised with exhaustion again, just as they had once been when O and Boy were first sleeping together.

O kissed these bruises and marks every night, as he had done when he found the marks of another man's passion on his Boy's body during that earlier period of their life. When he kissed him, all over his body, he saw that Boy was not being consumed by all this work, but was getting stronger, especially his back and his beautiful arms.

This was mostly from lifting Father in and out of the bath, which he had to do several times a day now to keep him clean. Boy would undress him, and then, when the old man was naked, he would stand close behind him. Then he would slip his hands under the old man's armpits and grasp his forearms; then he would tell him to lift his left leg and step into the bath, then the right, and then Boy would bend his knees and gently lower him into the bath. All this was done just as the book said it should be. Boy also sometimes did it facing him, with Father's hands clasped behind his neck, using his hands to lift his legs into the water. Often Boy used to take his shirt off so as not to get it soaked; when O saw these two men through the bathroom door, one naked and one half naked, holding onto each other, and when he heard the very deliberate instructions, *lift your leg, that's it. Higher. Lift it higher,* he was reminded of the times when Boy and he had made love in the bathroom just like that, when he himself had given instructions not unlike those. He thought it strange that the old man should accept this treatment; he was often sweaty or incontinent, and must have been embarrassed to have his genitals washed daily by a younger man, surely he must be embarrassed, O thought, even if he doesn't show it. Has he accepted the way in which this young man, this young man in particular, is touching him, or is he just too ill and old to be able to fight back any more?

O would watch them together; he was very moved to see Boy doing what he was doing. He said:

'Can I help?'

and Boy said, holding the old man to his breast (he had just lifted him from the bath) and giving his lover a rare smile (rare these days):

'It's alright, suddenly I feel very strong.'

'Strong enough?'

'I think so.'

And he was; he never hurt the old man, not once, never slipped when he had him in his arms, never dropped him.

He was strong enough; but some nights he would let himself collapse into exhaustion once he had got Father to bed. He had enough strength for the days, but not for the nights any more. They had always held on to each other as they had fallen asleep; now Boy often just lay there exhausted, and then O would hold him and kiss his body everywhere, saying over and over again, very quietly so that not even Father would hear, *I love you, I love you, I love, I'm here, I'm here, I'm here, we're going to live, we're going to live, we're going to live.*

As he pushed himself to perfect his new role, Boy began to use a set of gestures that came from nowhere, weren't learned from anyone he knew. Perhaps he got them from watching all those old films. He would push his hair up from his temples with the back of his hand—or rather, he would make the gesture of a washerwoman pushing back her grey and lank hair with a wash-reddened hand, stretching her aching back—but Boy had no real hair to push back, since O still clipped his hair short for him every week, except for the lock at the front. He would also twist the ring on the work-roughened second finger of his left hand when watching the television. This was a gesture which O had only ever seen in widows. Boy even seemed to somehow acquire skills he had not had before. One morning Father clutched suddenly at his arm, fearing that he was about to slip on the wet bathroom floor; he tore the sleeve of Boy's shirt. He wore it torn for days (he would just get up each morning and put on yesterday's clothes, there was no dressing up now). But then one night when they were watching television Boy took his shirt off without saying anything and sat there bare-chested in front of the television and neatly repaired it. O didn't even know he could sew.

It was amazing how much work he found to do in such a small flat; cleaning, ironing, dusting, even re-painting—he started painting even though all the paintwork was still fresh and new from when they had moved in. O had heard that pregnant women sometimes had a compulsive need to clean. He had read about the Jewish ritual of throwing out all the food in the house; he had read in one of Boy's books that in the moments before death you may see the dying person's hands frantically plucking and smoothing the sheets, as if tidying them. But still he did not actually know what compulsion Boy was obeying when he did all this. Sometimes the intensity of Boy's gestures was such that O wondered if he was in a fury of revenge; if he was revenging himself on some previous, hated life by repeating its gestures in a bitter parody, doing it all more diligently than it had ever been done, knowing full well that he, a young man, should never have been doing these things in the first place. He would scour the bathtub as if he was scouring away blood, wash the walls as if he had to be rid of some terrible infection, slice the vegetables with a great knife and boil them for too long. But he never took his anger out on the old man. He did have dreams of actually prising words out of him, dreams of actually cutting him open to see his heart, but he didn't ever hurt him. He wanted him to live. If he'd been asked, he would have said that he was fighting for his Father's life. Sometimes, in certain lights, O would catch Boy looking like a mother with a baby; his face slightly swollen with tiredness, flushing easily. He smelt all the time of food and piss and creams; he was extraordinarily sensitive to sound, always ready to attend to a cry for help or of hunger.

O did as much as he could. He would get the afternoon off whenever he could so that he could sit with Father by the gas fire. That was all the old man did now; lie in his bed or sit in his chair. O would bring home videos from work, because Father still liked to have the TV on all day every day. He didn't talk any more about what he enjoyed and what he didn't enjoy watching, but O got to know what he liked, because there were some tapes he would watch over and over again with evident interest, keeping his eyes on the screen, not turning to stare at the wall which is mostly how he would indicate discomfort or displeasure at this time. He liked the stranger Hollywood musicals, *The Pirate*, for instance, and he especially liked Vietnamese, Indian and Chinese tapes; musicals, operas, police thrillers and ghost stories; silk flowers, white-faced women, gongs, cymbals and sickening violence done both for real and as farce.

When he couldn't stand the television any more O would put on records that he liked and that Father liked too, so that they could listen to them together; Stuart Burrows singing 'Dalla Sua Pace' (the sleeve notes translated the first line of the lyrics as 'When she is beside me'); then Billie Holiday, Brenda Lee and Sarah Vaughan, the albums on which they sing their versions of 'All of Me'. When he did that Boy would come out of the kitchen and stand in the doorway and listen. He would ask O to put the song on again, and again, and all three of them would sit there in silence listening to the song four or five times over.

Father was so small and frail now, sitting there listening to the song, that Boy could have picked him up.

> *All of me, why not take all of me*
> *Can't you see,*
> *I'm no good without you.*

Often when they had been listening to her song O would go out and telephone Mother. He used to call her regularly at this time.

Once, while they were listening to it, Boy was cleaning the bath. O left Father alone in the living room; he just wanted to be with his Boy for a moment. They both remembered their first time together in the flat. It was the same song, but a different singer; and this time it was Boy who pushed O up against the wall, pushed his knee between his legs until it hurt him, bit him gently on the face. When they got to the line *when I am beside . . .* Boy balled his left hand into a fist and pressed it hard on O's chest, right over his heart, so hard that the ring marked him, made a small bruise, like a branding mark.

Father sickened. He couldn't go to the toilet by himself or eat easily now; Boy even chewed his food for him sometimes. His senility was so extreme that they had to fight the feeling that he was doing this deliberately; that he was somehow lying. But when the doctor had called he had told them that it would be just like this. To reassure himself, Boy looked up the description of angina again in one of his books; *the patient will often try and describe his sensations by referring to a steel band tightening around his chest, directly above his heart; or he may clasp his hands over his heart and push inwards, like an actor making the traditional gesture for avowal.* No one really slept any more, and even when the days were superficially calm, there was the constant anxiety; they were waiting for him to die. Both of them had flashes of feeling very close to murderous rage, the rage that makes people want to kill their children. O wanted to cram the old man's mouth with food and choke him, to tuck him into bed with too many blankets and smother him, lift him gently into the bath and drown him.

The very last time that they managed to get him to the breakfast table, Father was in evident distress. Usually he would point at something on the breakfast table when he wanted it—if he needed milk in his tea, he would just point at the jug and say *milk*. This morning he pointed at all the things on the table in turn; but when he pointed at the milk jug he said, out loud, *Boy*; when he pointed at the toastrack he said *Man*; when he pointed at the sugar bowl he said *Wife*. And then he sat there with both hands on the table and said *boy, child, mother, sister, wife, darling, baby*.

The next stage was just as the book described it; the old man became aphasic, which means that even when he knew what he wanted, he couldn't say what he wanted.

Then he sickened to the point where he couldn't communicate at all, not even by looking or pointing; and when he got to this stage they knew it was nearly the end and they called Mother and asked her to come. The night she came he wouldn't or couldn't stop crying, and O was going out of his mind because he could see that his Boy was hurting so much. She arrived in a taxi, still wearing the silver dress and carrying a small bag with everything she needed. When O opened the door to her he whispered:

'He's just gone off.'

She came in, and kissed O on both cheeks. He whispered, 'Boy's in the kitchen. And I'm watching TV with the sound off.'

And then he took hold of her hand and said:

'And now Mother's here.'

They both laughed, quietly, and she said:

'One: where can I change? Two: where do I sleep?'

Boy was so busy, scouring the kitchen sink, that he hardly had time to greet her. O and Mother just got on

with it and made a bed up on the sofa and laid an extra
place for dinner.

There wasn't actually much that Mother could do; she
helped with the vegetables and the dishes, but basically
Boy did everything. He kept on saying, *I can manage, I can
manage.* What she did do, quietly and unobtrusively, was
to get O out of the house; she took him to The Bar. Then
she'd leave Gary and the Stellas and me to look after him,
and she'd go back to Boy. Also she got Boy to eat and
drink; he was so busy providing and caring that he often
forgot to feed himself. She would bring him cups of coffee
in the night without asking him if he wanted them. One
night she put a bottle of champagne on the table, saying,
it's your anniversary, it's eight months now. The next night,
when Boy was so tired he could hardly eat, she kept him
talking, poured out another bottle of champagne, saying,
*well tonight is my anniversary, a private one, If you knew
what we were celebrating even you would blush, boys, now
drink up.* The way she could get Boy to eat and drink
without noticing it made O think that maybe Mother had
been a nurse at some point in her varied career.

And her biggest contribution was of course the money;
she was still keeping them.

She kept herself immaculate even though she was
sleeping on a made-up bed and had to do her makeup
in the bathroom mirror. She went to work every night
having had dinner with O and Boy at six o'clock. She
changed into the dress and called a taxi and went to work
with her cigarettes and her hair up. She said:

'Goodnight Boys.'

And every night O said:

'Goodnight Mother,'

and every night Boy came wet-handed out of the
kitchen and kissed her and said:

'Goodnight, Mother.'

For the last three days of Father's illness, this routine broke down completely; Mother didn't even come into The Bar. The three of them did nothing but watch over Father. He had stopped eating, Boy had stopped preparing food, and no one slept. They were just waiting, Boy waiting for Father to die, O waiting to support Boy when it finally came and Mother waiting to hold the two of them up should she have to. The television stayed on all the time with no one to watch it. It was almost winter; they kept the heating on day and night as the first frosts came.

When the death finally came it came quickly and was not expected, even though they had been waiting for it for so long.

After three days Boy was so exhausted that even he had to sleep. He woke at three in the morning; Mother and O were asleep as well; but Boy had set his alarm to wake him up at hourly intervals so that he could check on Father. As soon as he got out of bed he knew that something was wrong; the flat was freezing cold. He went straight to the kitchen; the pilot light on the boiler was out. He went quickly to Father's room, where he found that the old man had dragged the duvet off himself, and was sleeping uncovered. His skin was pale and cold, his breathing slow and shallow. Boy immediately pulled the duvet back over him and shouted to wake O and Mother.

Boy knew it was hypothermia, and he gave Mother and O quick and accurate instructions while he himself wrapped himself around Father under the duvet, trying to warm him with his own body.

Mother called for an ambulance; it took thirteen minutes to arrive.

O put on his red towelling robe, then went straight to the kitchen and filled every saucepan they had.

Boy couldn't actually remember if the correct way to restore body temperature in cases where the patient is not capable of taking a hot drink is submersion in a hot bath. He was afraid that the book in fact said, *this is a dangerous and possibly fatal remedy, since it draws all the remaining body heat to the surface.* But there was no time to find the book and check. He had to act.

In the kitchen, O found that they had run out of matches; he carried a piece of flaming newspaper from the gas fire in the living room to light the gas rings, and when he extinguished the newspaper under the kitchen tap the flat began to smell of burning.

He and Mother carried pans of steaming water to the bath; there was a pool of spilt water in the hallway.

When the bath was full (it took eight minutes) Boy began to lift Father out of the disarranged and dirty linen of the bed, to take him to the bath. He got him up in his arms and sitting on the edge of the bed all right; but then as he lifted him to a standing position he realised that something else was wrong; he could feel the sweat, he heard the change in the breathing, and he realised that the old man was in the middle of an angina attack. His eyes suddenly opened wide with pain and he was clearly terrified. His skin was now grey and his face began to discolour.

Force yourself to act quickly and decisively, the book said. *You only have three minutes. Leave the door open and turn all the lights on so that the ambulancemen can locate you.*

Boy called for help again.

By the time he got out into the hallway, he could carry the old man no further. O fetched Mother's wedding-present bedspread from their bedroom; they laid him down on that.

Mother took up a position at the door, watching for the ambulance.

All the lights were blazing.

The patient will probably turn his head towards the light, the book said.

Boy didn't think; he bent over his Father and began to heavily, deliberately hit him as hard as he could over the heart. He hit him again, and again, and again, striking for his Father's heart.

As death approaches, the patient will feel mortal dread; hold him as hard as you can, let him know that you are still there, let nothing frighten him. Turn off the television, the book said.

Then Boy did the last thing you can do; he leant forward as if in a passionate final kiss, he placed his mouth over his Father's and he tried to give him his own breath.

When the ambulancemen arrived, at four in the morning exactly, what they saw, framed by the open front door of the flat, with all the lights blazing, was this:

In the centre of the hallway floor, the naked bulb shining directly above his head, was a young man, holding a body in his arms. At first sight, the body looked small enough to have been the body of a child, though it was in fact the body of an old man. And the young man, because of the body cradled in his lap, and because someone had thrown a blanket over his shoulders which looked like a blue robe, and because his face was cast down in the traditional posture, looked like the Virgin.

The Virgin is conventionally portrayed as being unrealistically young and beautiful. All the lines and bags of exhaustion are gone, suddenly erased from her face now that the labour is over (or the agony, for it is hard to tell if this is a nativity or a pietà; the traditional grouping of figures is the same for both scenes). In this version, the Virgin is cradling her miraculous child in the simplest of settings; her resting place is a blanket spread roughly on the humble ground. Kneeling by her side is an older man, sober-faced and draped in a scarlet robe. This is Joseph—wondering now whether this is indeed his child, his responsibility, wondering what their life will be like now, watching over the tableau with strange, sad, half-doubting yet loving eyes. His posture, leaning slightly forward with upraised hands, acknowledges that his role is to support the Virgin at this moment, but makes it clear that, although he is her husband, he may not at this moment touch her. The Virgin looks down at the face in her lap; Joseph gazes on the face of the Virgin.

Around these central figures, in this particular version, there are no assembled saints or angels; the artist has imagined that the scene takes place at the dead of night and for your eyes only. There are no saints, no hermits, no knights of the Church Militant, no confessors or prophets, no ranks of faces; but as always in these compositions there is one face which turns to look out of the picture at you. This is the figure of the donor (the person who paid for the picture) standing in the foreground of the work with a strange mixture of pride (for this figure is wealthy, well-dressed, and proud of it) and humility (for it is acknowledged that wealth alone could not buy the role of witness at this scene, which is a privileged one). The donor both intervenes and intercedes between the holy figures and you, the spectator.

The donor in this version also doubles as the other traditional attendant figure in the composition. This is

St Anne, the Mother of the Virgin, the woman who rejoices in her own child's great role in history with a half-seen smile of maternal wisdom. Her smile is also full of pain, for she has seen both childbirth and death before, beginning and ending. She stands right on the edge of the central family grouping. But now that she sees the ambulancemen have arrived, the donor has stepped back, stepped away, taken a place right at the edge of the composition. This is the moment at which she turns to look out of the picture. Look, she is turning now. Mother is turning towards you in her silver dress, Mother is turning to welcome the ambulancemen, Mother is turning to look at you, you, one of the arriving crew or gathering crowd; turning in her silver dress, which in this light and at this hour of the morning does indeed look strangely like a robe embroidered with seed pearls; and the scarlet bathrobe, in this light, does indeed look like a robe worthy of a saint; and the bedspread on the hall floorway looks like a carpet rich, rare and costly enough to be a worthy resting place for the Virgin and her child. Mother turns, and in her dual role of donor and St Anne, indicates the tableau on the hall floor with a small movement of her hand.

She says, *Look at that. The Holy Family. Virgin and Child with St Joseph and Donor.*

She says, *you can look now, it's finally finished.*

She says, *look, there's nothing more I can do.*

And now Mother walks away, she shuts the door; she shuts the door in your face, she shuts out this strange sight from the eyes of the gathering crowd of neighbours. She shuts the door from the outside, not from the inside. She shuts the front door and she goes along the walkway and down the five flights of stairs and away into the city at dawn without even taking her bag or any money.

Cupboards, shelves, cabinets, papers, you can keep them. I leave you my toothbrush and my nightie and my overnight bag; and I leave you my words of advice and my generous allowance and my maternal wisdom; I leave you my sense of humour and my years of experience and my feminine guile; I leave you our early evening suppers and my late night drinks and your uncleaned baths and your unwashed dishes and your two weeks of ironing; I'm taking all the jewels, both the real and the fake.
Mother

The ambulancemen dealt with everything quickly and carefully. Surprisingly, even when they realised that these three men had lived together as a family, though unrelated by blood or marriage, they said nothing and apparently did not think the situation worthy of comment.

O made all the arrangements on the phone the next morning.

And when they were left alone, these two, who had such a sense of occasion and had invented so many ceremonies, hardly knew what to do. For how long should you sit in mourning, for how many nights do you watch when you are unsure of what it is you are trying to let go of or say goodbye to or keep hold of?

Boy pulled off Father's ring before they took him, and wore it with his own. He didn't eat for three days. This seemed appropriate, but hardly adequate as a sign of mourning.

It was a miserable funeral; miserable and quick. There were only a few of us there. I saw Boy crying like I had seen the man crying at their wedding. O held onto him, but Boy said, *don't try and stop me from crying.* Boy said, *I am not crying because he's dead. I am crying for the life he led. And it isn't my fault and it wasn't his fault but I wish there was somebody to blame, if he wasn't to blame then who was to blame, who was it, oh I want to hurt them, I want to hurt them, I want to hurt them.*

As I said there were only a very few of us there—after all, we had never even met this Father. The really strange thing was that Mother wasn't there—but as we found out later, she didn't even know when the funeral was or where. O had left a message for her at The Bar, but they didn't know yet that she hadn't got it.

I made myself go but I shouldn't have. I am not good at funerals. Sometimes when I remember, I remember there

being so many and so close together . . . This was not one
I needed in addition to all that. Weddings, divorces we
could do in style and no trouble, but it's hard for me to
have a good funeral. Other people at that time used to
try and tell me that funerals were good, were good for
you, that it was good to say goodbye in public, but I could
never feel it myself, I was always so angry. I just used to
stand there listening to the crying and I always thought
I could hear someone swearing under their breath. People
say I should not be so sad and in fact I have seen friends
smiling and embracing as they cry and be glad somehow
that our boys had such lives. But I don't see it. I suppose
I can't forgive any of it. And so I couldn't cry with Boy,
but I was used to crying like that, I knew what he was
crying for, that woman knew what she was crying about.
When I heard Boy saying what he said I promised myself
I'd remember his words and use them myself sometimes
later, *I won't cry because he's dead, I'll cry because of the
life that he led, and I know, because he told me.*

On the afternoon of the funeral, a teacher who was going out on his own to celebrate his forty-second birthday had his face cut open. At exactly the same time. What is the sense of those two things happening at the same time I thought, those two ceremonies, just what is the sense in that, just when . . .

Sometimes I think I no longer know what love means, I said. But I know one of the things it means; it means the way O stayed with Boy in the six days after this man's death, not just standing beside him at the funeral, but standing by him for each of those one hundred and forty hours. And the way O never, in all that time, never said to him, 'Are you alright?'

The morning after the death itself, when it was so cold, and the water was still spilt on the hall floor and the smell of the smoke was still clearing, he sat with him in the living room and held his hand all day, for Boy was in some kind of state of shock, as if he hardly knew what he had seen or done. As if he could not face whatever the next thing might be after all that was over. They sat there in the cold side by side, O made some toast and tea but Boy could not eat anything; it just sat there and went quickly cold. The flat seemed empty, whereas before it had felt full with just the two of them in it; and it felt wrecked in some way. Boy was certainly not doing any housework now, in fact it seemed necessary to leave the place exactly as it was for a while, as if preserving the evidence of what had happened, the proof. They even left the bedspread in the middle of the hall floor. In the panic of trying to fill the bath with near-boiling water, the small bathroom mirror, the one they used for shaving, had got broken, so that there were dangerous silver splinters in the bath and on the bathroom floor. They were still there. The day after the funeral (four days after the death), white faced and tightlipped and barefoot, Boy went into the bathroom, but not to clear up; without asking O's permission or explaining himself, he got up from his chair in the living room and walked purposefully into the bathroom, not caring if he cut his feet open. There, using a fist wrapped in a towel as his weapon, he broke the other mirror, the big one, too. Then he went and smashed the full length mirror in the bedroom, the one

they watched themselves fucking in. Then he went to the
kitchen and yanked open the fridge door and with both
hands scooped the food off the fridge shelves and onto
the kitchen floor, all that pointless food he had bought,
and he went on without stopping and broke the plates,
the milk jug, the butter dish and the sugar bowl which he
had bought especially for those elaborate breakfasts. He
did all this in silence, though he was breathing heavily
through his clenched teeth.

Then he got the two binliners and the shoe box and
the packing case from the bedroom, and he carried them
into the hall, and emptied them in the middle of the
bedspread, in the middle of the hall floor, in the very
spot. And then he set fire to the heap of letters and to
the bedspread and he stood there and he watched them
burn. When they were well and truly alight he did not
stay to watch but went back into the living room, as if
so satisfied by the act that he did not need to witness its
completion.

O followed him while he was doing all this, but did not
try to stop him; he was just watching to see that he did
not cut himself on any of the shards of mirror and china.
When the fire in the hallway got dangerous and started
to scorch the walls O brought saucepans of water from
the kitchen and threw them over it, so that there was
more foul-smelling smoke and a wet mess of charred and
blackened paper.

Not everything was destroyed in this fire, but most of it
was. Even Boy's own original and precious collection of
letters and photos was burnt. O saw the photo of the First
World War soldier lying in the black mess, only burnt
along one edge, and he saved that.

That night Boy opened their bedroom door wide, he
threw open all the doors inside the flat, turned on all the
lights, and turned the television off, so that everything
that happened in their bedroom could be heard and

everything could be seen in every other room, and he took O into the bedroom and when they made love he cried out just like a boy of sixteen, he cried out in his pleasure just like he used to before there was anyone to hear.

And then, only then, having done all that, did Boy throw open all the windows, and then go and throw open the front door so that there was a bitter draught coming in from the front door, he let the cold come in and begin to clean the house.

At the end of the week, working together, they swept the broken mirror from the bathroom floor, and O called someone and had the boiler fixed. He turned the thermostat right up. The gas came on with a great thump and the flat began to heat up again, room by room, as the hot water flowed from each cold radiator to each cold radiator. When the water was scalding, O turned the bathroom taps on full, and to the sound of that gushing water he stripped Boy and carried him bodily into the steaming bathroom and lowered him into the almost unbearably hot water, then washed him, dried him and dressed him and took him out for the night. Took him out to The Bar, where else.

And on that night, of all nights, it was O and Boy themselves who were assaulted.

They never even made it to The Bar. Not even to the appropriate bus stop. They were halfway there, on a street with plenty of cars going past, and plenty of streetlamps, a safe street, a street where there usually wasn't any trouble, when they heard people talking behind them, laughing, and then people overtaking them, jostling them, and then it had already started to happen, there were five men standing in front of them and four men behind them.

It was ten o'clock on a Friday night, a public holiday had been declared (the Christmas lights were going on), so people were out and a bit drunk; there was more shouting than usual. But I have to say that Boy and O were not in any way in the wrong place at the wrong time. Normally they would have seen it coming and crossed the road and gone another way; but on this night, the seventh night after being witnesses to a death, seven nights after Boy had had a man die in his arms, Boy's whole attention was taken up with the simple act of walking down the street, practising being part of the world again. And O's whole attention was on Boy; he was apparently walking calmly and normally by his side but in fact he was waiting, always ready to catch him should he fall, or to fold him in his arms should he suddenly cry out and crumple to his knees. That is why neither of them noticed what was happening until it was too late. All their senses were straining to accomplish this ordinary task of walking up the road to the bus stop and thence to an ordinary Friday night out at The Bar, and when they looked up from the pavement and saw the five men in front of them they were taken by surprise, they were surprised to see that it was already too late, that they hadn't seen it coming, that they were already in trouble.

Boy had read lots of thrillers. Often they had contained the phrase 'You're in danger of losing your life', or descriptions of how cold a gun muzzle is when pushed between your teeth by a man who's saying, *now do you get the idea or do I have to explain the whole situation to you?*—but he had never expected to feel just like the books say that people feel like in these scenes, that is, very calm. It didn't occur to him for one moment that he might get killed. This despite the fact that he knew that two people had been killed that year, he knew, because I'd told him.

He felt very calm and was watching everything very closely as it happened and felt that he had time to notice almost everything.

He noticed their fashionable clothes. Their jewellery. Especially the gold chains. Their smiles; how cheerful they were, not sinister. Their looks which meant, *oh I could enjoy hurting you. I could talk about that with my friends afterwards, I could watch a film about you getting killed on the TV or a documentary about you dying and I would probably laugh if I was having a beer, if I was with the kind of friends who'd laugh at that then I'd laugh too, I would.*

O was waiting for the first move. Without having to turn round, he was as aware of the men behind him as he was of the five in front. His back was waiting for the first push between the shoulder blades. Without thinking, he took hold of the scruff of Boy's jacket with his left hand, and just held on to it. He knew that two men are harder to push down than one.

No one was saying anything. O could see his own breath, it was so cold.

Then he heard them starting, someone was saying, *oh excuse me boys,* someone giggled and said, *oh excuse me girls,* they even used the most stupid old lines, one of them actually said, *backs against the walls boys.* To them it was not a serious situation at all.

O thought it was coming any minute now, so he looked down (he remembered Stella telling him that this was the right thing to do if things got this bad), looked down for a half brick or a piece of wood to use, trying to imagine as he did so what it would feel like to slam it into the side of someone's face, that one who was grinning; but then O looked up, there wasn't anything close to hand, O looked up and saw something out of the corner of his eye, saw a movement of an arm, something metal; O spun round, O turned and saw one of the young men reaching out his hand to touch the back of Boy's head.

There was no knife coming down this time—there was no knife, O saw that at once; the gleam of metal which had alerted him to this movement was from a heavy gold bracelet. The man had a delicate wrist, an elegant hand O thought, and as he lifted his gold-braceleted hand slowly to the back of Boy's head O realised that what the man really wanted to do was just to touch him, that he was was going to run his fingers across Boy's precious black hair. The young man was saying, quietly, *oh, oh such a pretty boy.*

After what they had been through, not just the death but also the courtship, the engagement, the wedding and all their nights together, all their ceremonies, O could not bear it that anyone should touch his Boy for so slight a reason as petty hatred.

And so he did the only thing he could do to express his outrage. Without thinking, O opened his throat so that the cold night air dropped into his lungs in one single, massive breath, and then he shouted, roared, he shouted right in the man's face, without thinking, shouted right at the top of his voice, but in a voice which he had never heard himself use before, something that sounded more like a car crashing than a human voice, and what he cried out in the man's face was *not a hair upon his head you fucker.*

Then there was silence again; nobody moved; the man held his braceleted hand in mid air, six inches from the back of Boy's head; and then O shouted again with all the breath in his body, *go home.*

And the young men realised that these two men who they had assumed would be afraid were not afraid, or seemed not to be, and they began to back away. The man who had reached out his hand to touch Boy from behind pulled it back as if from the bar of an electric fire.

They backed away, saying nothing, and, inexplicably, it was over.

It was over quickly; no one had been hit.

But when they had gone O felt just as if he had laid into them with his bare hands; he even looked down at his knuckles, expecting to see them split open and bleeding. Then he took Boy in his arms and felt him all over, as if checking for broken bones, and he examined his face, tenderly, for cuts or bruises. He touched his own lips with a quick touch to make sure that they were not split or swollen. And then his arms suddenly ached as if it had been a big fight or as if he had been swimming too long, too far out at sea, at night. And then he hugged and held onto his Boy just as if he had actually hauled him dripping from some deep, freezing and dangerous water.

They held onto each other until they were warm again, and they kissed.

Then they started walking again, not to escape from further threat or because they wanted to get to The Bar, but because they had to do something to work off the extraordinary anger that they felt. They knew that they had to keep moving. They walked fast, sometimes even broke into a half run, saying nothing. But then when they passed a phone box, O stopped, panting, and said to Boy:

'Do you have any change?'

'Yes—why?'

'I'm going to call Mother.'

And they didn't smile, but it felt like it, and Boy said:

'Well tell her that we were perfect.'

*

But Mother was not there; the phone rang and rang and rang, but she was not there. She just was not there when they needed her most.

And they didn't smile all that evening, and they never made it to The Bar, and they never talked to Mother, but they stayed out late amongst the crowds that night, brave-faced and apparently unshaken, for it was as I have said a public holiday and the crowds were out in their fine clothes to see the Christmas lights turned on, even though it was a cold winter's night, and for four more hours after this attack on them O and his Boy did not go home but they made their way slowly through the city hand in hand, holding hands in public all the night. They went through the city as if inspecting it, having escaped unharmed from this immediate threat, having escaped, it seemed, from almost everything and being able now to walk down the streets almost in freedom; for in their strength, as they walked side by side that night, as they walked hand in hand, they felt that the city could not touch them and could not hurt them now. And this was not folly on their part and it was not ignorance; for they did still on that night hear, see and feel everything around them, O and his Boy, it is not true that they only had eyes for each other. As they walked the night streets of the city they saw all the great plate-glass windows shining, they saw all the money and the lack of money, they heard the contemptuous voices of the noisy and the eager, the arrogant and the stupid and the vain, the too-rich young men driving their too-fast cars down the narrow streets at night with their music on too loud, they saw the too-young men sleeping half-mad with alcohol under the bridges, the floodlit and empty churches, the begging children at the railway stations, the crowds assembled for the public holiday, just as they had seen on other nights crowds gathering on the streets for all the city's other reasons, the genuine rage, the useless violence, the pleas for justice, the demands for payment, the acts of arson, the insults, the underpaid teachers and nurses and the confident buyers and sellers of everything and the words BLACK and VICTIM in bold type on the front page of the newspapers, and the handsome young blonde policeman trying to do his job. They heard all of the city's one hundred and four languages and all its slang, its argot, filth, radio stations, its music, advertisements and sirens, and they also heard the calm, educated voice which rose over everything saying, *a lot of our people, many of our people who are gathered together here tonight understand that tonight we celebrate the fact that this great city of ours is once again on the way to being great again, and we can say that with pride, we can celebrate, and, you know, they are glad to join us now in this celebration; this is surely a time for us all to join together, to enjoy and admire. But let us also remember our future and think of our children and the city which they will inherit, I would just say that, and may you all have a splendid time, thank you,* and they saw the lights going on all over the city, the fireworks, and the great crowds cheering, and plenty to see and plenty to buy everywhere, and amidst all this they felt entitled to walk the streets these two, they felt entitled to stand side by side, to be as remarkable as they were and yet go unremarked.

Inexplicably, no one looked at them, though they must have looked as striking as they always did when they were together. Inexplicably no one stared at them when they paused to kiss under the strings of coloured lights by the river. The waiter did not look at them twice when he brought them their drinks. The band did not stop playing when they started to dance with all the other couples, a slow waltz; for some reason no one turned to watch when they left the dance floor hand in hand

and went on through the crowds and into the night to begin their journey home.

And when they got home at four a.m. the night did not end there for them, but went on until way past the dawn, and they were for that night and for several other nights of that remarkable year perfect, perfect, perfect.

The reason why they couldn't get hold of Mother that night was that she wasn't at The Bar. And the reason why someone else at The Bar hadn't answered the phone was that The Bar wasn't open any more. Boy and O were the last ones in town to know that The Bar had been shut for the seven days of their mourning, and in fact was never to open again, at least, not to open in the same way, with Mother running it. When they heard that, they realised that Mother wasn't just leaving them alone for a few days with their grief or shock, as she had once left them alone with their happiness; she was gone. She had walked out of the door and she was gone.

A week later, the cheques began to arrive.

The first one just had written on the back, *So you see, I still love you both.*

The next one came with a postcard enclosed; it said, *Darlings, I just couldn't stand it any longer.*

A second postcard, which arrived the very next morning, as if Mother was eager to explain herself, said, *And I realised that you didn't need a Mother any more.*

The third cheque, a week later, expanded on this point further, or rather the letter which accompanied it did:

> *Darlings,*
> *I realised that leaving was one solution. I feel that*
> *I've done my time, you've all heard my song by now,*
> *you've had all of me, and if The Bar has to close,*
> *well, there are others. And God knows I've set you*
> *two up. I hope that Gary and co. have organised*
> *the selling off of my books, feathers etc properly*
> *like I asked them to, some of them were worth quite*

*a lot. I want all the money to go to the annual
collection; can you make sure my instructions are
being followed, O, god knows we need every penny
this year of all years.*

*You should be very proud of me boys and not
sad at all; all I took was the makeup, the Vechten
photographs in a big envelope and all the jewellery,
which of course I can't wear here.*

*It's beautiful; I can't remember the last time
I could properly use that word of a place instead of a
person.*
Mother

Mother wrote with very small, precise handwriting; economically, as if she meant every word she said. Boy said that it must be all those years of doing the books. Also she chose her postcards with great precision; she meant them, too. She took particular pleasure in postcards of ruins, especially ruined monuments. O and Boy received a postcard of a giant face from a monumental stone statue, its once handsome stone lips cracked open, the inscription across its forehead, which had once announced a heroic career of military exploits, now illegible, the giant stone curls of its hyacinthine hair now the nesting place of feral pigeons, that country's commonest bird; then one of a classical garden in which the paths appeared to be made of raked gravel, but were in fact (you couldn't see this in the picture, but Mother explained this on the back of the card) made of tesserae in eighteen kinds of marble, glittering, costly fragments which had once composed a mosaic map of the known world, with the Emperor's capital city in its centre, and, of course, many portraits of the Emperor, of whom no known statue or even portrait on a coin is now known; then one of the greatest castles ever built, its eight massive rings of walls preserved intact in the desert, preserved unscarred by war for five centuries because it was never manned, but left uninhabited the year of its completion when its wells mysteriously failed; and one of a fascist stadium with statues, where the heroic figures, contrived to look like marble, had crumbled and split, revealing the cheap iron armatures beneath the concrete of their straining thighs and ostentatiously upraised arms.

Though there was clearly a reason for this sequence of cards, it did not seem to mark the sights or resting places of a journey, like postcards from abroad are meant to. If there was a journey, it was untraceable from the clues provided; the locations of the ruined monuments on the front of the cards didn't match the provenance of the postmarks on their backs. However, Mother clearly was on some kind of journey; all the cards had been sent from cities with major airports or railway stations.

Dear Boys, I'm fine, how are you? I had no idea it would be so easy to leave. Now I'm on an island quartered by alleyways, with flowering trees, staying in what seems to be half a palace . . . the men are so beautiful, such teeth, and everyone has black hair like ours, perhaps you two would feel at home, who knows, love,

Darlings; jasmine, vines, roses, bougainvillea, oleander, hibiscus, anemones, cedar, my love as always,

I am the woman without jewels, the minister without portfolio, the gigolo without a dictionary, a duchess stranded without her car. I wanted to send you a map with this place marked on it but cannot find one, (this was written in a shaky script, as if it had been written on a moving train).

Mother's cards were all put in Boy's box of papers, the original shoebox with the scarlet ribbon, though it was almost empty now after the ritual burning. The few letters and pictures which had survived had survived by accident, (they had got stuck in the bottom of the box when he'd emptied it into the flames). Only the portrait of the soldier had been deliberately rescued, and O had done that.

Now when he got it out and looked at it Boy thought that the picture looked not so much like himself, but like a young and handsome version of the dead man, of his 'Father'. For a while he kept it out of the box, on the chair by the bed, but face down, as if he didn't want this man to see the two of them making love. Then after a while he turned it face up on the chair. Then he put it up on a shelf in the bedroom. And then he hung it on a wall in the spare room, the room that had been the old man's room. Sometimes he'd stand in front of it before he went to bed, before he went to join O in bed, he'd look up at it and return its gaze and say, *Goodnight, Father.*

And even though Boy of course had O now to talk to in the evenings he would still sometimes go into their room and shut the bedroom door and get all of Mother's postcards out of the box, and the surviving letters and photos too, and begin to lay them out like a game of patience, just like he used to. He might have said, *I still want to see how it comes out.* And when he had laid out his papers quietly in a circle around their bed, he would talk quietly to them; but whereas before it had always been questions, requests for advice, now he would often talk back to the people in the pictures or those whose names were on the letters, and to Mother too, via her postcards. He would lie there on the bed and tell them quietly about his life, not just asking questions now but telling them things, giving them all the details of a particular problem, or cataloguing all the events of a day from its beginning to its end. And at the end of his recital of the details of his life he would pause, and say to his papers and cards, *well, what do you think?*

They got some of us queens round to help redecorate the flat, and we painted out the scorch marks in the hallway with white emulsion and got the last of the broken mirror and china up out of the cracks between the floorboards. And we had the radio on all the time, or one of O's records, and I think that all this wasn't just to do with redecorating the flat but also with somehow fumigating it with laughter and loud passionate music. A couple of the boys, who were actually at that time a couple—but very young, very in love in a demonstrative sort of way, always showing off how much they fancied each other, you know how they are, with their matching moustaches, as if no one had ever done this before, as if they had invented love, as well as sex—well this couple stayed on after the decorating was finished one night, and were snogging on the sofa while O and Boy were in the kitchen fixing dinner. And they got carried away (this is what I heard anyway), and when O came in with the food he asked them to carry on, and O and Boy watched while these two relative strangers (both of them were working out every other day and dancing every night, they were that sort, so they were quite into this exhibitionism, they thought they were so damned special having a handsome boyfriend), O asked them to carry on and O and Boy watched these two young men making love right there. I expect the boys thought that this was some kind of sexual perversion, that O and Boy liked to watch rather than do it themselves.

I expect they thought that since O and Boy had been living together for a while they no longer did it with each other and so liked to watch other people; I don't expect they guessed that Boy was still younger than them, because what he had been through and his status as O's partner made him seem an older man to them. I don't expect that they realised that this wasn't a sexual moment for O and Boy at all, but a tender one, that this was somehow and in a strange way a sort of housewarming to them, or a dedication of the hearth.

After they had gone, Boy said to O, *what are we going to do with his room? Maybe we could put a note up somewhere or in the paper, if The Bar was still open of course we could just ask around. We should put a note up somewhere and find some boy who hasn't got anywhere to live, you know how hard that is when you first get here. We could phone round and see if anyone needs somewhere to live. I don't see why we should have an empty room and I don't think it's right we should. And we need the money.*
They did need the money; the cheques had stopped arriving. The very last one (and this was the very last time that they heard from Mother) came in an envelope with a postcard, a few notes on torn scraps of paper, and a photograph. The postcard was a very beautiful altarpiece from a museum, a *Virgin and Child with St Joseph and Donor,* with Joseph in scarlet and the donor (or is it St Anne?) in a dress with a silver hem; she must have chosen it specially. And this was the message on the back:

> *Dear Boys, in haste. I need the money more*
> *than you do now. Do make sure that you get a*
> *job as soon as possible, Boy, so that you have*
> *two incomes; remember that money is the most*
> *important thing. I will get an address to you*
> *soon, as there are some things I need for people*

*here, and some new books. I am starting a new
library.*

and this is what she had written on the scraps of paper
also enclosed;

*The Family—penetrates the interior—'what country
friends is this'—love, Miss, Missie, Mademoiselle, M.,
Madam, Madame, Mother, Anne.*

And the photograph, which I now have, is the last known
image of Madame; a polaroid of her with a monkey.
However this is not the usual tourist picture—the monkey
is not perched on her shoulder, and she is standing on the
edge of some desert, not on a promenade. Madame has
tied a kind of golden, silky scarf across her eyes; in her
right hand she is holding, instead of the usual scales,
her feathered evening bag, and it is bulging with paper
money. She has no sword; on her left hand (both her
arms are stretched out straight, just like the statue) is
sitting the tiny, grinning monkey, showing its teeth and
screaming with anger or some kind of laughter. Her pose
is exactly that of the great golden statue which was seen
to rock and sway in the storm on the night of O and Boy's
engagement. She has kicked off her shoes.

On the back of the photograph Madame has written,
JUSTICE.

After that last picture of her, let me show you a final picture of these two.

You want to know, of course, what happened to them after Mother left. You want to know what happens next to these two. You recognise that what really matters is what happens when two people try to hold things together. You do not believe that love is enough, and you think that what happens after love (if you see what I mean), the practice and not just the principle of love, that is what matters. That is what you want to know how to do. That is what you want to see a picture of.

Here it is:

Boy looks slightly older, but O does not; his face will remain that of a man in his prime and pride of his life for some time, that fixed, stylish and indeed stylised beauty of The Older Man. He will always be handsome. And Boy will always be beautiful I think. He spends the evening or night with a younger man sometimes now, a man younger than himself, a boy really; and these boys he chooses are always very excited to be chosen by such a beauty, and of course are even more flattered when someone like me tells them that they have been with half of such a famous couple, almost a legend or institution in our circle.

But for the purposes of this picture which I said I'd show you, there are just the two of them. They are not holding hands, they are not even looking lovingly at each other, I suppose because I want you to understand that this is no simple or obvious coupling. But they are very definitely together.

Boy has his shirt off. Someone who slept with Boy just recently told me that he now has a tattoo on his left breast, that is, over his heart. It is quite strange to have had that done at his age; it's usually done when men are still trying to prove something. I will include that tattoo in the picture for you. When Boy is older that mark on his breast will assert a pride that the rest of his body will no longer justify. The blue lines will have spread under the skin of his breast as the pectoral muscles have fallen and flattened; but they will still spell the same word. And when some young man asks him why he had it done, I hope that Boy (we will still call him that) will say that he had it done as proof that he was once admired, and that though men may have lied to him, they did not lie about that. They admired and adored him, and left the marks of their teeth on every part of his body. I know there was one who would groan aloud at the touch of his hair. And more than all these infatuations this body of his, this body of his belonged to another man (yes, I will use these words here, I will); the man who we all agreed was the handsomest man in town, the one love in whom all the others came to rest, the prince amongst men. And it was for him and at his request that Boy made this mark on his body, and not for any whimsical or ordinary contract but as a sign of his faith in the love of men, in the fact that it is indeed possible to choose a man, or men, and you be quiet now and sleep and don't ask me any more questions.

Oh how I wish there really was a picture like that for me to give you, oh how I wish there was one final picture of them I could show you, some last kiss or concluding image, the three of them together would be best, or the two of them would do, a picture of them kissing or fucking or a real proper wedding picture, or a kiss bravely silhouetted against rising flames. I wish this last picture of them could be staged against the backdrop of some grand historical event. I have just read this book in which *the terrible story of their fated romance comes to its stunning climax, played out against the flickering flames of the Siege of Krishnapur,* and having read that I wish that Boy could look out from their fifth floor balcony one night and see something like that, see this city once again in flames. Let it be a night with fire, let it be a night at least with fireworks, let it be a night with car horns, but not just a holiday, let it be the night of the sacking of the palace of John of Gaunt, when the looters in their pride and their fury cast a whole dinner service of solid gold into the dark river; let it be the night when the war was over and men kissed in the streets; let it be the night Franco died and the two Spanish queens I was with got drunk and started making out right there on the dinner table, let it be Riga, let it be Budapest, let it be Berlin, but let it be in our own country, right here in our city, this city, let it be a night to remember, a night to say, *I was there.* Let it be the night we raised a hundred thousand pounds, let it be the night they changed the law and we danced all night, spilling out of The Bar and dancing our way into the street, and nobody stopped us, let this be a night when the Strand and the Embankment are solid with people crying and cheering and cheering, cheering as Madame walks out into the arclights illuminating the makeshift stage in the middle of the square, as she walks into the lights, walking with a silver-headed cane now but still, just for old times' sake, still wearing the silver beaded dress, those same old sequins blazing out under the arclights as if she was burning or shining, a very grand lady, and look, there are Boy and O helping her up the six steps and across the stage, this is the picture I've been looking for, this is the picture of the three of them together again, arm in arm on that historic night, and now everyone is going very quiet, for everybody knows that it is at least thirty years since she last sang; and her voice is cracked, and her breasts have gone and are sagging, but her hair is still defiantly raven black, and a great hush spreads over the crowd now, people begin to light the candles they have brought with them and to hold them up; and Madame steps forward just like she always used to, steps up to the microphone, and she puts her hand over her heart. And there is silence, you can hear the hush spreading through the crowd, and then she sings, or rather half speaks, the words which we all know, the words we all knew and loved so well:

> *Your goodbyes,*
> *Left me with eyes that cry,*
> *How can I go on, dear, without you?*

and from the great crowd comes rising the whispered chorus, a great, strong, slow, gentle sound, everyone now holding up a candle or just a hand or a photograph of a person who couldn't be here tonight:

> *All of me,*
> *Why not?*
> *Take all of me;*
> *Can't you see?*
> *I'm*
> *No good,*
> *Without you.*

Boy wishes sometimes that there was a phone number for her.

He would often sing her song to himself when O was at work, mimicking her voice with considerable skill; but what he really wanted was to be able to pick up the phone and speak to her, or to hear her singing down the phone; or just to be able to play a tape of her singing it, *all of me, take all of me.*

That's Boy's song now; and that's the song I'd choose, that's the song I always ask Gary to play when I see him at the new place where he's working now, I say, some music for the ending please, Gary, something to sweeten and elevate the ending of this story, something to celebrate the fact that they are still together, thank you, that's it, and the last words of this story are *Goodbye Boys. Goodbye Mother. Goodbye Father. Goodbye, and Thank You, Thank you and Goodnight.*

Somehow, when I read ... I never used to really believe what I read, but only thought it very strange, and a good deal too strange to be altogether true; though I never thought the man who wrote the book meant to tell lies.

Herman Melville, Redburn, 1849

This novel contains fragments from and reworkings of *The Picture of Dorian Gray* (Oscar Wilde, 1891), *Hadrian The Seventh* (Fr. Baron Corvo, 1904), *Maurice* (E.M. Forster, 1914), *Our Lady of the Flowers* (Jean Genet, 1943), *The Heart in Exile* (Rodney Garland, 1953) and the screenplay of the film *Victim* (Janet Green and John McCormick, 1961). The line 'Buddy, will you take me home?' is from Stephen Sondheim's musical *Follies*. The novel entitled *Lady Into Fox* which Mother gave Boy to read was written by David Garnett and published in 1923. The lyrics of 'All of Me' were written by Simons and Mark (copyright Bourne and Company, New York, 1931) and are quoted by permission of Francis Day and Hunter Limited, London WC2H 0EA and Marlong Music Corporation, New York.

Neil Bartlett, Ghent, Newcastle, Cardiff, Edinburgh, Toronto, Amsterdam, London, 1986–90.